A Perfect Weakness

by

Jennifer A. Davids

SMITTEN
HISTORICAL ROMANCE
LIGHTHOUSE PUBLISHING OF THE CAROLINAS

A PERFECT WEAKNESS BY JENNIFER A. DAVIDS
Published by Smitten Historical Romance
an imprint of Lighthouse Publishing of the Carolinas
2333 Barton Oaks Dr., Raleigh, NC, 27614

ISBN: 978-1-946016-56-0
Copyright © 2018 by Jennifer A. Davids
Cover design by Elaina Lee
Interior design by Karthick Srinivasan

Available in print from your local bookstore, online, or from the publisher at:
ShopLPC.com

For more information on this book and the author visit:
https://www.jenniferadavids.com/

Brought to you by the creative team at Lighthouse Publishing of the Carolinas (LPCBooks.com): Eddie Jones, Pegg Thomas, Linda Yezak, Shonda Savage, Brian Cross, Judah Raine, Jenny Leo

Library of Congress Cataloging-in-Publication Data
Davids, Jennifer A.
A Perfect Weakness / Jennifer A. Davids 1st ed.

Printed in the United States of America

PRAISE FOR *A PERFECT WEAKNESS*

Jennifer A Davids' newest novel, A Perfect Weakness, is a beautiful story of regret, redemption, and romance. Filled with intrigue, culture clashes, a dashing and haunted hero, and a compassionate, wounded heroine, Davids adds an endearing lesson about God's unfathomable forgiveness. A Perfect Weakness shows that the truest love shatters the most impenetrable walls.

~ **Pepper Basham**
Author of the *Penned in Time* and *Mitchell's Crossroads* series

A wonderful picture of redemption on so many levels. A Perfect Weakness is an enchanting Victorian tale that invites the reader to taste the rural English countryside and fall in love with its very authentic characters who each take their own journey toward healing—and meet each other on the way. Rich with historical detail and emotional impact, this story will draw you into its pages and make you want to linger long after the thrilling conclusion.

~ **Joanna Davidson Politano**
Author of *Lady Jayne Disappears*

What a beautiful story! In A Perfect Weakness, author Jennifer A. Davids takes readers into the depths of redemption and God's love through two hurting characters searching for purpose. A unique author voice blended with humor and heart, a strong hero and heroine, and an English setting make A Perfect Weakness just right for those who enjoy Downton Abbey and other period dramas. This novel is one I will return to often, and Davids is an author whose future stories I'm eagerly awaiting.

~ **Marisa Deshaies**
Editor

A Perfect Weakness will carry readers away to Victorian England with a wonderful story that blends romance, family drama, and heart-tugging secrets, all while exploring the power of God's grace to overcome past failures and bring redemption. I was captivated by the intriguing characters and cheering for them to find a path forward through their struggles. Jennifer A. Davids includes several twists and turns that will keep readers turning the pages until the very satisfying ending. Reminiscent of Jane Eyre, this novel will delight readers who enjoy English historical romance. Well done!

~ **Carrie Turansky**
Award-winning author of *The Governess of Highland Hall* and
Across the Blue

A fresh new voice for historical romance readers, Jennifer weaves a beautiful story of consequences, principles, and redemption while reminding us of God's abundant love.

~**Diane T. Ashley**
Award-winning Fiction Author

Dedication

This is for all those who fear they've fallen too far.
You haven't.
Let Him help you back up.

Acknowledgments

This book has been a long time in the making and it certainly didn't happen in a vacuum.

To my husband, Doug, thank you for your patience with your crazy writer wife. I would say that I'll never get behind on the laundry again, but we both know that's not going to happen. Love you.

To my children, Jonathan and Grace, our inside joke 'it must be cholera' is one of my fondest memories of writing this book. You are the best kids a mom could have.

To Linda Yezak, editor extraordinaire, this book is a thousand times better for your input. I owe you about a dozen cups of coffee. Bless you.

To Pegg Thomas and those at LPC who decided to take a chance on this book: thank you, thank you, thank you.

To my writing sisters, Carol Moncado, Joanna Davidson Politano, Stacy Zink, Kristy Cambron, and Jessica Keller, for your critiques and prayers over this book and the life events that went along with it, I cannot thank you enough. I am truly blessed to be doing life with you all.

Finally, to God, my Abba. When I asked You what would happen with my writing in 2017, You said I wouldn't believe it if You told me. I still don't. Thank You for knowing how to run my life better than I do. Don't ever stop reminding me.

Author's Note

Researching the nineteenth century is a daunting task. As a writer of historical fiction I try my best to thoroughly research my work. However, I am neither a professional historian nor, in regard to this book in particular, a doctor. Any errors either historical or medical are entirely unintentional, and I humbly pray they can be overlooked.

CHAPTER 1

Hampshire, England, July 1868

Penelope Howard stood before a mound of earth in the church graveyard.

Had it really only been a few months since Uncle William's passing? It hardly seemed possible that the warm, caring man she had loved since childhood now lay interred in the cool soil beneath. But then that was only his body, the outer shell. Her uncle's soul rested with God, finally free of the sickness which took him far too soon. How unfair that she couldn't have attended his funeral. Such a silly custom, not allowing women to attend funerals. To the county, he was Lord Renshaw, the baron of Ashford Hall, but to her, he was a dear uncle whom she'd deeply miss.

"I'm glad Uncle William and Aunt Amelia are together now. There is comfort in that," she said to her brother beside her. "How soon until they replace the marker?"

Her brother, Thomas, laid an arm across her shoulders. "A few more months. The ground needs time to settle, and they will have to add Uncle William's name and the dates."

"I'm so glad the funeral was well-attended."

"Indeed. I felt quite justified turning down the extra mourners the undertaker suggested. Half the county showed up," he said.

"No surprise there." Penelope knelt and skimmed her hand over the recently disturbed earth. "I'll bring some flowers to lay here in a day or so."

She would try to visit more often than she had in the past and bring flowers when she could. It wouldn't be too difficult. Their parents' resting places were just a few rows over. And there was one other, the one closest to her heart, though it didn't really need care. It should be here. But that would not be proper. Or safe.

"Mr. Howard, Miss Howard." Mr. Phillips and his wife, tenants of their late uncle's, stood off to the side.

Penelope rose as Mrs. Phillips stepped forward with a sympathetic smile. "I hope you don' mind if we extend our condolences to you both."

"Of course not, Mrs. Phillips, it is most kind of you."

"Lord Renshaw was a fair-minded man. It's a loss he's gone and no mistake." Mr. Phillips shook Thomas' hand. "I'm wonderin' if I might have a word. There's a matter I need to discuss."

"Of course." Thomas took his duty as Ashford Hall's estate agent seriously, but he had set aside today to take her to their uncle's grave and then relax. No doubt he would have rather avoided the conversation.

As the men moved away, Mrs. Phillips said, "It'll be pretty once the marker's back."

"Yes it will," Penelope replied.

"And when the grass grows over."

"Of course."

Mrs. Phillips finally quit stalling and came to the point. "Is there news of the new lord? Do we know when he'll be here?"

Her thinly disguised curiosity was understandable, all things considered. Ashford Hall would not be inherited in the usual way. Under normal circumstances, a son or nephew would be groomed to bring about a seamless change. Not so in this case.

Penelope toyed with the strings of her reticule. Thomas had told her to inform the tenants. If she told Mrs. Phillips right now, they all would know by next morning. A dear woman, but one did not tell her anything which should be kept a secret. The chief concern lay in how the tenants and the village of Woodley would react.

"We have had a letter from Mr. Smith, the solicitor. It would seem Lord Renshaw's heir is an American."

"An American!" Mrs. Phillips' jaw hung slack for a bare moment. A hopeful sign. "That's unexpected."

Unexpected. Not a wholly bad reaction and encouragement enough to continue. "He is not foreign to our ways. He's a doctor and trained in London and Edinburgh. Lord Renshaw himself sponsored his education."

"A doctor? Is he a physician or surgeon?"

"I do not know."

Mrs. Phillips tapped a finger to her mouth. "Oh, but he must be a physician if he is gentleman enough to be his lordship's heir."

"I am not certain. I do know there is less distinction between the two in America."

"Hmm. Could be worse I suppose." She placed a hand over her heart. "He will come take care of the estate, won't he? Make his home here?"

"I am confident he will take care of things properly." If he could be found. The solicitors were having a problem tracking this Dr. John Turner down. The address her uncle had left was incorrect, and the city in which he was supposed to live, Philadelphia, was large. But Mr. Smith had assured them they would find him in quick order.

"We'll have to see then, won' we? And let's hope he doesn't come with a wife." Mrs. Phillips leaned toward her. "We would miss your visits."

This wasn't the first time that particular issue had been raised. Hannah, their housekeeper, had voiced the thought just the night before. If Lord Turner were to bring a wife or even a sister with him, she would become the lady of the Hall and be expected to take up a certain role in the community, such as visiting tenants and those in the village. The role Penelope had been performing for several years now. The duty had fallen to her under unique circumstances and was accepted by most, but there were a few in the community who thought it unconventional.

Hopefully, the new lord would not take their view—wife, sister, or no. Nothing was fixed yet. He had to be located first, and even then he may decide to leave things in Thomas' hands. He was a doctor and in all likelihood had a thriving medical practice. Besides, even if the worst should come about, it was certain the woman in question would be in want of a friend, being in a new country.

And if that should fall through, Penelope's visits were by no means her only link to the estate or the community.

"I'm sure things will work out for the best, Mrs. Phillips."

Thomas approached and took her aside. "I'm sorry, old girl, but there's a problem at their farm I must see to."

His tone sounded flat. So much for his day off, poor man. "Do you want me to come with you?"

"No, but I need to go with them now. Would you mind driving back? I am sorry."

"Don't be silly. I'll be fine. I'm sorry you won't have the day to yourself as we intended."

"Hall matters can't seem to wait. Mr. Phillips said he would drive me home when we're through."

"Should we wait luncheon for you?"

"Probably not." Aggravation melted from his face as he turned to the farmer. "I'm ready when you are. Miss Howard is willing to drive herself home."

Penelope lingered at her uncle's grave for only a few minutes more before leaving. As unfortunate as it was that Thomas had been needed elsewhere, it gave her time to stop someplace which had haunted her thoughts since their period of mourning had confined her movements. She guided the small horse-drawn dogcart down a tree-lined path which gradually rose until she cleared the shade and a tall, crumbled ruin greeted her.

It had fascinated her since she was a little girl. Part of the Ashford Hall estate, it lay at the top of a hill which overlooked the entire property and the village of Woodley. Known locally as "the Castle," it had been the home of the original baron, built in the era of knights, their ladies, and holy quests. She could almost hear her and her brother's youthful laughter as they pretended the fairy folk lived among the broken rocks. And the sketches Thomas had drawn of their musings! If only he still had them.

Those times were long since gone. The Castle was different now.

She halted the cart before the stone bridge that had been built across the old moat and climbed down. Perhaps this had been a mistake. Perhaps she should stop coming here and put it all in the past. To return week after week, year after year was irrational. But a primal urge pulled her forward, across the bridge and into what once had been the courtyard.

A green swath of grass had replaced the flagstones, and all that lingered of the stronghold were the remains of the great hall and two other towers. An ancient stone wall, which time had worn down, loosely connected them.

Not far from the wall, she ran her fingers down the bark of an oak tree as she knelt at its base. She swept back tall grass and found it. The stone marker engraved with the image of an angel.

Her angel. She would be nearly five now. Old enough to help Hannah in the kitchen, old enough to squeal in delight whenever her Uncle Thomas swung her up in his arms, and yet young enough to still be afraid of thunderstorms and run to Penelope to be comforted.

Why had she come here? It was like this every time, and what good was it? It wouldn't bring her back. Her angel nestled safe in the arms of the Lord. He had kept her for the past five years and always would.

Penelope strode away. She had little time for heartache. Hannah needed help preparing the luncheon and would notice any hint of emotion, then ask questions Penelope couldn't answer.

But as she walked, the marker called to the maternal part of her that could never fully abandon her child.

CHAPTER 2

Philadelphia, August 1868

Dr. John Turner sat in an elegant parlor, sipping tea as if nothing disastrous had happened. A sort of soft numbness had stolen over him, despite the fact that just a few hours ago, he had fallen on his own sword. How long this anesthetizing effect would last was uncertain. That his actions had been necessary, however, was without a bit of doubt. He stared into his cup. The amber liquid released tendrils of steam which melted away into the air.

"You know members of the press were there." Dr. Robert Matthews, his oldest friend and colleague—no, former colleague—frowned, his arms crossed like a reproving father.

"So, you're finally speaking to me?" John asked.

Robert ignored his question. "How did they even know to be there to begin with?"

"Probably an anonymous tip."

His friend ran a hand through his hair. "Every newspaper will publish the minutes of that meeting—including your statement!"

He hoped so. Yes, he could have quietly removed himself from the Philadelphia Medical Society, but what good would it have done? The Society was a nicety, a glorified club, not a legal entity. They couldn't bar him from practicing medicine. Laying bare his sins to the whole world by letting the vultures of the press pick apart his reputation was the only way to keep another innocent soul from falling into his grasp.

He set his cup and saucer on a marble-topped side table and walked to the fireplace. "Don't worry. I never mentioned your name." As he studied the intricate scrollwork of the clock resting on the mantelpiece, he could feel Robert's eyes on the back of his head.

"Do you really think I care whether or not my name was mentioned?"

"You should. You and Sarah have done enough for me. I won't have your reputations damaged now that this is coming out." And that would be soon. The evening editions would be on the streets in a matter of hours.

"Neither of us care. You are more important than all that." Robert squeezed his shoulder, and he jerked. The numbness had begun to bleed away. "You made a mistake."

"I attended to a patient while I was drunk!" His words ricocheted against the parlor's walls and flew back at him. They found their mark, and he winced. "And not just any patient. The woman I was going to marry trusted me with the life of her sister. And I betrayed that trust. A young woman is dead because I couldn't lift myself out from the bottom of a bottle."

Robert's hand dropped away, and John took the chance to move to the window. The grayness of the day gave the glass a mirror-like quality. His brown hair and eyes looked black as if a skull stared back at him. How appropriate.

"You have to appeal the ruling. I have connections with one of the reporters I saw, perhaps—"

"No, Robert."

"John, please reconsider."

"It's time for me to go. I packed before the Medical Society meeting this morning and had my bag sent to my old office." Defeat dulled Robert's gaze, so John softened his tone. "I want to thank you and Sarah for taking me in."

"You don't need to thank us." Robert dropped into a chair. "You were ill."

"Ill? Ah, yes. I forgot that's what you told everyone. If being too drunk to see your patients qualifies as ill."

"I said that because as far as I was concerned, it was the truth.

You were and still are ill. Your body may be free from alcohol, but your soul is still sick."

Robert didn't understand. Did the man even have any demons? He hadn't seen what John had seen, heard what he'd heard, and—thankfully—done what he'd done both during and after the War of the Rebellion. Unlike John, he'd served in Washington, in a recovery hospital. After the war, he went on to develop a successful practice and marry the woman of his dreams. But he was right about one thing. Sickness had invaded John. He was sick of thinking himself worthy of being called doctor.

"You know you're welcome to stay," Robert said.

"I know, but I can't."

"Can't or won't?"

"Both. I'll let you know how I'm doing." He strode toward the parlor door.

"Where will you go?"

"I'm not sure," John replied. He paused. Robert's fingers were steepled, forefingers resting lightly against his lips, eyes focused elsewhere. Apparently, he had an idea. He had never been one to give up without a fight.

"What?" John regretted the edge in his voice. After all, Robert was only trying to help.

"You could go out west. Start over."

Something about the notion stilled John's rejection. The idea had merit. Though not in the way Robert was thinking. He wanted him to go and doctor there, where no one knew him. Completely out of the question, the doctoring part anyway. But why couldn't he go west? Grow cows or corn or something? How hard could it be?

Robert joined him at the doorway. "Sarah has an old family friend in the Colorado Territory. She had a letter from him that mentioned they need a doctor."

"Let me think about it. Don't do anything yet, please."

"You need to take this chance. Don't throw it away."

"I'll let you know." He tried to push a note of hopefulness into his voice. He failed.

Robert reacted to his attempt by shuttering his emotions like a statue.

"Well," he said, holding out a marble hand. John barely touched it before he withdrew it. His voice was a dull echo as it followed him to the window on the other side of the room. "Goodbye then."

"Goodbye, Robert."

The gray sky was turning slate by the time John arrived at his former office. He had taken the horse trolley from Robert's Chestnut Street home as far as Fourth Street. From there he walked to his neighborhood close to the docks and to the door of his tiny trinity house. He fished out his key and let himself in. His carpet bag sat just inside the door, the only object in the room not covered with dust. Not that there were many. Without Robert and Sarah's knowledge, he'd sold or donated his equipment. The only items left in the room were a desk and chair and a small washstand.

He pulled off his coat and vest, laying them across the desk before sinking into the chair. He dragged a hand over his face and dug fingers into his temple. The narrow, curved stairway in the corner invited him to climb to his bedroom and sleep. But sleep rarely helped anymore. Some nights he slept soundly, only to wake, strangled by guilt for being able to do so. Other nights … Well, other nights the dreams came. Guilt had choked his mornings of late, so he was due for a bout of nightmares.

No, he'd sit here for a while, perhaps think about this business of going west. Leaning back, he let his head rest against the wall. He could disappear out there. A number of veterans from the war were doing it, so the papers said.

Yes. Right. What a good idea. He could see it now. He'd move out there and run into one of those veterans. And it would turn out that particular veteran would be a fellow he'd treated—butchered, to be accurate.

Eventually, his back ached. Night had fallen. Time to see what tortures his mind had in store for him. He rummaged through the drawers for a match to light the oil lamp he could just make out on the desk. Pulling out the large lower drawer, he reached in—and stiffened as he brushed his fingers against supple leather.

He slammed the drawer shut, found a match in the next one, and lit the lamp. The chair skidded in protest as he stood. He flung his coat and vest over his arm and grasped the lamp. He took a few steps. He didn't need to see it. What good would it do? It was just a thing, and it meant nothing. Less than nothing.

But his heart dragged him back to the desk.

Fine. But seeing it wouldn't change his mind.

He threw down his things, yanked open the drawer, and withdrew his medical bag. He set it on the desk and took a step back, cupping his hands over his mouth.

Engraved on the brass placard below the handle, his name flickered and gleamed as the lamplight played across it. He hadn't been able to sell the bag with the rest of his medical equipment because of that placard. It was attached in such a way that its removal would ruin the bag. He released the clasp, revealing the tools of his trade. He'd forgotten to tell someone to sell the contents. The warm, rich scent of leather hadn't diminished despite its many years of use.

You could go out west. Start over.

Start over. Could he? Could Robert be right?

His heart pounded so hard, his hands shook as he reached into the bag. A shingle with his name on it. No, not his name, his mother's. It could work. And he could re-grow his beard. He would be careful. Keep to himself. He could make things right.

He touched an instrument at the exact moment someone knocked on the door.

He jerked his hand back and curled his fingers into a fist. What had he been thinking? Who was he to think he could have a chance start over, much less deserve it?

As the knock came again, he snapped the bag shut, gathered his garments, and picked up the lamp.

"I'm not seeing patients," he said through the door, but he made it only a few steps more before the knocking resumed. Scowling, he spoke louder. "I said I'm not seeing patients!"

A muffled voice answered back. "I have no need of a doctor. I'm looking for a Dr. John Turner on a matter of business."

The heat of anger rapidly cooled. "Business" could only mean one thing. There would be charges after all. Stumbling over to the door, he opened it with wooden fingers.

At the threshold stood a man only a year or so younger than he. "Dr. John Turner?"

John raised his brow at the man's cultured English accent. "Yes," he replied.

The stranger touched the brim of his hat. "My name is Miles Warner. I'm a solicitor with Smith and Stewart in London."

"You're here at the request of Lord Renshaw?" Such a weight settled over him he barely had the breath to speak the words. How had William found out?

Mr. Warner's countenance sobered. "Not exactly. I'm very sorry to inform you that Lord Renshaw passed several weeks ago. I've come on behalf of his estate."

CHAPTER 3

Penelope sat in the cart on the side of the road by herself as she cradled her injured hand in her lap. Of all the days for this to happen, it would have to be the day of the new lord's arrival at the Hall. Her horse shook its head.

"I won't say it's *all* your fault, Bessie," she said. "But throwing a shoe did not help."

The animal snuffed and stretched her head in reply.

Thank the Lord for Hannah. If her housekeeper had not been with her, she'd still be at the Castle, and there would now be no one to go for aid.

All that business at the Castle with her failed rescue attempt. A kitten had gotten stuck inside one of the towers, and she managed to reach it, but when it wriggled out of her arms, she had fallen on the wet stones, muddied her dress, and sprained her wrist. The cat, in turn, had run off. She agreed with Hannah. It had been silly of her to try to rescue it in the first place. But how could she have ignored those tiny mewlings? Especially when they at first sounded like the cries of a babe.

She shouldn't have stopped at the ruins, especially with Hannah. But the pull to go was too great. They were early returning from their errand, and she had only meant to steal a glance at her angel as they took a quick turn along the wall. She needed to stop these sentimental visits and just forget. If she didn't, someone would put two and two together.

Bessie shifted. The cart shook, and Penelope grabbed the seat. Poor girl. She must be uncomfortable. She climbed out, careful to guard her injured hand. Hannah had told her to stay put in the cart, but the horse's behavior spoke of more than just a thrown shoe.

Penelope walked to her head and soothed her, then stepped back to see if she could assess the problem. There was the bare hoof, the right rear leg. Had she lamed it too? Bessie shifted again, and the cart lurched. No, it wouldn't be safe to check and risk spooking her. She planted herself at the horse's head. "There now, girl, don't fret," she soothed.

The clop of hooves directed her attention to the road. A coach drew near. And not just any coach. It was from the Hall. The new lord? Oh dear. She had planned to meet him at the Hall with her brother. Not standing along the side of the road with a lame horse. Perhaps he wouldn't stop.

No such luck. The coach came to a halt right next to her.

At least she wore Hannah's cloak over her muddy dress. And her bonnet shaded her face. If the conversation went quickly, perhaps there would be no need for introductions.

Before either coachman could alight, the door swung open, and a man climbed out. She gripped Bessie's harness. How could this be the new baron? He was younger than she'd imagined, Thomas' age perhaps. And far too handsome.

"Good afternoon," he said. Curious toffee-brown eyes regarded her. "Are you all right?"

An American accent. It had to be him. "Good afternoon. I'm fine, sir. But poor Bessie has thrown a shoe, and I fear she is lame as well."

"Do you live close by? I could take you home." He gestured toward one of the coachmen. "One of these fellows here could stay and watch your horse until you send someone."

"That is very kind, but I could not think of leaving Bessie in such a state." Nor could she contemplate a coach ride of any length with him. Give her wounded animals or distressed children to deal with any day. Handsome men turned her insides into putty. He could at least have the decency to wear a proper mustache and mutton chops, not those short sideburns which just reached his jaw.

He smiled, and her insides pooled liked melted wax. "That's kindhearted of you, but I can't just leave you here on the side of the road."

Kindhearted. As if being handsome weren't bad enough, he had to have a silver tongue as well? No. Enough of that. The last time a man made a favorable first impression, the results had been disastrous.

"I will not be alone for long, I assure you," she said. "My traveling companion has gone for help. She should be back at any moment."

He hesitated. "I don't know."

Voices drifted from farther ahead on the road. Hannah and Mr. Briggs, no doubt. "There, I hear her now with one of our farmers. It was very kind of you to stop."

He glanced up the lane. Mr. Briggs and Hannah rounded the corner. His face relaxed. "All right. I guess I can leave now with a clear conscience."

"Yes, indeed. Thank you again for stopping."

"My pleasure." He touched the brim of his hat and climbed back in the coach. As soon as he closed the door, the coach moved on.

She released her stranglehold on Bessie's harness. Not the sort of man she expected, but at least he hadn't asked her name. By the grace of God, he wouldn't recall any of this, and they would have a proper introduction.

John hadn't asked her name. But what business did he have asking for a woman's name? None. He'd come to England as his cousin's heir to settle down quietly and mind his own business. And he intended to do just that. This village of Woodley might be small, but if all went as planned, he probably wouldn't ever see her again.

Now if only everything would go as planned.

He hadn't anticipated a stay in London to settle legal matters, nor had he expected a final letter from William. *You will soon learn of the opportunities I have arranged for you. I know your heart is in medicine, and I would not have your new station in life completely wrench that from your capable grasp.*

Opportunities. They'd come clothed as chairmen of several of London's most prestigious hospitals. All offered the same thing, an invitation to be a consulting physician when he was in London for the Season. And all were turned away disappointed. The new baron's time in London was temporary. He would reside permanently at his country estate in Hampshire.

The coach flew over another bump, and John grabbed the coach strap. Again. The constant shuffle and vibration were draining. London cab rides were smoother than these country roads. The coach turned and ceased its pitching. At last. He peered out the window. Pea gravel. This had to be it, the road to Ashford Hall.

He wiped his hands on his pant legs. Mr. Smith's description of the place gave him the idea it was something of a monstrosity. When the white Palladian mansion drew into view, his suspicions were proved correct. He'd left America to keep to himself. From what he'd seen, he would have plenty of room to do it in. Granted, it was beautiful, but why did it have to be so large?

The coach pulled to a stop, and the door opened before he could grasp the handle. He alighted, and a man in a dark morning coat, vest, and tie came forward.

"Welcome to Ashford Hall, Lord Turner."

Something about the man struck him as familiar. He was the same height as he, but several years older, with carefully combed black hair and a slender, hawkish face. John knew this man from somewhere.

The man glanced back at the rest of the servants and then back to him. "Is there something amiss, my lord?"

"No, not at all. My apologies."

"No need, my lord. I am Parker, the butler."

Even the name sounded familiar.

Parker gestured toward a woman at the head of the line. "Mrs. Lynch, the housekeeper."

The housekeeper? She was younger than he was. The housekeeper at Ashford House had been old enough to be his mother.

Parker sensed his confusion. "Mrs. Lynch is new to Ashford Hall, my lord."

"I see. And does Mr. Lynch work here too?" John asked her.

She gave him a shallow curtsy and a bare dip of the head. Her frosty manner lent a slight chill to the air. "'Mrs.' is a title of courtesy, Lord Turner. I am not married."

"I see. I'm sorry."

"Again, apologies are not necessary, my lord." Parker's words thawed the moment, and he motioned to the man standing next to Mrs. Lynch. "This is George Avery, your valet."

George stood at attention with a brave, determined look plastered on his face. Like any good soldier, he wouldn't look John in the eye. Was he the valet, or was John back in the Union Army? John sought to reassure him.

"Hello, George." John should call him "Mr. Avery," but he seemed far too young for the title to stick comfortably. "It's been a while since I've had a valet, but I'm sure we'll get along fine."

A grin appeared until Parker cleared his throat. John hadn't meant to get him into trouble.

So he was back to having a valet. While he had trained in London, one of Lord Renshaw's footmen had served him. William had even offered to send the man to Edinburgh with him but—

That's who he is. John gave Parker a quick glance. He was older now but definitely the same man who valeted for him all those years ago. Did he remember him?

Parker introduced the rest of those assembled, with the

exception of the cook and her staff, who were preparing dinner. Once he'd introduced the last housemaid and John had thanked them for welcoming him to the Hall, they walked away along the outside of the house, save a footman who strode up the front steps and waited by the door.

"Wouldn't it be easier for them to go through the front door?"

"They'll enter through the servants' entrance at the back of the house," Parker said. "You always were one to question our customs, my lord, if I may be so bold."

"So you do remember me."

"It is hard to forget a man who refused to let me do my job for the first two weeks." He tilted his head. "I trust that won't be the case now?"

"I'm still an American, Parker. I can't promise to do everything as an Englishman would, but I'll do my best not to start another revolution." He extended his hand, but Parker frowned at it. "Please."

As if a weight were attached, Parker offered his in return, and John gave it a quick shake. "It's good to see you."

"And you, my lord."

The warmth in his voice hinted to the less formal man John had once known. "When did you become butler here?"

"Mr. Gates, my predecessor, retired about a year after you left the country. The butler at Ashford House was still in his prime, and so Lord Renshaw decided to give me the position."

"It's good to see a familiar face."

"If I'm not mistaken, this is your first time seeing Ashford Hall," Parker said. "The estate agent, Mr. Howard, and his sister meant to be here when you arrived, but they've been delayed. Allow me to show you the house while you wait."

A tour? No. Couldn't he sit without being bounced around every few seconds?

"Actually, I'm tired. Can it wait? I would really just like to find a quiet place to sit."

"If you wish, my lord." The butler smiled. "In fact, I know the very place."

"Thank you."

Parker extended his arm, and John preceded him up the steps and through the double doors.

His hands clenched. An airy front hall paved with marble and edged with engaged columns frowned on him as if challenging his right to take ownership.

Parker led him to a door to their immediate left. He opened it and stood back for John to enter.

There were no walls, at least not in the traditional sense. Instead, there were shelves upon shelves of books broken only by windows which offered a view of the front drive. To the right were more books and a fireplace banked with wingback chairs and a comfortable sofa.

"This first section is for more leisurely reading."

John started. "The first section?"

"Yes, sir. Beyond those columns and around the corner to the left is the section devoted to more scholarly pursuits."

Beyond the smooth, marbled pillars stood more shelves of books. The next section beyond the columns was considerably larger.

By a whole second story.

The length of the room was almost equal to that of the gallery and boasted shelves so tall a spiral metal staircase in each far corner rose to the narrow balconies running along its sides. A long carved wooden table with matching chairs dominated the center of the space, like a dining room table. More wingback chairs dotted the margins for good measure. Parker opened a set of double doors which divided the shelves at the rear of the room.

"Another section?" John asked.

"A study. It was, of course, Lord Renshaw's before he passed. He did all his estate business here with Mr. Howard."

John walked in. There were more shelves filled with books, but they did not encompass every inch of wall space. A large wooden desk stood before a window that looked out to the rear of the house, and paintings lined the upper portion of the wall. What a grand library.

"Will this do, my lord?" Parker asked.

"Yes, very much." This would more than do. He'd sleep in here if he thought he could get away with it.

"I'm sure you will be pleased to see this as well, sir." Parker gestured to his right. "Before he died, Lord Renshaw asked that these volumes be moved here from the outer room."

Medical titles both old and new filled the shelves. The latest edition of *Gray's Anatomy*. Bound past issues of *The Lancet*. And there on the desk sat the most recent edition of the medical journal.

He closed his fists. "Move them back where they were."

"My lord?"

He picked up the medical journal and handed it to him. "And please see about canceling this subscription."

The butler paused for the barest of moments before taking it. "Will that be all for now, my lord?"

"Yes, thank you."

Parker didn't understand. How could he? It was clear William had told him what to expect from his heir, and he wasn't living up to it. Nothing he could do about that. Parker and the staff would have to accept it.

But he could see what novels this library contained. He ambled back out to the front section and perused the shelves. Mallory, Hawthorne, Whitman, Carroll, Dickens, Thackeray, Bronte, Austen, Blake, Shakespeare, Wordsworth, Tennyson—a man could read for a solid year and not get through everything this one section contained. He reached for *A Tale of Two Cities,* then paused. He'd never read it, and nothing kept him from doing so right now. Except the *Lancet.*

No. He wasn't going to ask Parker to bring it back. He wasn't. He snatched the Dickens and read and re-read *It was the best of times, it was the worst of times* ... before snapping the book down. He jumped from the chair and left the library. That tour sounded better after all.

CHAPTER 4

The look of concerned irritation on Thomas' face was the first thing Penelope noticed when they pulled up in front of Fairview. But the irritation vanished the moment he got a good look at them.

"What on earth happened to you? Where's Bessie?"

"Never mind Bessie. Miss Penelope fell trying to rescue, of all things, a cat," Hannah blustered.

"What? Where?"

"The Castle," Penelope replied as her brother helped her down. "Bessie threw a shoe, and her leg is lame. Mr. Briggs kindly lent us his mare."

"Why were you there?"

"Never mind that." Hannah rounded the cart and took hold of Penelope's arm. "You need to get yourself to the Hall to meet the new lord. She needs to give this wrist a good long soak."

"Word came from the Hall almost twenty minutes ago that Lord Turner arrived," Thomas said. "I sent a note to say that we would be late. But I imagine you won't be coming with me as planned, old girl."

"I'm afraid not," Penelope replied. "Hannah, thank you. I'll come to the kitchen as soon as I've changed. I'm sorry if I scared you." And she had scared the woman who took such good care of her and Thomas. Color only now returned to her cheeks.

"Humph." But the noise held a note of warmth. "Just you watch yourself next time." She walked inside.

"Change?" Thomas asked.

Penelope lifted the edge of the cloak and revealed her muddy dress. "But first I want to add a note of apology to the welcome basket I prepared for Lord Turner." When Thomas glanced at his pocket watch, she added, "I won't take long, I promise."

In the study, cheese, fresh bread, and last fall's jams sat in a basket she had prepared earlier that morning. After pulling paper from a drawer, she dipped Thomas' pen into the inkwell. It didn't take long to scratch out her regrets, though she lingered as she folded and sealed her note.

Should she tell Thomas she met him? No, there was little point in that. She could just imagine that conversation at the Hall. "Oh, by the way, that bedraggled woman you met along the road earlier today was my sister. So sorry she couldn't come." Not the impression she wished to make. She would meet him neat, cleaned up, and ready to make a good first impression.

His arrival still didn't seem credible, though. That or the fact he had left America so soon after being located. Mr. Smith's message a scant two weeks ago had been sparse on detail and left her, at least, with questions. What had the doctor done with his practice, and what about his patients? What sort of doctor would or could just pick up and leave? Mr. Smith mentioned he had registered him with the General Counsel in London, so he must mean to practice here.

Her brother lifted the cloth on the basket and read the label on a jar of jam. "You know this wasn't really necessary. This all gets sent over anyway. Mrs. Lynch already has jars of this in the Ashford Hall stores."

"I doubt Parker will be taking him through the stores when he shows him the house." She placed the note in the basket. "My aim is to show him what the Home Farm does by giving him a sample of what it produces for the use of the Hall. He may have lived in England before, but that was in London, and he won't know anything about our country ways. I only regret I won't get a chance to see him taste that jam. He's sure to be hungry after his long journey."

Thomas rolled his eyes good-naturedly. "He's a man, old girl. I doubt jam will be the first thing on his mind after traveling thousands of miles by both land and sea."

"Oh? You're always glad for your tea and biscuits after your trips to Somerset." She attempted to give him the basket with just her good hand, but it was too heavy.

"I won't leave it, don't worry." He sorted through the satchel on his desk with a deep "v" between his brows. This was going to be a hard day for him, all things considered.

"I'm sorry," she said.

He waved his hand. "Don't worry about it. I won't be that late."

"That's not what I mean. I know you were angry about the estate."

"The estate? Why?"

"Uncle William didn't leave things exactly as you hoped." She'd noticed his clenched fists when Mr. Smith went over the will.

"Ah, Uncle's will. I was never angry."

"You seemed to be."

"I didn't mean to. I'm sorry if I made you think so."

"Are you certain?"

"Why should I be angry? Uncle William left me Fairview and a good job. I'm just worried you might be angry."

"Me?" She gaped at him. "How could I ever be cross with Uncle William?"

"You were given nothing. The entirety of Ashford Hall and its assets are unentailed, his to give as he chose, and he left you nothing."

It had been odd, Uncle William not leaving her anything. But then he had done so much for her already. If it weren't for him, where would her angel be resting? The bottom of the Thames? She cleared her throat. "Not 'nothing.' I still get to serve the Hall. That is inheritance enough."

"Assuming the new lord hasn't brought a wife with him."

"Yes, of course." He hadn't. He had been the only one in the coach. However, that did not mean someone wouldn't follow later. "But I assume even if Lord Turner has a wife or sister, I will still be permitted to remain living here in your grand home. Uncle knew you would never turn me out into the cold."

"As you're my sister, I suppose I must allow it." He dodged her playful slap on the arm. "Why do you do so much? Seeing to the Hall's tenants and helping Mr. Gregory with the boys' school and the church festivals, not to mention the cottage hospital."

"Thomas, you know I can't help it. I need to, like Mother always did."

"You'd curl up and die if you didn't, I suppose." He nodded at her hand which she held close to her waist. "Hopefully, that won't slow you down."

"This? I'll be fine in a day or two. It won't even keep me from doing my regular visits tomorrow."

"'Regular visits'? What were you doing today?"

"I wanted to call on Mr. Fletcher and make sure he was doing all right."

"Why did you stop at the Castle?"

Her mouth went dry. "No particular reason. We were a little early, and I wanted to stop."

"I haven't been there in ages. Is that huge tree still there near the wall?"

"Yes." Before he could ask more, she went on, "At any rate, this poor kitten wandered into the square tower and got itself stuck." She told him the rest.

"Hmm. The paths are slippery in there when it rains." He raised his brow and gave her a grin. "Good thing you're a tough old girl."

"Yes, good thing." She rubbed her sore wrist. There was a time when he would have shown more concern. That time she had fallen in front of the house when they were children. Who had cried more? At least he still had faith in her. That was something. Wasn't it?

She drew a little closer. Where was his tie pin? "Where is the tie pin Uncle William left you? I thought you meant to wear it today."

"I know," he said. "I lost it yesterday trying to get the cart out of a rut."

"How awful! Where did it get stuck? I could look for it tomorrow."

"I doubt it. I was just south of Highclere. I'll send word I lost it in case it's found."

Highclere? "What business did you have being there when you needed to get ready for Lord Turner's arrival?"

Her brother's blue eyes darkened slightly, and his Vandyke beard bristled as he set his jaw.

"I'm sorry, Thomas. You know I didn't mean to sound like Papa."

Paper snapped as he rolled up his map of the estate and meticulously placed it in its leather tube.

"You run the estate as well as he did, if not better. If he were here, he would be proud."

Thomas stilled. "Would he? He would *say* that?"

Silence hung about them heavier than a London fog. She traced a finger along the edge of the desk. "He was never one to give praise lightly."

"He was never one to give praise at all." Hurt edged his rigid voice. "Especially to me."

Why hadn't their father been able to accept Thomas for who he was? The quiet, fastidious man had striven to make his life like a well-oiled machine. But Thomas had been a faulty part, and Papa had never hesitated to remind him of that fact. His sharp words and criticism were meant to be tools to set her brother to rights. Instead, they reinforced the notion that while Papa might have loved Thomas, he never really *liked* him.

Penelope went about righting the mess she'd made on Thomas' desk. A leather-bound book revealed itself from beneath a spare sheet of paper. Was that what she thought it was? She brushed her fingers across the cover. She started to open it, but his hand suddenly came down on top of it, his face soft yet inscrutable.

"I had time yesterday. You were off visiting Mrs. Reynolds."

"I'm sorry. Could I see what you have done? Or is it not ready for mortal eyes?"

The fanciful phrase from their youth eased the tension. His mouth twitched before a small smile appeared.

"No. Not yet." He scooped up the book and stuffed it in his satchel before taking hold of the basket. "I need to go."

Penelope followed him to the door and watched as he drove the cart down the drive. *Let Lord Turner be pleased with Thomas and bother to tell him so.*

CHAPTER 5

"Are you sure, my lord?" Mr. Howard asked John as they rode down the lane from the Hall the next morning. "It's rather unconventional."

"I'm an American. Lord Renshaw once told me being unconventional is one of our defining characteristics." John shifted in his saddle. "We're about the same age, and calling you Mr. Howard or Howard doesn't sit right with me."

"Call me Thomas."

"Good. And you may call me John." He adjusted the reins in his hands. "Thank you for taking me around to see some of the tenants on such short notice. I hope I didn't make trouble for your wife."

"My pleasure, but I'm not married," Thomas said. "My sister helps me run Fairview."

"And Fairview is the Home Farm?"

"Correct."

His breath caught in his throat. It was still incredible he owned so much. Aside from the Hall, he had property in Somerset, the town of Southampton, and the Isle of Wight. And then Fairview, the Home Farm, raised all of the Hall's food. Though he owned the farm but not the house. That had gone to Thomas. And his sister, it seemed.

"What else does your sister do?"

"The question is what doesn't she do," Thomas replied with a snort. "Aside from helping our reverend, Mr. Gregory, with a number of projects, she also visits the tenants on the Hall's behalf."

"She visits on the Hall's behalf?"

"It's all very proper, I assure you. She's at an age that there is really no need for a chaperone, especially here in the country. Although our housekeeper does accompany the old girl sometimes."

So she was his older sister then. Good. "I'm sure everything is done appropriately. But is there really a need for someone other than you to visit them?"

"Maybe not as often as she does, but then she likes to be helpful. It's tradition for the lady of the manor to call on those tenants who are ill or less fortunate. My mother did it in my aunt's place since her health was poor, and my sister inherited the responsibly from her." He cocked his head at John. "You are aware my aunt was the late Lady Renshaw?"

"Yes, Parker mentioned it."

"It's not the usual arrangement. If you had a wife or a sister, she would be expected to take it on. There are those who say my sister should be turning her attention to something more suited to her age, but as I said, she draws such satisfaction from everything she does for the Hall and for Woodley." He shrugged. "I haven't the heart to stop her."

"Do some of the tenants have a problem with her?"

"Oh, no, the tenants and those who rent from you in Woodley couldn't be happier. But Mrs. Baines of Hartsbury Manor has complained to me before. It's nothing to concern you."

"Are you sure? I don't want to make things complicated." That was the last thing he needed.

"Mrs. Baines is in a very small minority." Humor edged his voice. "You should worry more that she has a niece, a Miss Isabella Abbott, whom she and her brother, Sir James, want to get married off."

John rubbed the back of his head. That was the greater concern indeed. "Thank you, I'll keep that in mind."

It was a good day to visit. A cloudless, cerulean sky and a coolness to the air which hinted autumn was not far off. Color already inched its way onto a few trees. No wonder William had taken so many trips back here while John studied in London. A restfulness lay here, which meant it might be worth trying to get a handle on the enormity of his inheritance.

Thomas snapped his fingers. "Two of the Apostles."

"What?"

"I knew our names reminded me of something. I'm not sure how I feel about being the Doubter. At least you're named after the disciple Christ loved."

His cautiously happy mood melted away. The disciple Jesus loved. That was his name, but was that how he saw himself? Loved by God? He wasn't so sure.

Before he left the Hall, Parker had informed him of William's custom of assembling the servants in the front hall for Scripture reading every morning. He tried to decline, but the butler had already assembled the staff and told him they were waiting. Before he knew it, he was standing in front of them with William's Bible in his hand. Not knowing what to choose, he'd allowed the book to fall open in his hand and read the first thing his eyes landed on. "But whoso shall offend one of these little ones which believe in me, it were better for him that a millstone were hanged about his neck, and that he were drowned in the depth of the sea."

He reached up to his neck as if he could already feel the rope there. No. After failing so miserably, how could the Divine Father still love him?

They rode all morning from one tenant to another. All were happy to meet him. Each farm, large or small, was well kept and neat. Wherever someone held a concern, Thomas listened carefully and jotted it down in the small notebook he kept in his breast pocket.

John took note of what he was told of Miss Howard. She was "a dear thing" and "such a kind woman," but how sad she hadn't made a good match. The more he heard about her, the more eager he was to meet her. He couldn't help but admire her kind nature and hard work for his tenants.

But the tenants were eager to see him "settled," as they put it. Upon discovering he wasn't married, many of them hinted how the young Abbott girl had come out just last Season and that Hartsbury Manor would one day be hers, there being no entail upon the estate. Hartsbury's and Ashford's estates adjoined, making the match even more advantageous in the tenants' eyes. By the end of the morning, dodging their nudging had become an art form.

And Thomas suffered from their matchmaking efforts too. Several mothers made an effort to have their elder daughters on hand to meet them, and all of them eyed him with undisguised admiration.

By early afternoon, John and Thomas had visited all the largest farms save one. They rode down its manicured lane to find the farmer giving orders to one of his laborers. He gestured at them, and they waved at Thomas, then he took hold of the horses' bridles as they dismounted.

"Good morning, Mr. Howard." The farmer pumped his hand. "I didn't expect to see you again so soon."

"Good morning, Mr. Cole. I've come to introduce Lord Renshaw's heir, Lord Turner. Lord Turner, may I introduce Fredrick Cole."

The man's jovial manner became respectful as he offered a bow. "My lord, welcome to Oak Hill Farm."

John suppressed a groan. The bows and curtsies were beginning to wear on him. "Good morning, and thank you." He looked around the courtyard. "You have a fine-looking farm here."

For the next hour, Mr. Cole showed them the barns and animals, and they also walked out to the edge of the man's fields. John slowed as they returned, a hand on his left leg. His old war injury always came back to haunt him whenever he walked or rode too long.

Mr. Cole noticed he was lagging behind. "Are you all right, Lord Turner?"

"I'm fine." He caught up with the two men. "Please, let's continue."

Thomas asked Mr. Cole about next year's planting. John tried to listen, but the dull ache in his thigh began to grow. *Not now.* His tenants needed to see a healthy, capable man, not a wounded cripple, but he'd need his cane for a few days if he didn't sit down. He'd hated using the blasted thing after his leg had finally healed. The practical part of him, knowing he'd need it again from time to time, kept him from feeding it to the fire once he could walk without it.

He leaned to rub the point where the stray bullet had entered his leg. Piles of limbs filled his thoughts. His leg should have been among them.

Straightening before the two noticed, he forced himself to ignore the pain and concentrated on the conversation, even adding to it at some points. But by the time he shook hands with Mr. Cole and their horses had been brought out, he felt as if his leg were on fire. Somehow, he managed to swing himself onto his horse and wish the farmer a good day. He followed Thomas until they rounded a corner and the farm was out of sight. Then he reined in and rubbed his thigh.

"Are you all right?" Thomas' voice rang with concern. "Did you take a bad step back there?"

"I'm fine." He tried to shift himself in the saddle to make his leg ache less, but his movements didn't sit well with the animal beneath him. His horse sidestepped, and he gritted his teeth. "I injured my leg in the war. It's healed, but if I ride or walk too much, it acts up."

"And we've done a good deal of both today," Thomas replied. "We're quite close to the Home Farm. Why don't we stop? We can have tea, and you can go on to the Hall from there."

Within a few minutes, they were riding up to Fairview's door. John's leg protested as he slid to the ground, but the pain had eased somewhat. If he could just sit down. He made his way over to the benches on either side of the front door.

Thomas took charge of his horse. "There's no place to leave the horses, and our stable boy seems to be missing. I'll lead them back and send someone to the kitchen to fetch Hannah, our housekeeper. She'll be at the door shortly."

John didn't mind waiting as long as he could sit.

A minute or two after Thomas left, the door opened. "Lord Turner! We were told you'd injured your leg. Can you walk, sir?"

John stared. This was Thomas' housekeeper? The woman he'd tried to help yesterday? Her bonnet had hidden her youth. And her beauty. No, it had to be his maid. Did they have one? She wore an apron but no cap on her burnished gold hair, and her brows constricted over summer blue eyes. Most likely she wondered why he hadn't said anything yet. Whoever she was, he needed to stop his gaping and stand up.

"Certainly, I—" He took a step and stumbled.

She slipped her arm around his waist and splayed her fingers across his lower chest, supporting him. How, he couldn't explain. She was the size of a pixie, and he towered over her.

A warmth spread through his chest at her touch, like a cup of his mother's tea on a cold day. No, it was a purely physical reaction to not being near a woman since Maggie. Yet, the warmth spread to his cheeks as he grasped the hand that burned into his chest. What on earth was wrong with him? She was just trying to help him. That shouldn't affect him at all. Except it did.

"Please, I can manage. I—"

"Nonsense. I've managed taller and heavier men than you, my lord." Her hands remained locked in place as she opened the door wider with her foot. The ease with which she supported him into the house spoke of nursing skill. Was that sort of training normal for English housekeepers?

They made their way into a parlor, and soon she had him settled into a chair. She tucked a pillow behind his back. "Shall I get a hot compress, sir?"

He stretched out his aching leg. "No, thank you. It simply needs rest."

She brought a side table closer to his high-backed chair. As she did so, an older woman entered, scanning the room. "Where did that little stool get off to?"

The housekeeper said, "Oh, of course. The cushion tore, and I took it to my room to mend it. I'll go get it. We must elevate that leg."

She left before he could protest. All his leg needed was a few minutes rest. That would be enough to get him back to the Hall. Once there, he could keep off it for the rest of the day and not have to resort to that ridiculous cane.

The other woman had stayed behind and managed a stiff curtsy.

This was Thomas' sister? She had to be, with her officious manner and her age. And Thomas constantly referred to her as "old girl." She was much older than John had imagined, too old to be running all over the countryside and Woodley on a regular basis. No wonder Mrs. Baines complained. What could Thomas be thinking?

"You must excuse us, my lord. My hip isn't what it used to be, and I'm afraid I wrenched it recently." She limped over to him.

If it weren't for his own leg, he would have jumped up and helped her. No, she shouldn't continue doing rounds for Ashford Hall. If Thomas wouldn't curb her other activities, he could at least put a stop to that. Surely Thomas could find someone to replace her if needed. And the sooner, the better.

"Is there anything else I can get you, my lord? Tea?"

Tea sounded wonderful, but it would be best if this were dealt with first. He took a deep breath. "In a moment. Won't you please sit down?"

"You want me to sit down?" The uncertainty in her voice was unmistakable.

"Yes, please. We need to talk."

She lowered herself onto a sofa across from him and perched on the very edge.

He clasped his hands, gathering the right words. "I understand you are a hard worker, and I admire everything you do for my tenants and in Woodley. Everyone speaks very highly of you."

"Thank you, my lord." Her voice sharpened.

Of course, the matter must have been approached before. "I hope you won't see me as some ignorant American riding in to change everything just to change it. But I truly feel this particular change would be for the best."

Her mouth twitched. "My lord—"

"This is as hard for me to say as it is for you to hear." He laid his hand over her folded ones. "I'm worried you may be spreading yourself too thin, Miss Howard, and in light of your injury, I think it would be better if you stopped your visits to the tenants." She slipped one hand from his grasp and covered her mouth. He grimaced, wanting to take back what he said. But how could he? "I'm very sorry."

Miss Howard's large form shook and her face glowed red—with barely suppressed laughter.

What on earth was the matter? He had imagined disappointment or even tears, but not this.

The woman pressed her lips together and tried to compose herself by flapping the edge of her apron like a fan across her face.

"Miss Howard?"

A peal of laughter was her only response.

"Oh dear!" The young housekeeper stood in the doorway, her brow creased with consternation. "My lord, I am so sorry, I should have made the introductions before I left the room."

She strode forward and set the stool down. "Hannah, please, compose yourself." Hannah nodded and, with a deep breath, covered her mouth with her hand. She managed to school her features, although her eyes still twinkled.

The younger woman grasped the skirts of her now apronless dress, bowed her head, and curtsied. "My lord, if I may be so bold, I am Penelope Howard."

CHAPTER 6

Which was worse? Meeting him disheveled and muddy on the side of the road, or meeting him like this? Etiquette demanded Penelope be introduced to him by her brother, but the need to rectify the current situation was far greater. She laid a hand on her housekeeper's shoulder. "This is Hannah Trull, our housekeeper and cook."

The new lord of Ashford Hall shifted in his seat. "Mrs. Trull, I apologize—"

"Please do not apologize, Lord Turner. In light of the unusual circumstances, I should have introduced myself as soon as I opened the front door." Why hadn't Thomas sent for someone to take the horses and waited to make the introductions? Then again why had she gone to the door in the first place? She hadn't thought. All she'd heard was Lord Turner was injured, and off she went.

She turned to Hannah. "Why don't you rest your hip and keep Lord Turner company while I help Fanny prepare the luncheon?"

Hannah rose, albeit stiffly. "With all due respect, I've rested enough for one day. I didn't wrench it that bad. You, literally on the other hand . . ."

She took hold of Penelope by her bandaged wrist and pulled her toward Lord Turner. "You're a doctor, my lord. Look at the state of her hand. Sprained this only yesterday. Had no business helping you into the house, but would she send Fanny or let me do it? No! Shot straight to the front door." She extended Penelope's hand toward him for his inspection.

Now less than two feet away, Penelope was forced to do what she'd been avoiding the instant she'd first seen him at the side of the road. She looked at Lord Turner full in the face. Her heart began to run races around her flip-flopping insides.

His slender face colored as his strong, capable hands grasped her wrist. He turned it from side to side before letting it go, embarrassed by Hannah's forthrightness. "It does look swollen, Miss Howard."

She nodded as she drew her hand back to her chest. Why on earth had Hannah put both of them in such an awkward position? She sought her head for something to stop her thumping heart and found it. *Handsome faces seldom are.* Yes, she should know that well enough by now. Her heart slowed, and she prayed it would be easier to look at him with that maxim—as well as the memories behind it—in place.

"Let's set ourselves back to our proper places, shall we?" Hannah took her by the arms and pushed her into her seat on the couch. "*I'll* go to the kitchen, and *you* see to Lord Turner. Master Thomas will be joining you shortly, I imagine." She placed the stool where Lord Turner could make use of it. "My lord, *she* is the one you want to speak to about spreading herself too thin."

She dipped her head and made her way out the door.

Penelope smoothed her skirt. "I hope you will excuse Hannah, Lord Turner. She has a tendency to be a little brusque." She tipped her head up. There, that was better. Her insides were settled. Until his face relaxed somewhat and he swept a few loose strands of cinnamon spice hair away from his forehead.

"Don't worry about it. I used to know a woman a lot like her back in Philadelphia." He directed his attention to her wrist. "Unless you're in more pain than you're letting on, it doesn't look that bad."

"It's not bothering me, my lord." And it wasn't. She had only mildly strained it.

"I take it Miss Trull was your traveling companion yesterday?"

"*Mrs.* Trull, and yes, she was."

"Why didn't you just tell me who you were?"

Her face warmed. "I hoped to be formally introduced to you under better circumstances." How ridiculous. Better circumstances? She raised a hand to her mouth, but Lord Turner laughed, and she joined him.

"Thank you, Miss Howard," he said. "I haven't had a hearty laugh in a long time."

Penelope dabbed at her eye with her knuckle. "I'm sorry to hear that, my lord."

"That's all right." His expression cooled. "War isn't very cheerful."

"Of course. You served, did you not?"

"Yes." He entwined his fingers, and his attention drifted somewhere far away from her parlor.

She rose and stepped over to the tea service. How foolish to have mentioned the war. And he'd already somehow hurt himself. A cup of tea seemed like a small thing, and as an American, he probably preferred a strong cup of coffee, but perhaps it would help ease his melancholy.

She poured him a generous cup, added milk and sugar, and took it over to him. "Here, my lord."

He looked at her, then at the cup and saucer she offered him. A light came to his eyes that she wasn't sure how to place. He accepted the cup, and she resumed her seat. After taking a sip, the glint in his eyes intensified.

She shifted in her seat. Had she made it wrong? "I'm sorry, my lord. Would you prefer it different?"

"Not at all. In fact, if I didn't know better, I'd say my mother had made this herself." He lifted the cup and breathed in the scent of the brew, then released his breath with a sigh. "This is the first cup of tea I've been offered since arriving in England. People think I want coffee since I'm American, but my parents were English and raised me on tea. I don't even like coffee."

"That is a blend from a company in Andover, not far from here." She would send a supply over to the Hall the next time she ordered some for the farm.

"It's wonderful. Thank you." He took another sip, and his light mood restored. He asked about her wrist. "How did it happen?"

"It's rather silly, I'm afraid. I was rescuing a trapped kitten."

"Trapped?"

"Perhaps your lordship passed by ruins on the way to the Hall yesterday?" They were visible from the road that led to the Hall's main drive.

"Yes, I did see those. I meant to ask Parker about them, but I didn't have the chance. What are they? An old abbey?"

"No, the remains of the original Hall, known as the Castle. It was built by the first Baron but destroyed during our own civil war. A few of the towers are still standing, and the kitten was trapped in one of them." She related the rest of the story to him. "It was a silly thing to do."

"Why would you call that silly?"

"It is, isn't it?" Hannah had said so yet again while Penelope soaked her hand.

"Rescuing something small and helpless? I think it's admirable. Not silly."

Penelope tidied the lightly soiled strips of cloths covering her wrist. "You are too kind, my lord."

"I mean it."

"Thank you," she murmured.

Admirable. As if yesterday's compliment hadn't been bad enough. What could she do with those words and the danger they posed? They needed to be buried so there would be no lasting harm. But already, more than just her cheeks were warm. His praise had slipped past her defenses and begun to kindle a cold place in her heart. It had been an age since anyone spoke to her like that or had seemed so pleased with her. Not since Mama passed. Oh, Thomas had faith in her and Hannah fussed, but to hear a simple, kind word?

Lord Turner cleared his throat. "Are you all right? Does your hand hurt?"

Her emotion must have shown on her face. Her heart jumped at his concern, and she forced it to be still.

Thomas strode in. "Oh, she's a tough old girl. Nothing slows her down, does it, Pen?" He sat next to her on the sofa. "Actually, I'm surprised to find you here. I thought you were visiting today."

Thank goodness for Thomas; his timing couldn't have been better.

"Hannah insisted on going with me to handle the cart. But then she slipped and wrenched her hip. It isn't serious, but I thought better of going out." She addressed Lord Turner. "I assure you, I do plan to make my visits tomorrow."

"If, of course, you are agreeable with her continuing to do so," Thomas added.

Lord Turner set his cup on the side table. Here it was. He was going to tell her not to continue with her visits. She straightened her spine.

"I heard nothing but your praises all day, Miss Howard," he said. "I can't imagine a better person to see to the tenants." Traitorous delight coursed through her, until he continued. "However, I will allow you to continue on one condition. You must promise to go for help if you come across another kitten that needs to be rescued."

"Of course, my lord." Was it relief or his teasing that caused her heart to pound so? Mercifully, Thomas spoke before she could decide.

"So she told you about her adventure yesterday. Tough old girl, isn't she?"

"Well, I wouldn't call her old."

So that was why Lord Turner had mistaken Hannah for her. "That is merely my brother's unfortunate nickname for me, my lord." She didn't mind Thomas using it between the two of them, but did he have to refer to her to others that way?

"But accurate," her brother retorted. "Papa always said you went from a babe in arms to responsible young lady practically overnight. And he was the first one to use it, not me."

"I hated it when my mother called me Johnny," Lord Turner said to Thomas. "Did your father have an embarrassing name for you?"

He couldn't know what a precarious question that was. Their father hadn't had any pet names for him. Just long-suffering sighs, annoyed looks, and a sharp word or two. She held her breath as her brother tapped a fist against his knee. "No. Just Thomas."

"Let me get you some tea, Thomas." She rose and changed the subject as she poured another cup. "How do you like the state of things, Lord Turner? My brother works very hard to make sure the estate runs smoothly." By the time she returned with his cup, much of the tension had left Thomas' face.

"I agree. I don't know much about running an estate, and it's good to know I have someone as qualified as you helping me."

"Thank you." The slight pink in her brother's cheeks spoke volumes.

"But I can't help but wonder why you haven't married. I'm surprised you haven't courted any of the young ladies we saw today. They certainly were interested."

"A question I've often asked him, my lord." Penelope gave her brother a gentle nudge.

Thomas' fingers shook, and he fumbled his teacup just enough for it to rattle in its saucer. "I don't think my marital status is as interesting as yours. None of the tenants could quite believe you were unmarried."

"Thomas!"

"No, it's all right, Miss Howard." Lord Turner swept off a bit of dust from his trouser leg. "I was serving in the American Army up until a few years ago. Not exactly droves of young ladies there."

"What about afterward? Surely your medical practice left you time for romantic pursuits."

Penelope leaned forward. Whatever his reply, it would turn the conversation toward medicine and how often he planned to visit the cottage hospital. The war was an understandable sore spot, but he wouldn't mind being asked about his practice. But her questions slipped away as a distinct tension filled the room.

"Not as much as you might think." Lord Turner took a deep sip of his tea and plowed forward. "Now, what about these ruins? The Castle. Is it open to anyone who wants to go see them?"

Thomas set his cup aside. "Yes. Lord Renshaw always made it known people can visit whenever they please."

"I'd like to see them for myself. In light of your sister's injury, I want to make sure no one else can get hurt."

"One of the Ashford Hall gardeners is in charge of tending to it. We can see what he recommends."

He leaned forward. "I wonder if it might be better to completely seal them off somehow."

"But … s-surely, my lord." The words tripped as they left her mouth. She swallowed and forced her heart back down into her chest. "I beg your pardon, but surely something that drastic isn't necessary. I mean, Mr. Truett could simply close off the tower where I slipped and fell. Uncle William—Lord Renshaw—was exceedingly proud to show the county the origins of the barony and the Hall." It was unfair to play on his emotions, but the need to be free to visit the ruins overrode all else.

He rubbed the back of his neck. "Well, I suppose closing them off completely might be a bit much."

Her muscles tingled as the tension left them. "Thank you, Lord Turner."

"Of course. I don't want to change anything that was so important to William."

As the two men fell to discussing the proper raising of sheep, Penelope fixed herself a cup of tea. That had been a near thing. Not just the closing of the Castle, but her outburst. Maybe she shouldn't have spoken. Wouldn't it be best if she were forbidden from visiting? She could go on with her life. Her secret angel would rest safely.

Pain rose in her chest as the ghostly echo of a child's laughter slipped through the corridors of her mind.

She moved back toward the men and forced her thoughts to their conversation. But that only served to turn her attention to Lord Turner, a subject nearly as unsafe as her angel.

Handsome faces seldom are.

Yes, of course. And hadn't that already proved a little true? Why had he gotten so uncomfortable about Thomas' mention of his medical practice? Or had the subject of marriage agitated him? No, it wasn't until the mention of his practice that he had gone so cold. Why? Did it have something to do with how he had managed a swift arrival? But as she tried to reinforce her imaginings on the man who spoke words of encouragement to her brother, they refused to stick and fell in a heap at her feet.

A quarter of an hour later, Lord Turner set down his empty cup and rose. She and Thomas followed suit.

He rubbed his leg. "I think I can make it back to the Hall now."

"Are you sure, my lord? We could send a stable boy with you," Penelope suggested.

Thomas shot her a flat look. "Of course he's sure."

"No, your sister is just being thoughtful." Lord Turner caught her gaze. "You're very kind, but I'll be fine."

"Then I shall go and send someone for your horse, my lord." She made for the door before the warmth she felt showed in her cheeks.

CHAPTER 7

As soon as he was out of sight of the Home Farm, John nudged his horse into a canter. Best to get as far away from Penelope Howard as possible. She was kind, considerate, and beautiful—the type of woman who was far too risky for him to be in close proximity to. He urged the great bay beneath him a tad faster. Why had he continued to praise her as he had? Because it was too ingrained in his nature not to. Yet even as the distance between him and Fairview steadily lengthened, it was difficult—if not downright impossible—to erase her image from his mind. What was it Thomas had said about that first tenant they visited? Something about the sheep? Or was that where Miss Howard had said that tea was from?

Blast it! He gave the horse its head. This would not happen again. He would not make the same mistakes with that sweet young woman as he had with Maggie. He had not come all this way for that. He meant to live a quiet life taking care of William's legacy and, for once in his life, not be the cause of trouble. And he would. By God, he would.

No matter how boring or tedious it became. If his conversation with Thomas were any sample of what the day-to-day running of this estate was like, he would soon get bored out of his mind.

The Lancet. Had Parker seen to canceling it yet? It wouldn't hurt to keep abreast of the latest—

No! He wouldn't even dip his toe in those waters again. Too much danger of simply picking up where he left off. People would get hurt, and he would end up breaking another heart. And he'd nearly done that just an hour ago. For whatever reason, Miss Howard felt strongly about The Castle, and he didn't want to be the one to disappoint her by closing it.

Who could do that to a woman such as her? She radiated kindness like the first warmth of fire on a cold day. Which made her large eyes, pert nose, alabaster skin, and honey-gold hair twice as appealing.

A savage growl escaped his throat, and he urged his horse faster.

The searing ache in his leg had returned by the time he reached the Hall. A young groom jogged up to take the horse's bridle as he halted at the front steps. John swung down and clutched the saddle for a moment. He shouldn't have pushed himself.

"Are you all right, my lord?"

"I'm fine. At least I will be once I get inside."

The groom nodded, and the gravel crunched beneath the horse's hooves as he led him away.

John's chair in the library called to him. But the front doors were shut tight and no footman waited to receive him. All right. He'd have to let himself in. But how? He had no key. Was it locked? There was a distinct ridiculousness in the situation, but he would have to find the humor in it later.

"Where has Joseph got to?" the groom said. He and the horse were only a few feet away. "Shall I help you, Lord Turner?"

"What about my horse?"

The groom wrapped the reins around a balustrade. "Fortis is one of our best horses. He won't go nowhere, your lordship."

He strode up and John took his arm. As they reached the door, it opened. Joseph stood there, mouth open like one of the many fish John and his father used to catch.

"Sir—Lord Turner—my lord! I'm so very sorry."

John waved him off as they crossed the threshold. "Don't worry about it. If you would, open the door to the library for us."

He raced ahead of them. "Yes, my lord, of course."

The groom helped John into his chair, while Joseph hovered. He then turned on the footman. "I've a good mind to box your ears, Joe. What do you mean leaving your post like that?"

"It wasn't my fault, Arthur." Joseph managed to turn three shades of red. "I had to . . . you know ..."

"Mum will be furious when I tell her. She wants to see you as butler here one day, and you won't go far abandoning your post, no matter what the reason."

John wouldn't mention the incident to Parker. But he would ask him to assign another footman in the hall. "Joseph, as I said, don't worry about it. You're not the first man who had to answer nature's call at the wrong moment. I made it inside. Now, why don't you go back to your post before Mr. Parker comes along?"

Joseph couldn't move fast enough. Arthur, on the other hand, had walked trance-like to the wall of books behind him.

"It had the same effect on me too," John said.

The groom started. "I'm sorry, my lord. I'm partial to books."

"No reason to be sorry about that. I am too." He gestured for Arthur to take the seat across from him. Arthur perched on the very edge, back as straight as a board. "What do you like to read?"

"I read part of one of Mr. Dickens' stories once. Never got a chance to read the rest."

"Which one?"

He named it, and John squinted as he scanned the shelves. "Right there on the other side of the fireplace toward the middle."

Like a skittish colt, Arthur rose and found the book.

"Just bring it back when you're done."

"Really? Thank you. I'll take care with it." He opened his mouth to say more but shut it again.

"What?"

"I was wondering, Joseph told me one of the maids told him the late Lord Renshaw had medical books in the library." John's sigh caused Arthur to back toward the door. "I'm sorry, my lord. I've overstepped."

"No. It's true." He couldn't believe this was happening. Like it all had been planned out somehow. Had William engineered this too? It wasn't possible. "You're interested in medicine?"

"Yes, my lord." He rushed through the next sentence like a rabbit running from a dog. "I like being a groom here, but I don't want to take care of horses all my life. I want to help people." He snapped his mouth shut, and his face reddened again. Arthur was about nineteen and every bit of awkward. His dark blond hair stuck out at odd angles, his nose dominated his face, and he was a head shorter than John. John should deter him, tell him he was better off in the stables. But how could he? He recognized the eagerness and hope in the young man; it mirrored his own when William had insisted on sponsoring his education.

"What kind of a doctor do you want to be, Arthur ... "

"Wilcox, sir. Arthur Wilcox." He shifted from foot to foot. "What kind of medicine did you do in America, my lord? Did you set bones or tend to the sick?"

Ah, the English tradition that put doctors in two different boxes. A physician attended the sick, while a surgeon set bones and stitched people up. "In America, doctors generally do a little bit of everything."

"Oh. I'm not quite sure, my lord. I don't think I care all that much, so long as I help people."

Help people. There were other ways to help people. He should say as much, but instead he said, "Come on. I think I know where we can find the books to help you decide."

But Arthur glanced out the window. "Begging your pardon, my lord, I should see to Fortis. If I'm not back soon, I'll catch it from the head groom."

"Of course. But when your duties permit, come and find me. I'll make sure Parker knows to admit you."

Arthur left with a light step. Helping him might be the right thing to do. John had taken himself out of the world of medicine. Maybe he'd help replace himself with someone who could do better.

He made his way over to the medical section and scanned the titles for some basic texts. William must have spent a fortune for such a diverse collection. He snagged a rare edition and opened it, unable to take in the words fast enough.

He categorized books in piles, according to what Arthur would need and at what point in his education he would need them, then sat at the massive table.

"My lord?" Joseph said from the doorway.

"Hmm?" He turned the page.

"Dr. Royston, sir."

The spell broke, and a ball as hard as India rubber took up residence in his gut. Behind Joseph stood William's physician when he died. John had wanted to speak to him about his cousin's passing but had intended to call on him—not have the man find him here, surrounded by all these books.

"Lord Turner, how do you do?" The older gentleman offered his hand. "Dr. Henry Royston, at your service. I'm sorry to come uninvited, but I have been so looking forward to the day when I am not the only doctor in Woodley—well, I couldn't help myself."

The man's eyes drifted toward the books.

John rose and took a step forward. "How do you do, Dr. Royston? Won't you sit down? I've been meaning to ask you about my cousin and his final days."

"I'm not sure what I can tell you." Dr. Royston settled into a chair in front of the fireplace. He clasped his hands in front of him. "I presume Mr. Smith told you it was consumption. You know the symptoms and progression of the disease as well as I."

"Yes." He'd seen several cases in Philadelphia when he worked among the poor. "I really just wondered if his passing was peaceful." *And had he known about me?* Despite his last letter, John was still haunted by the notion that William had somehow found out about his downfall.

Understanding softened the man's gaze. "Of course. He passed during the night. So as far as I could ascertain, he slipped away quietly."

John frowned. "There wasn't a nurse sitting with him?"

"He wouldn't allow it. His niece, Miss Howard, tried to convince him to let her stay during the evening hours, but he insisted she return to her room and rest."

"Miss Howard? She nursed him?" Of course. It was just the sort of thing she would do.

"Yes. All but ran the place for those last couple of months. She did see him that last day. I know she would be more than happy to tell you how he was."

"Thank you. I will be sure to ask her." He would, at some point. A delay of a week or so would not change anything. He would have some time to prepare himself, harden his resolve.

Dr. Royston gazed at the bookshelves that flanked the fireplace. "I've long been an admirer of this library." He rose and returned to the books piled on the table. John followed. A tourniquet bound his chest as the doctor picked up a tome. "This must be one of the newer books. Renshaw said he was going to invest in the latest editions." He glanced down at the article John had been reading and grunted. "So what do you make of Pasteur and his germ theory? Rubbish if you ask me."

John flipped the journal shut. "I haven't formed an opinion."

The man arched a brow. "Really?"

"Yes." He cleared the edge from his voice. "I'm sorry if this is rude, Dr. Royston, but I've had a long day."

"Of course. It wasn't very good form for me to come here uninvited in the first place."

"That's all right." The pressure in his chest lessened. He started for the bell pull to summon Joseph but paused when the doctor spoke again.

"But before I go, I want to issue an invitation for you to join me at the cottage hospital whenever you can." Dr. Royston placed the book back in the pile. "Not the most interesting of cases, but we keep busy. There are few such hospitals in this area at the moment."

The tourniquet re-tightened. A cottage hospital? He'd read about them when he was still in the States. William had mentioned the need for one, had even hinted that he would donate the necessary funds. So he'd gone and done it. And in doing so had created another "opportunity" for John. But unlike the ones in London, this one would be far harder to get away from.

"That you are trained as both a physician and a surgeon means your services would be extremely valuable to us," the doctor continued. "The man we usually call to perform surgery, a Mr. Albert Worth, resides an hour or so east of here, which can be tricky when there is an emergency."

He managed a deep breath, releasing it as he spoke. "Unfortunately, the estate will be taking up a good portion of my time."

"Really? I was under the impression Thomas Howard is very adept at his job. You shouldn't worry for anything."

"And I'm sure I won't." John started back toward the bell. "But Ashford Hall and its concerns will be my priority."

"But the hospital is one of the Hall's concerns."

"What do you mean?"

"I mean you are now the patron. The board makes most of the decisions, but you have the final say." He cocked his head and regarded John. "Lord Renshaw gave me the impression that you would be very much involved."

"Well, he was mistaken." He yanked on the bell pull. "If you have any needs or concerns, please inform Mr. Howard. I will let him know to expect to hear from you."

Joseph entered, but Dr. Royston didn't move an inch. "I heard you visited your tenants today. Lord Renshaw, I understand, was always mindful to do that from time to time. But he came to visit the hospital at least once a week. I hope we can count on you do to the same." He gave him a nod and followed Joseph out the door.

CHAPTER 8

Not even Hannah was up when Penelope made her way to the kitchen. She put on the kettle and slathered a slice of bread with jam. Once her tea was prepared, she took her simple breakfast into the parlor and opened the curtains. Through the small rectangular glass panes, the predawn sky glowed orange-red, a warning of rain later in the day. Good thing she had risen early. She could make her visits before the weather broke and still be back for tea with the teacher for the new girls' school.

She yawned. Warm chestnut eyes and a teasing half-smile had haunted her during the night. No, it hadn't been as much that as it had been his praise. *Kindhearted … admirable … I can't imagine a better person … you are very kind …*

Handsome faces seldom are, but in this case—oh no, what if, in this case, that maxim were wrong?

It had to be wrong, it simply had to be. What about his reaction to Thomas asking after his medical practice? Or despite his encouraging manner, how bored he'd clearly been as they spoke of the tenants and the estate? His questions were intelligent and thoughtful, but they were belied by his flat tone and the way he focused on a far corner of the room as her brother answered.

Those two points pruned back his effect on her, and she had finally been able to sleep. But now, as the light crested the hill outside, it threatened to grow. And that would never do. Best get her emotions in order.

She slipped up to her room and returned with her mother's Bible. The well-worn book opened naturally to the passage in John now. She no longer needed to mark it, as Papa had asked. Did she even need to have the words before her? His insistence she read it daily had written them on her heart, if not her very soul. But its meaning was no longer bitter. It was a comfort now. God and the passage of time had changed its meaning as well as her view of the token Papa had given her which rested on the mantel in her room. Even so, there were consequences to every action. Consequences she would live with forever.

She pressed the book shut and, laying it on her knees, spread her hands over the cover. Mind and heart were made up and in order. She would do her best for the Hall, as she always had. Lord Turner could keep his secrets. So long as he did his duty, they were no concern of hers. Besides, how often would she really be seeing him? She could avoid him at the cottage hospital when he visited and had no need to meet with him over her visits to the tenants. She could voice any concerns to Thomas, who would pass them along.

She rose. It was time to get the day started. She would visit the Hall today but did not have to present herself to Lord Turner to pick up the basket Thomas had delivered. Her need for it was sentimental as it had belonged to her mother. Penelope made her way to the stables, ordered the cart, and drove away from Fairview a quarter of an hour later.

She drove to the rear of the house and let herself in by the servant's entrance, as was her habit on her informal visits to the Hall. She navigated the few steps down to the linoleum floor and made her way down the white-walled passage leading to the caverns of the house.

This late in the morning, the staff had already left the servants' hall, but she heard the cook, Mrs. Long, laying down her orders for the day. Penelope peered around the corner into the kitchen. The cook's back was to her as she guided the newest kitchen maid in the intricacies of properly scrubbing a copper pot. Mrs. Long had been the Hall's cook for as long as Penelope could recall and ran it with calm efficiency. She had yet to hear her raise her voice to any of those in her charge, a trait she greatly admired.

Mrs. Long caught sight of her. "Miss Howard, we have not seen you for an age. Would you care to sit down for a minute or two? I find myself with a generous amount of coffee on my hands this morning." She nodded toward the silver tray on the work table before her.

Penelope stepped into the kitchen. "Coffee? You sent up coffee for his lordship this morning?"

The woman crossed her arms over her chest. "Mrs. Lynch was quite adamant he drank it, but this is the second morning that we've sent it up, and he's barely touched the stuff. He's an American, isn't he?"

"Indeed, but I happen to know he prefers tea." She lifted the lid, and its rich brown scent wafted out. "I had it from his lordship himself yesterday."

"And here Mrs. Lynch goes and orders tins and tins of coffee." Mrs. Long shook her head. "I haven't the slightest notion what the state of our tea is like. If it's no good, she won't order more, not until the coffee is gone."

"Not to worry, Mrs. Long. His lordship so enjoyed the tea we served yesterday that I thought I would order some for the Hall as well."

"Order what for the Hall, Miss Howard?" Mrs. Lynch stood at the kitchen door.

"Tea, Mrs. Lynch," Mrs. Long replied. "Miss Howard has it on good authority that Lord Turner is partial to it rather than coffee."

The housekeeper's frown deepened. "Does she? And how did you come by this, Miss Howard? That is rather personal information for a young lady to know about his lordship."

Penelope fought the urge to glance heavenward. Mrs. Lynch was, perhaps, only two years older than she. "Lord Turner stopped by with my brother while they were out visiting tenants yesterday, and he happened to mention it."

"I see," the woman replied as if forced to admit it. "I suppose

I shall have to remedy that, but I haven't a clue as to what to do with all that coffee."

"Why don't you send some of it over to the Home Farm? I'm sure Mr. Howard would appreciate having something other than tea for a change."

Mrs. Lynch's face softened at the mention of Penelope's brother. "Well, I bought quite a bit. I hope he enjoys it." Ice slid back into her voice. "But please remember I am the housekeeper for the Hall now, Miss Howard, and it is *my* responsibility to order the supplies we need for his lordship's comfort. Not yours." She strode down the hallway toward the still room.

Mrs. Long shook her head. "That woman has been after your brother since she was nothing but the head housemaid at Hartsbury Manor. Though why she has it in for you is beyond me."

"I wasn't in favor of her being hired." Penelope watched her retreating figure and sighed. "She overheard me saying as much to Mr. Parker, and we've been on uneasy ground ever since."

Mrs. Long leaned toward her conspiratorially. "I 'spect your disfavor was based on her youth—much too young to run a household, truth be told. But I'll wager you're a little uncomfortable with her attraction to your brother too."

The woman didn't know how right she was.

"Well, at least I know what to do with the coffee." Mrs. Long picked up the pot and started for the sink, then paused. "Unless you still wanted some. I have some time before I have to start on luncheon."

"No, thank you. I only came by to pick up my basket. I sent over a few things with Mr. Howard when he came to visit Lord Turner."

"A basket? Oh yes, I do remember that. I'm sorry, but I don't recall what became of it. We were quite busy preparing his lordship's first meal at the Hall."

A young maid looked up from her work at the far end of the table. "Mrs. Lynch might know what became of it, Miss. I saw her take a basket into her room yesterday."

Penelope overcame the temptation to take a look in the woman's room. Not the best idea if she wanted to make peace with her. Her need for it was purely sentimental.

"We'll keep an eye out for it," Mrs. Long handed the pot to a maid. "I'm sure it's around here somewhere. I'll send it along to Fairview when I find it."

Penelope thanked the cook and bid her goodbye, leaving the pleasant kitchen to return to her cart. She should swallow her opinion of Mrs. Lynch and find a way they could become friends. How could she smooth out the roughness between them? Should she ask her to luncheon with her and Thomas? That would certainly please Mrs. Lynch, but not necessarily her brother. Despite the housekeeper's efforts, Thomas seemed less than interested, although he never failed to act the gentleman. Then again, after his time in London, he had made an effort to seem disinterested in any young lady.

She turned the cart from the lane onto the road, which ran alongside some of the wilder portions of the Hall's land, and caught sight of Lord Turner. He and the Hall's head woodman were walking their horses toward the gate in the estate's fields, close to the roadside hedge. After all that bother with his leg yesterday, and he went out to meet Mr. Gibson on horseback?

They turned toward her as she approached, and Lord Turner raised a hand in greeting. While Mr. Gibson mounted his horse and headed back over the field, Penelope pulled to a stop.

"Good day, my lord."

"Hello. Out on your rounds, I see." He gripped the top of the gate with such strength his knuckles turned white. "No injured animals yet?"

"No, sir, none. But it is early." She gave herself a mental jab. Where had that teasing tone come from? "I see you were with Mr. Gibson."

"I wanted to explore the rest of the grounds beyond the

gardens." He winced as he shifted his weight. "It's bigger than it looks."

"Yes, it is. Even though I grew up here, I always find myself on the grounds without even realizing it."

He studied the ground as if it fascinated him, but his brow held a deep crease. His leg must have been bothering him far more than he cared to reveal.

Perhaps a little impropriety was in order. "Your horse looks a bit winded. Would you like for me to drive you back, my lord?"

"Yes, Fortis could use a break." He reached for the latch in the gate.

Once his horse was secured to the back of the cart, he settled in next to her. If only her heart were as easily controlled as the tired mare she urged into a walk. She struggled to rein it in as he looked down at her with eyes like soft toffee.

"Thank you."

"You are most welcome, my lord."

"No, really, thank you." He shifted his bad leg in front of him. "It was stupid of me to think I could go riding again after yesterday."

"Thomas mentioned you injured it during the war in America."

"Yes. It always acts up when I do too much. I know better."

"They say doctors make the worst patients."

He said nothing, and the air grew as taut as it had yesterday in the parlor. So it *was* something about medicine that disturbed him. But why? According to Mr. Smith, he had the finest training. Why avoid the subject?

It hardly mattered, now did it? It wasn't really any of her business. Hadn't she settled that with herself earlier this morning?

"With your permission, I'll take the road the tradesmen use to deliver goods to the Hall. You could easily walk or ride to the main drive from there without being noticed."

"Thank you, Miss Howard."

The gratitude in his words relieved the tension, but she

struggled with what to say next. She shouldn't say anything, really. That would be best. Oh, but had he enjoyed what she sent over in the basket?

Before she could ask, he said, "Dr. Royston called on me. He said you were with William on his last day. Could you tell me how he was?"

She swallowed as her throat tightened. "As he always was, even considering his condition. Kind. Cheerful. Asking me about how this or that was coming along." Always a finger in every pot. Even in the end. "We watched the sun set that day and then he told me how much he loved Thomas and me. It was as if he knew."

Things will change once I'm gone, dear girl, he'd said. *I know you think your life is exactly as it should be and will be, but it's not. Embrace what's coming.*

"Did he say anything about me?"

She started. Had he? Was that what her uncle had meant by that enigmatic statement? Oh, Uncle William. Even from beyond the grave he still tried to plan and scheme and play the matchmaker. After his triumph with her parents, he apparently meant to duplicate the feat. No wonder he had left her nothing substantial. He intended Lord Turner to be her "inheritance." But why? He'd known how impossible that would be. He himself had all but said that no man would want her in her condition.

She flashed Lord Turner an apologetic gaze. "No, my lord."

For several moments, all that could be heard were the horse's hooves as she walked along to the tradesmen's drive, the gravel crunching and hissing beneath them. Trees dotted the path and seemed to whisper to one another as the wind lazily threaded through their branches. In between them was a stately view of Ashford Hall from the rear as it overlooked the rolling, hedge-lined hills beyond.

"So he was ashamed of me," Lord Turner muttered.

The weight of his words pressed on her, and she drew the cart to a stop.

"My lord, I knew my uncle well. I cannot believe he was ashamed of you." She knew how it had been when he was ashamed of someone close to him. "I'm sure there was no reason for him to be so."

A different sort of tension stretched the air, more perplexing than the previous uneasiness. His jaw clenched and unclenched, and his hand was fisted in an iron-tight ball. "Are you sure, Miss Howard?"

She blinked. "My lord?"

"I think William never told me or you about my being the heir because I was the poor relation." He stared at the Hall. "My father was William's cousin. His father was a landowner and expected him to marry well, but instead, he married a penniless orphan. Grandfather disinherited him, and he and my mother moved to a suburb of Philadelphia." He shrugged. "We lived a simple life, but a happy one."

"Do your parents still live there?"

He shook his head. "They're buried there. My father died in an accident and my mother a few years later."

"I'm so sorry."

"But don't you see? What else could William do when he discovered I was his heir but offer to educate me and make me respectable? And then not tell me for fear I would get too big of a head?"

After spending so much time with him, Lord Turner understood little of her uncle. Then again, he had not seen him for several years. He needed a gentle reminder.

"I'm sorry to be bold," she said, "but surely you recall Uncle William's devotion to his family. He would not have wanted the fact that you were his heir hanging over you."

"Of course. He told me himself he disapproved of my grandfather's actions. Family was more important than rank or position."

"Yes, exactly."

"Then why not tell you and your brother about me?"

"I cannot say." Indeed, she would not say. It would be too mortifying to confess her suspicions of her uncle's machinations. "But his last words to me were full of hope for the future of Ashford Hall. He would not have spoken so if he had been ashamed of you."

"He was a very forgiving soul," the lord muttered.

What a curious statement. "Yes, he was."

"Dr. Royston also said he passed in the night and that, as far as he could tell, it was peaceful. Do you think he was at peace?"

He would know far better than she. But he wasn't seeking a medical opinion. She whispered a yes. Her voice was not to be trusted.

"I miss him too." Uncle William had meant as much to him as he had to her. He laced his fingers with hers and gave them a squeeze, then quickly released her.

He tugged on his jacket while she shifted in her seat and shook the reins. The cart lurched forward, but they only rode for another minute or two before Lord Turner bade her to stop.

"Why don't you let me out here? I think I can manage the rest of the way."

"Of course, my lord," she murmured and set the brake.

He gingerly climbed from the cart and shuffled back to his horse, then drew the animal around to her side of the cart and peered up from the beneath brim of his tall hat. Thankfully, it shaded his eyes so she couldn't see if their chestnut-brown depths were as warm as his voice sounded when he spoke.

"Thank you for the ride. And thank you for taking care of William during his last days. You have a kind and soothing manner. I know now his passing was peaceful." He touched the brim of his hat, mounted his horse, and rode toward the Hall.

Penelope managed to turn on the wide lane easily enough and make her way back to the road and continue on her way. Her heart took much longer to sort out.

John rode until he could not help but look back. The cart shrunk as it continued down the road and the weak sun caught her golden head. His fingers still tingled while his heart pounded against his chest and his common sense. He urged Fortis into an easy walk.

He should have stuck to his resolution of waiting to ask her about William. If he had thought her beautiful before, she was twice so now he had discovered how easy she was to talk to. Not that she would have seen their conversation that way, with its tense moments and long pauses. But whatever she thought of their exchange, for his part he'd come a mere hair's breadth away from telling her ... well, telling her everything. What a disaster that would have been.

Or perhaps not.

His tale would keep her far away from him. She seemed trustworthy. His secret would remain safe with her if he asked it of her. But then, there was the other possibility.

What if Miss Howard chose to show him compassion instead? Maybe even forgiveness. What then? The weight on his heart shifted a fraction. Just as quickly, memory moved it back and somehow made it twice as heavy.

Compassion? Forgiveness? Never. He wasn't worthy of either and never would be. God himself couldn't forgive him. How could Miss Howard?

He must keep her at arm's length. He would find out from Thomas when she did her visits and keep to the Hall those days to avoid any chance meetings. And when they did happen to meet, he would curb his natural inclination to praise when praise was due. He hadn't failed to notice the flush in her cheeks when he'd done so yesterday.

Despite his better judgment, he nudged Fortis into a light trot. The sooner he got back to the Hall and the sanctuary of the library, the better. There he just might be able to purge her from his thoughts.

CHAPTER 9

The gray which edged the sky earlier covered it as Penelope concluded her visits. She called on Mr. Fletcher again to see how he was getting on, but he was not at home. His neighbor told her he went to the cottage hospital. But of course he did. If only she had sent a note to say she was coming. It was no short walk to the hospital from his home. She could have taken him to visit his son, Peter. The neighbor promised her to go fetch him, which set her heart at ease. But then he asked after the new lord, a subject she had been trying to avoid all day in vain. Her visits should have taken her thoughts away from Lord Turner. But with his arrival and the calls he made yesterday, it was "Lord Turner—what a nice new lord of the Hall," and "My! But the new baron is handsome." How was she supposed to put him from her mind amidst all their praise?

She rounded a corner in the lane as she guided her cart toward Fairview. Yesterday she was "admirable." Today, "kind and soothing." What had happened to her iron resolve from this morning? Melted by the warmth of praise and a fleeting squeeze of her fingers. And then to be further dissolved by the strong suspicion her uncle had somehow planned them to be together. How apple-red her cheeks must be at this moment. Had Uncle William known just how much she would be drawn to him? What a foolish question. Of course he had. He hadn't been blind to her behavior all those years ago. Not as she had been. That thought alone cooled her considerably.

At least she could look forward to teatime. She'd invited the school mistress for the new girls' school, a Miss Clara Bromley, over this afternoon. With any luck, she would not be interested in the new lord of Ashford Hall as she was not from the general area but from Bristol. Then again, that fact might make the opposite true.

Penelope made it back to Fairview just as the sky opened up in a light but steady rain. It grew harder as she and Fanny, their maid-of-all-work, were laying out everything in the parlor. Would Miss Bromley come at all? She had no conveyance, so it was entirely possible the wet would keep her at home. But at the agreed-upon time there was a knock at Fairview's door.

"Miss Bromley," Penelope said as Fanny led the school mistress in. "I thought the rain would keep you away."

"It wasn't raining when I left. I thought I could beat it."

The poor thing was soaked. "No need to apologize. I'm so glad you're here. Fanny, help her out of her cloak and bonnet and take them to dry in the kitchen"

Before long, Penelope had her settled in front of the fire. They had met a few days prior, and she seemed even younger now than she did then. She couldn't be more than nineteen. "How are you getting on?"

"Tolerably." Her small, soft voice grew smaller still as she went on. "As I was going to bed last night, I heard a terrible sound—like a woman screaming."

"That was only a fox." Penelope handed her a cup of tea. "Just a vixen looking for food for her cubs. They sometimes call like that."

"Oh." Her cheeks pinked as she examined her cup. "That is a relief. You must think me terribly foolish. I've only ever lived in Bristol."

"Not at all. It's quite understandable." She was no stranger to that sensation. Hadn't all the foreign noises in London frightened her when she first went there? "You said your situation was only tolerable just now. Is there something I can do to help?"

Miss Bromley took a long moment to answer. "If I may be honest, Miss Howard, this is the first time I've been away from home." She paused. "I hope this doesn't sound like I'm spoiled, but there are aspects of this situation which are new to me."

"Such as?" The girl had such a tortured expression. "Please, you may feel free to tell me anything."

She set her tea to the side. "I've never had to get along on my own before. My family is—was—well off." Her voice dropped to a whisper. "I was sent away to help earn money for our family. I'm not used to being without my maid."

She touched the low caramel bun at the nape of her neck. Her family's downfall must have been a recent event.

"You mean you did that yourself? It's very good and most suitable for a schoolmistress. As for some of the more practical aspects, I think we can get a woman from the workhouse to help you."

"Oh, but I could not pay her."

"Don't worry about that. The school is being funded by an annuity. I'm sure it is generous enough to hire a maid-of-all-work. I will speak to Mr. Gregory." If some poor soul could escape the workhouse to serve Clara Bromley, all the better.

"Thank you so very much, Miss Howard."

"You are most welcome." She took a sip. "And you must come to dinner here once a week. My brother and I would love to hear how you and your pupils are doing."

"Your brother is the estate agent for Ashford Hall, is he not?"

"Yes."

"What is he like?"

Hoofbeats sounded outside, and Penelope rose. "Come see for yourself."

Just because she didn't care for her uncle's matchmaking didn't mean she shouldn't have a try at it. Clara Bromley was the sort of person Thomas needed. And what a display her brother unwittingly made as he rode up and dismounted. The rain had eased considerably; in fact, he must have come from very close by indeed as there was hardly a speck of mud on him. What would

Miss Bromley say about him? She remained still as Thomas strode to the door and out of their view.

"He's very handsome." She raised a hand to her mouth. "Do forgive me. That was too forward."

"Not at all," Penelope said as she guided her back to their seats by the fire. "Especially as you are quite right."

Thomas entered the parlor a moment later and pulled up short when he caught sight of their guest. Penelope hid a satisfied smile by taking a sip of tea.

"Who do we have here?" he asked.

"This is Clara Bromley. She's to be the mistress of the new girls' school."

"Miss Bromley." He took a seat with them. "A pleasure."

"The pleasure is mine, Mr. Howard." Her soft voice strengthened as she spoke. A good sign.

"But I do apologize. I don't recall hearing about a girls' school," he said.

"Of course you do," Penelope replied. "Uncle left an annuity for its establishment. He left the responsibility for it all with Mr. Gregory."

"Ah yes, of course." While he spoke to Penelope, he kept his gaze fixed on Miss Bromley. He was as charming as Penelope had seen him in quite a long time. He hadn't been like this since before his trip to London so many years ago.

In a short while, he and Miss Bromley laughed as if they were old friends. Perhaps it was time to make him shine a little more in her eyes.

"Thomas' talents are not only in business and organization," Penelope remarked. "He is an artist."

"I'm not in the least surprised." She raised her chin an inch. "He has that look about him."

"A look?" Thomas leaned forward in his seat. "What kind of a look is that?"

"The look of pure genius, Mr. Howard. It's in your eyes."

Roses sprang to her cheeks. "I'm sure God has blessed you with a great deal of talent."

"Thank you." Sincerity warmed his voice. "Now I only wish He would bless me with a little more time."

The clock on the mantel struck the hour, and Miss Bromley rose. "I should be getting back before it gets dark."

"Are you sure?" The rain had started again, and Penelope couldn't send her back out into it. "It would be no trouble for you to stay for dinner."

"But it will be dark by then, and I don't think the rain will end soon," Thomas replied. "I could drive her back. We have that little trap in the stables."

Penelope hesitated. Yes, the business in London had been many years ago, and Thomas had changed since then. But he clearly had a regard for Clara, and it would not do for either of them to be exposed to gossip. "Why not have young Alfred take her instead? You've been riding all day, and I'm sure you're tired."

Only she noticed the way he stiffened beside her and the razor-thin tightness in his voice as he spoke. "I'm not quite as tired as all that."

"I wouldn't want to feel responsible for tiring you out, Mr. Howard." Miss Bromley's voice and eyes softened. "A true artist needs his rest."

The tension eased. Somewhat. "Perhaps you're right, Miss Bromley."

Penelope did allow him to see their guest to the door unaccompanied. That he disappeared into the study not to emerge until dinner did not surprise her in the least. He was silent through the first portion of their evening meal.

Enough was enough. "It was not because I do not trust you."

The sound of fork and knife against plate was the only reply. His face was rock hard and his movements equally stiff. How could he be angrier now than before?

"Thomas?"

"I was under the impression our father was dead and buried," he replied.

Penelope laid down her utensils. She may not have sounded like Papa this time, but she had acted like him. But in the end, she stood by her actions. "I did not want either of you exposed to gossip."

More silence. But it was easier this time. Eventually, he raised his head. "Perhaps you were right."

"Thank you."

"No, thank you. I wasn't thinking." They both resumed eating. After a few moments, he motioned toward her hand. "You didn't overdo it with your wrist today, did you?"

"I'm afraid I might have." It still needed to be re-wrapped. She should have waited another day before driving. Perhaps if the rain held, she would find some activity around Fairview tomorrow.

"Hmm. Well, I know you'll rise to the challenge."

There it was again. She was his tough old girl. His confidence was gratifying, but, "Thomas, what if I had done worse than sprain my wrist?"

"You didn't."

"But I could have. Doesn't that concern you?" She paused. "It used to."

"When we were children, yes. We're not little anymore, Pen. We're all grown up now." He pushed aside his empty plate and leaned forward. "I would never want anything to happen to you. I'm your brother, aren't I?"

"Of course." What else could she say to that? It simply wasn't his way to praise. Not in the way she needed.

But it did seem to be someone else's.

She pushed the thought away, but Thomas brought him back to mind as they moved to the study. "So how do the tenants like Lord Turner?"

"They are very pleased with him." She took up some mending from a chair in front of the fire while her brother began to sort through correspondence on his desk. "Though they would like to see him married. Most of them are for Isabella Abbott."

"Yes, they were quite taken with that idea. I heard in the village today Sir James and his sister are planning a ball to welcome the new master of Ashford Hall."

"Hmmm. I hope they won't be too disappointed when their efforts come to nothing."

"Why do you say that?"

"You have to admit, he didn't seem too keen on the subject the other day."

Thomas waved his hand. "He'd been dodging the same sort of question all morning. I probably shouldn't have brought it up."

Penelope directed her attention to Fanny's torn apron. Perhaps that had accounted for his cross behavior. But what about his indifferent attitude toward the estate? His leg and the fact he had been out all morning and part of the afternoon could account for that. But he hadn't acted tired at first, and what about his curious behavior earlier today?

What did it matter, and why should she care? Let him meet and marry Miss Abbott if he fancied her. It would solve a great many problems. She slowed her stitches. It would. No matter what her foolish heart believed.

"Blast!"

"What is it?"

"I have to go into Somerset tomorrow." Thomas folded up a letter and snapped it back down on his desk. "I hope this rain doesn't hold."

"I'm sure Lord Turner would lend you a carriage. Is there some sort of problem with the new bailiff?"

"Who? Oh, no." He drew a slow breath and looked down at the letter. "A problem with a tenant." He drew his sketchbook over to rest in front of him. "And I was going to paint something I sketched this afternoon."

She rose and laid a hand on his back. "I'm so sorry. Is there any way it could wait?"

"No, the matter is quite pressing." The clock on the mantel chimed the hour. "I better get to bed. I'll need to leave early."

"Do you think you'll be home for dinner?" she asked as he tidied his desk.

"I don't know, but just to be sure, don't count on me." His voice was tight as he finished and headed for the door.

Apparently, tomorrow was to have been a lighter day for him. It had been so long since he'd been able to escape into the attic studio Mama had insisted on creating. Papa had only agreed to please her. It was spacious and well lit, and Thomas would refine his craft for hours on end. But then Mama died. Papa said it was time Thomas learned a real profession. Thomas left for London and, instead of proving their father wrong, fell into the wrong crowd. Papa had been forced to ask Uncle William to intervene and clean up his mistakes. In the end, Thomas returned and learned the job well, but Papa never allowed him to pick up brush or pencil again. And he never let him forget why.

After Papa's death, how many months had it taken for Thomas to realize he was free to create again? Too many. His new work was lacking and didn't have the charm or the emotion it once had. And he knew it. And as lime will slowly eat away at a hide, so anger and resentment ate at Thomas. Would he ever forgive Papa?

Forgiveness is a process. She knew that better than anyone. It had taken a long time to forgive Papa's reaction to her mistakes. But that reaction had been warranted. The whole situation had been, in part, her fault. Papa had wanted to ensure she would never make that mistake again. His reaction had been disappointing but not unforgivable. No one was so far gone that they did not deserve either her forgiveness or—more importantly—God's.

She prayed her brother would one day come to see that.

CHAPTER 10

John had no business going anywhere near a church. Devils don't belong in sanctuaries. How ironic this particular devil had to attend to be a good example to his staff and the community. So here he was, parishioners parting like the Red Sea as he made his way down the aisle of St. Andrew's at the close of services. And all the bows and curtsies. As a doctor, he was used to a title. But he was just a man, a very flawed, very cursed man.

He made it to the door. Outside at last? No. Mr. Gregory stood between him and fresh air. He smiled upon seeing John and gave him a deep nod. "Lord Turner, thank you for coming. I hope you enjoyed today's sermon."

"Yes. It was quite eloquent."

"I hope you will forgive me if I teach frequently from the first book of Saint John. It's a favorite."

"I am more than happy to leave those kinds of decisions in your hands, Mr. Gregory."

Why had he agreed? Hearing more sermons based on 1 John 1:9? *"If we confess our sins, he is faithful and just to forgive us our sins, and to cleanse us from all unrighteousness."* He would choke on false hope. Some acts were beyond redemption. Even Christ Himself had spoken of sin that could never be forgiven.

A gentleman approached, followed by two other women. He had graying hair and a mustache, and while the younger woman was fashionably dressed, she wore an expression of displeasure at everything she saw. The other woman was much older, wore gray and a similar countenance. And the cane she held—was it a walking stick or a scepter?

Mr. Gregory greeted them. "Sir James, Mrs. Baines, Miss Abbott."

A pause ensued, and the older woman took the poor reverend to task. "Well, Gregory, are we to wait all day to be introduced?"

If she meant to fluster the reverend, she missed the mark. "My apologies, Mrs. Baines, I was not aware that you had not yet been introduced," he replied. "My Lord Turner, may I present Sir James Abbott, his daughter Miss Isabella Abbott, and his sister, Mrs. Dorothea Baines."

John bowed his head, which Sir James returned as the two ladies curtsied. "I'm pleased to meet you."

"Thank you, Lord Turner. The pleasure is ours."

So as to not block those exiting, the four stepped farther into the churchyard where other groups of people had gathered to chat. It had rained for the past day and a half, and everyone was eager to enjoy the fine weather. They passed a group of the Hall's tenants, who immediately paused their conversation to acknowledge John's presence with bows and curtsies.

A little girl peeked up at him with wide eyes from behind her mother's skirts. What was her name? He and Thomas had visited their farm. Instead of curtsying, she smiled and waved. What a relief. He returned the smile, but the mother noticed her daughter's lack of decorum and scolded her.

"Lily Elizabeth Smyth! That's Lord Turner. You do what's proper, now." But to her mother's horror, the child merely giggled and waved again.

"You appear to have your hands full with that one, Mrs. Smyth," Mrs. Baines said.

John fisted his hands. Did she have to sound so acidic?

The mother refused to meet his eyes. "I'm ever so sorry, m' lord," she murmured. "I'll see it doesn't happen again."

John wove a hand through his hair. "Mrs. Smyth, I would appreciate it if you wouldn't. In fact—" He raised his voice so those around him could hear. "I ask that you refrain from doing me such honor in the future. I'm just a man."

This set off a round of murmurs. Miss Howard and her brother stood nearby. Thomas bit back a grin, and Miss Howard raised her brow at him before continuing her conversation with Mr. Gregory. Mrs. Baines raised her chin. Her large, round eyes had somehow taken on the sharpness of a scalpel, which matched the tone of her voice.

"Are you sure that's wise, Lord Turner? Allowing them to be on equal footing with you?"

John's mouth twitched. "As an American, I believe that all men are created equal."

"In America, perhaps. Here it is a different story. You would do well to remember that." As she spoke, Miss Howard and Thomas approached and diverted her attention. "Ah, good morning."

The two greeted her, then Miss Howard drew up next to John. "I'm sure Lord Turner does not mean to start a revolution, do you, my lord?"

"No, of course not." He straightened the cuffs of his coat. "We've already won one of those."

Thomas coughed into his fist while Mrs. Baines took on the demeanor of a bottle brush.

He hadn't meant to say that quite so loud. Or maybe he did. Sir James either hadn't heard him or decided to ignore it.

"I understand you arrived in Woodley just this week, Lord Turner," Sir James said.

"Yes, I've been getting to know the Hall and the tenants, thanks to Mr. Howard. He and Miss Howard do an excellent job keeping up with everything."

"Yes, Miss Howard does keep busy." Mrs. Baines gave the ground a tap of her cane.

Of course. It was Mrs. Baines who disapproved of Miss Howard's charitable endeavors. "My tenants have nothing but praise for her, as do I. They couldn't do without her."

"I see." She arched her brow. "This is your first time in England,

I presume."

"No, I was here several years ago."

"Oh?"

John squared his shoulders. "Yes, I stayed with Lord Renshaw in London."

"And what was your business there?"

"Perhaps this is not the time or place," Sir James interjected. "My sister and I are planning a ball in a week's time, to welcome you. We hope you can attend."

He saw right through the invitation. This was not for his benefit, but for Miss Abbott's. She stood there and watched them like a disinterested cat. He wanted to refuse on those grounds alone. But like church, this dance was not something he could exclude himself from.

"Thank you, Sir James. I would be happy to come." He turned to Thomas. "I hope you enjoy dancing."

Sir James and Mrs. Baines glanced at each other.

"Well then, I will be sure to send invitations to the Hall *and* Fairview." She took her niece by the elbow. "Come along, Isabella. We should be getting back."

Miss Abbott caught his eye. Was she attempting to flirt, or was that a hint of amusement in her gaze?

"What did I do?" John asked once they were out of earshot.

Miss Howard watched the three climb into their carriage. "We will, of course, decline," she said, and Thomas voiced his agreement.

"Why?"

"My brother and I are not in the same social sphere as you and Sir James," she replied, her voice calm and firm. But the hint of regret was impossible to miss.

He shook his head. The same social sphere? What kind of nonsense was that? Especially since it was quite clear she wanted to go. "That's ridiculous. You're both going."

Miss Howard drew a deep breath. "Lord Turner, it would not be appropriate for us to attend. My brother is your employee. He is not a gentleman."

"What is that supposed to mean?" He looked at Thomas. Had her comment offended him?

But he was unperturbed. "She means that I have to work for my keep. You do not. And she's right. It would be best if we stayed home."

John fought back a growl. No wonder his parents had moved to America. "Where I come from being a gentleman has to do with a man's character, not how he earns his living."

"But, my lord, surely even in America the help are not invited to balls or evening parties," Miss Howard intoned.

"No, but that doesn't mean they couldn't go if they got an invitation," John shot back.

An edge rose in her voice. "But they have only invited us because—"

"I don't care. Both of you work extremely hard and deserve a chance to get out. You're going."

But Miss Howard had not quite exhausted all her excuses yet. "We don't have a proper conveyance."

"Then I'll send one." She opened her mouth, but he raised his hand. "Not one more excuse, Miss Howard. I won't hear of it." Before she could form another protest, he strode toward his carriage. It wasn't until he was a mile or so down the road that he realized what he'd done.

CHAPTER 11

For two straight days, irritation and excitement warred with each other. No matter how many times Penelope's ire rose at being ordered to go, her excitement immediately fired back with the heady prospect of going to a ball. The dancing lessons Mama had given to them would finally be put to good use. But Lord Turner really had no idea what kind of predicament he had put them in.

Hannah, on the other hand, had been delighted when the invitation came and sang Lord Turner's praises for engineering the invitation and his insistence they attend. While Penelope stewed over her carefully worded acceptance, Hannah pulled out Mama's trunk. In short order, she coerced Penelope away from her desk and buttoned her into one of her mother's old dresses. It fit perfectly but would have to be updated.

Miraculously armed with a recent copy of *The Englishwoman's Domestic Magazine* and *La Follett,* Hannah set to work. She was a talented seamstress. The dress would be nothing short of spectacular once she finished with it.

Now, as Penelope attended to a patient at the cottage hospital, her lips twitched. That she would be dressed so far above her station should not please her so.

"Why would you be trying to hold back that pretty smile, Miss Penelope?"

The patient, Mrs. Travers, took her in with rheumy but kind eyes. Penelope let loose her smile and set the water glass on the bedside table. What honest excuse could she give her?

The elderly woman winked at her. "It wouldn't be because

you'll be going to that fancy ball at Hartsbury, now is it?"

"How did you hear of that?"

"My neighbor overheard Lord Turner in the churchyard." Her hands danced over her blanket. "Told me everything, she did, when she visited yesterday."

She sought the floor for a hole she could crawl in. Mrs. Travers' neighbor was Mrs. Brody, the town gossip. If she knew, all of Woodley, along with more than several people in the neighboring villages, knew what had transpired.

Mrs. Travers patted her hand. "Now don' you worry. Not a soul feels badly about it." She looked down at the covers. "But, well, there's Mr. Davies and the Brown sisters. They feel you're reachin' above your station. And Old Mrs. Russell and her niece too. But don' you worry about them. It's *generally* seen as a good thing. You go and find a good man to take care of you instead of you fussin' over all of us."

"Now, Mrs. Travers," Penelope tidied the woman's light blanket. "If I don't, who will?"

The elderly woman took her hand in both of hers, the lines of her face deepening. "I knew your mother for many years, even before you started visitin' with her for the late Lady Renshaw. She wanted more than all this for you and would have been that pleased at this chance."

Penelope's role in Woodley was not what her mother would have wanted, but any hope of home and hearth had died along with her child five years ago. "Thank you, Mrs. Travers. I had best see to my duties."

The older woman pointed at the water Penelope had just given her. "That's from the village pump isn't it?"

"Yes, why? Was there something wrong with it?" She picked up the glass and examined the contents. Nothing seemed amiss.

"There's that new well near Felicity Oliver's little cottage at the edge of the village," she said. "My grandson has a farm near there, and he brought me some. Oh, Miss Penelope. It's so good. Those from the village are abandonin' the pump to get water clear out there. I was hopin' Matron Talbot might send for some."

The part of Woodley Mrs. Travers spoke of was farther out from the village green. Shortly before he became ill, her uncle had seen the sense in digging another well.

"As the village pump is so close, I doubt it, Mrs. Travers. But perhaps we can send word for someone to bring you some especially."

She smoothed the white apron that covered her black dress as she stepped from the women's ward to the front hall. Dr. Royston stood there with Miss Felicity Oliver.

"And I'm telling you it's the beginnin' of cholera, Dr. Royston." The spinster's querulous voice rose, and Penelope yanked the door shut. It wouldn't do for Miss Oliver to start another panic. She once sent the entire village into a tizzy because she swore she had the plague. "I was livin' in London in '54. I remember the signs."

"As I've recalled you saying many times, Miss Oliver," the doctor replied. "But this is a small Hampshire village, not a crowded London neighborhood filled with bad air and the noxious fumes associated with that disease. Perhaps you ate a bit of undercooked meat a day or so ago."

"Not likely," she replied darkly. "Prudence burns everythin'." She pounced on Penelope who now stood next to the doctor. "You recollect those biscuits she made, don't you?"

Indeed she did. The maid-of-all-work's biscuits had more in common with wood chips than anything edible. "Of course, but I must agree with Dr. Royston. Why don't I call on you in a few days? To be certain nothing is amiss."

The spinster's face creased. "I don't want to be a bother."

Dr. Royston coughed, and Penelope took the woman's arm and guided her to the front door. "It will be no bother whatsoever."

"But I truly am worried." Miss Oliver's face still registered distress.

She regarded the woman for a moment. She'd never seen Miss

Oliver like this, not in all their long acquaintance. It seemed too genuine. But her fears had to be ungrounded. Cholera, even in London, was rare these days. It would take more than she and Dr. Royston to convince her this time. She squeezed the spinster's arm. "I am very sure when I see you again you will still be the picture of health."

"I hope you're right."

Penelope opened the door for her, assuring her once again she would see her in a day or two. As she walked back toward Dr. Royston, the door to the matron's office opened.

"What was she dying of this time?" Matron Talbot walked over to them, bonnet in hand. Miss Oliver possessed the talent of being able to frazzle her considerable patience in a matter of seconds.

"Cholera," Penelope replied.

The woman yanked on her bonnet ribbons as she tied it. "Here? We have some of the cleanest streets in the county. There's nothing here to foul the air enough to bring on cholera."

"Ah, but Matron," Dr. Royston said, "Miss Oliver is an expert. She was in London during the Soho outbreak in '54."

The matron pulled a face as she put on her bonnet.

"Her sister just returned to Southampton, Matron," Penelope said. "You know how she gets when she's lonely. I've promised to visit her in a couple of days."

"Thank you, Nurse Howard. And do try to keep her from voicing her worries. We don't need another panic on our hands." She checked the watch pinned to her bodice. "I must fly. Can you stay until I return?"

"Of course. I've just checked on the patients, so I'll finish your filing."

"Thank you." She left, and the doctor excused himself to make his rounds.

Penelope had finished the filing and was taking it upon herself to answer some correspondence when someone knocked on the door. Lord Turner stood on the other side. While her heart danced, she curtsied. "Lord Turner, what a pleasure."

"Miss Howard." He peered around the room behind her. "So in addition to visiting my tenants, helping run my farm, and the numerous other things you do, you're also the matron of the cottage hospital?" His mouth curled upward on one side. "You *are* an amazing woman."

Amazing. Another word she would have to deal with. But digging her nails into her palms did not help. "No, sir. Matron Talbot had to step out for a while, and I'm performing some clerical duties in her absence. I'm trained as a nurse, and I volunteer my services here a few days a week."

"I see. Where did you receive your training?"

"St. Thomas'."

"I'm an admirer of Miss Nightingale. Very impressive." Tension feathered across his face. "I came to call on Dr. Royston."

"Of course." She stepped around him into the hall. "He is doing his rounds at the moment. I'm sure he would appreciate you joining him."

"Oh." He tugged on his frock coat. "I wouldn't want to disturb him."

"I cannot see how you could do that. He would most certainly appreciate the help of another doctor."

"I still don't wish to disturb him. I'm only here as the hospital's patron. Nothing else."

Clenched hands and a voice that might snap at any moment. What on earth? "Very well, my lord. If you will come this way."

He strode among the beds of the men's ward, pausing every so often to ask a patient if he was comfortable. He offered his hand to those who were able to greet him but otherwise held both behind his back as if keeping himself from consulting a chart or checking a bandage. And his questions were ones a layman might ask.

But when he stepped around the screen which separated Peter Fletcher from the rest of the ward, he stopped. He pulled back the sheets to look at the bandage covering the stump that had once been the boy's left leg. Peter murmured in his sleep. He re-covered the lad and stepped away, motioning for her to follow. "How did this happen?"

Had his voice shaken? "A cart accident. The axle broke, and the cart tipped over into the ditch with the boy underneath. The break it caused was clean, but Dr. Royston and the surgeon, Mr. Worth, could not get it to set properly. They felt the best option was to—"

"Amputate." He'd all but spat out the word. "What about his family?"

"He and his father are—were—carters for Fairview."

"Carters?"

"They cart grain to the market or fertilizer to where it's needed in the fields."

"You said were. What happened to the father?"

"He's still working for the Home Farm, but Thomas cannot see it lasting much longer. He's older and getting on in years." She gestured to the boy. "Peter did a great deal of the loading and unloading."

Lord Turner's eyes turned black as coal. "There's got to be something else the man can do at Fairview. I will speak to Thomas." Penelope only just caught him muttering under his breath. "Why?"

"My lord?" He looked at her, startled that she'd heard him.

She took a deep breath. "My lord, everything possible was done. As I said, they could not get it to set correctly, and it became gangrenous. There was nothing more they could do."

He shook his head and with a light growl brushed past her to the door.

She'd heard of the forced amputations in the field hospitals during the war in America. Horrors he must have witnessed if not participated in. Was that it? After all the time and effort her uncle had taken to help him become a doctor, was it the war that forced him to keep himself in check? Because that's how he acted. Like a finely bred horse being held back in a race. *Lord, what happened to him? How can I help?*

They had just stepped back into the hall when the front door opened and Matron Talbot entered. Penelope introduced them.

"A pleasure, Lord Turner." The matron dipped him a curtsy. "I hope you are finding the hospital satisfactory."

"Yes, thank you, Matron. Nurse Howard has been giving me a tour while Dr. Royston makes his rounds."

"Oh. I understood you are a doctor as well, sir. You did not wish to join him?"

"No. Thank you."

"I see." She backed away, tugging off her gloves. "Unfortunately, I have some pressing business to attend to. I hope it will be convenient for Nurse Howard to continue to escort you?"

"Of course."

"Do be sure to visit Miss Oliver sooner rather than later, Nurse Howard. She was right outside the door earlier, waiting on me. I was late to my appointment."

"I will, Matron."

As the matron shut herself into her office, Lord Turner asked, "Miss Oliver?"

"An elderly lady who is something of a worrier, always coming down with something or other." Could two goals be accomplished at once? He couldn't be pushed back to where he belonged, but perhaps a gentle nudge? "Actually, she rents a cottage from you, my lord. Would you have the time to come with me when I visit?"

His face took on a guarded expression. "Why?"

"She currently believes she is coming down with cholera." She spread out her hands. "Which you must know is impossible with our fresh air and clean streets. But if she were to hear your opinion, not only as her landlord but as a doctor, she would certainly give up that notion."

Lord Turner crossed his arms. Was he at least considering it? "Has Dr. Royston voiced his opinion to her?"

"Yes, of course, but—"

"Then I'm sure between the two of you that will be more than enough to make her see sense." He strode ahead of her to the doors to the women's ward.

"Lord Turner—"

Penelope gasped. Cold, dead eyes locked on to hers.

"Exactly, Miss Howard." The edge to his voice was jagged. "I am *Lord* Turner. *Not* Woodley's doctor."

He didn't seem angry as much as hollow. Empty of what mattered most to him. Like Thomas. How many times had she seen that same look in her brother's eyes when a painting or sketch had not met its potential?

The hall clock chimed the hour. They both started, and Lord Turner cleared his throat. "I'm due to meet with a tradesman at the Hall. Please make my excuses to Dr. Royston."

He darted around her and strode out the door.

As she drove home later that afternoon, his empty eyes refused to leave her alone. She shouldn't have prodded him. But how could she have known it would injure him? She pressed her fingers to her eyes. If she kept on like this, it would end in a headache, and she would be no good to anyone. There was little she could or should do. It wasn't her place to pry into his affairs, and he didn't want her to anyway.

But there was no reason she shouldn't pray for him. *Lord, please bring peace to his soul.*

As she passed through Woodley, she saw her brother standing outside The Baron's Arms, the local public house. Who was that with him? He moved slightly. Mrs. Lynch? She urged Bessie a tad faster. Best to rescue him from her advances.

As she drew closer, she noticed she handed him a basket. Her mother's basket. Well, that explained things. She must have been on her way to the cottage hospital and happened upon him. Thomas said something to her—the street noise was too loud to hear what—and she laughed. Curious. He didn't seem as put out as usual. Mrs. Lynch caught sight of her, and her expression stiffened. She said something to Thomas and was gone by the time she reached him.

"Hello. I didn't expect to see you today," he said. His cheeks were a tad too pink. "I thought you were doing your weekly rounds."

"I did that yesterday. Was that Mrs. Lynch I saw a moment ago?"

"Yes. She asked me to give this to you." She reached for the basket, but he held it back. "It's heavy. Apparently, it contains some tins of coffee for me." He set it in the cart near her feet.

"Yes, she mentioned she was going to send it over." She should ask him why he seemed so at ease. He was never so after his encounters with the Hall's housekeeper. But courage failed her. "I'm headed back to Fairview. Would you like a ride?"

"No, I have something else that needs seeing to. But I will be home in time for dinner for a change." He strode off.

She followed his progress for a moment or two, then directed her attention to the basket. Beneath the cloth lay the tins of coffee. An expensive brand. She should pay for at least a portion of it.

A small cloth pouch caught her eye. She opened it. Thomas' tie pin, the one he lost near Highclere. What on earth was Mrs. Lynch doing with it? Her stomach pitched. No, please don't let him be reviving his London habits here in Woodley. She set the basket down and snapped the reins. It couldn't be. He'd been far too taken with Clara Bromley, and he barely touched a drop of what little spirits they kept at home. There must be a simple explanation to all of it. But his pink cheeks spoke of him imbibing too freely in the pub, and what of his easy manner with Harriet Lynch? And the tie pin—how could she ignore any of it?

CHAPTER 12

The visit to the cottage hospital had been a disaster.

His meeting with the tradesmen long over, John prowled the grounds. He never should have gone. So what if Dr. Royston's words would have nagged him until he did? That would have been preferable than the nightmares he would undoubtedly encounter tonight. They had lessened since coming here. Even if the guilt hadn't.

Pea gravel crunched beneath his feet, and he paused to stare at a clump of rose bushes. Perhaps he should visit the boy's father. If he met with him, he might figure out a way to help them.

The word "help" instantly brought Miss Howard to mind. How could someone so gracious be so nosy, over-accommodating, and pig-headed? He recognized her request for his medical opinion for what it was, a nudge to dip his foot back into medical waters. What right did she have to prod him? Or deny her and her brother an evening of enjoyment? Because of some ridiculous notion that they were outside the correct "social sphere"?

Finally, a blemish on her flawless veneer. Or could all that be counted as one? She was only trying to do the right thing in both instances. The ball was one thing. They would go like it or not. But he couldn't excuse his behavior today.

He hadn't meant to be harsh. She couldn't have known how much it pained him to walk the ward as a mere observer, as the patron and not the doctor. And yet something told him she did. Had she sensed it and imagined asking him to give a medical opinion would encourage him? The thought warmed him much more than it should.

He made his way back to the Hall. He should apologize. But seeing her would not be the best idea. The clock in the front hall told him she wouldn't be home yet, not if she were as busy as Thomas led him to believe. A note would do. He would drop it off at Fairview and ask there where the Fletchers lived.

When he arrived at the farm, a stable boy greeted him and the door opened as he approached. How had they known he was coming? He hadn't said where he was going when he left the Hall. A young maid stood just inside the door. She curtsied, took his coat and hat, and led him to the parlor.

"Lord Turner, miss." The girl disappeared, leaving him with Miss Howard.

"Thank you, Fanny." She rose from her seat. "Good day, Lord Turner. I hope you aren't too surprised to be met at the door. I'm training our maid to be more vigilant about listening for visitors after our misunderstanding."

"I see."

"My brother is still out at the moment. Did you need to see him?"

"No, I came to see you." Her mouth dropped open, and he rushed on, "I mean I didn't think you would be home, and I wanted to leave you a note." He studied the pattern of the carpet for a moment. "I'm sorry, that sounded rude."

She let out a soft, musical chuckle. "Not at all, my lord. Won't you sit down? Would you like some tea?"

"No, thank you." He sat opposite her in the same chair he'd used last time. She kept her hands clasped in her lap. The bandage was gone. He'd been too distracted at the hospital to notice before. "I take it your wrist has healed?"

She rubbed it. "Yes, it's nearly good as new. It wasn't as bad as it looked."

"Good." Silence gathered around them. It should have felt awkward, but for some reason, it was calm. Easy. Too easy. Time to make his apology, ask where the Fletchers lived, and leave. "I came to apologize for the way I acted earlier today. I'm sorry."

"No, I am the one who should apologize, my lord. You gave me your answer, and I should have accepted it."

"I still shouldn't have behaved so badly." He stood, and she followed suit. "I don't mean to stay long. If you could tell me where the Fletchers live, I'll be out of your way."

"You mean to visit," she intoned, her voice low and soft.

"I do. I want to meet with him myself and see what I can do. Why?"

She didn't answer immediately. "Dr. Royston sent Peter home after you left." Another pause. "I could not help but notice the way you looked at him. Perhaps visiting would not be best if he brings back too many memories. Of the war."

She knew. Yes, of course she knew. She could see right through him. No, that was foolish. The war ran in the papers over here. "I should go."

"Why does the war stand between you and your calling?"

A dozen heartbeats passed. "So you've heard about the battles and the wounded."

"Yes."

"And you know about my role in it."

"You were a field doctor, I think. You saved lives."

"A field surgeon for the Union Army." He released a mirthless chuckle. "Oh yes. I saved lives. I cut off limbs, Miss Howard. Hundreds. Some days it seemed like thousands. All to—as you say—save lives."

"Then you did right. And I am sure many wives and families owe you a debt of thanks."

"You would think that. And it's generous of you." He fought against his pounding heart. His next words would deaden her soft eyes. "But no. I may have saved lives, but in the end, when it came to my own leg, I chose the coward's way out."

"I do not believe you are a coward, my lord." How were her eyes still gentle? Why did her voice have a tender quality?

"Do you know what a minié ball is?" She shook her head, and he continued with a grim explanation. "It's a bullet. Do you know what happens when a man's bone is hit by one? It shatters. And the only way to save the man's life is to cut off his limb. And while I hacked away, I eased my conscience by telling myself that what I was doing was a good thing. I gained a reputation. They wanted to promote me, but I wouldn't let them pull me from the men I was 'saving.' I even told myself if it were my arm or my leg, I would do the same thing. And then a stray bullet made it to my leg. And instead of letting them take it, I begged them to save it."

"You were human."

"I was a *butcher*." He would cut through her compassion. "I discovered that's what the men called me when I was sent to a hospital in Washington. I had chopped off the arm of the man in the bed next to me, and he didn't hesitate to tell me."

It was as if he had never spoken. Her gaze, her empathy never wavered. He saw in her exactly what he feared he would see. Forgiveness. And worse than that, a forgiveness that threatened to loosen his tongue further and tell her the rest in all its shame and horror. "No."

"My lord?"

"No. I've already said too much." He strode from the room and rode away from Fairview as quickly as Fortis would carry him.

CHAPTER 13

Mrs. Reynolds' new baby arrived early, and Penelope felt obliged to visit despite the fact it was not her day to make calls. And despite the fact they'd welcomed a little girl into their family. She hadn't held a baby girl—or any babe—for five years. How was that? Had all the mothers in and around Woodley ceased to have children in that length of time? No, she had been able to contrive excuses before. She had no way of inventing one now. Especially with the Reynoldses being such near neighbors.

When the woman greeted her at the door looking like Death itself with a wailing newborn in the crook of her arm, Penelope wasted no time in setting things to rights. She promptly helped her climb into her bed to rest with her child and set about tidying the little cottage. Molly Reynolds had no business being up so soon. Her labor had come early and lasted far longer than the midwife liked.

"I feel like the queen herself, so I do, Miss Howard," Mrs. Reynolds declared.

"It is well deserved, I assure you," she called from the little kitchen. "I only wish I'd had the sense to come sooner." Which was true. Misgivings or no, the woman had needed help, what with her husband out working their small farm and their only other daughter, Sally, off at the girls' school. She stepped to the doorway of her room. "What else can I do?"

"Nothin' for the moment 'cept keep me company. Though I wish you'd speak to Fred. He's that hard-headed about Sally goin' to that school." Mrs. Reynolds adjusted her nursing daughter. "Said he was comin' in to help, but we haven' seen him yet, have we?"

"I'm sure he just may have gotten caught up with something,"

Penelope soothed. "And it's good for Sally to attend and learn all she can, surely."

"Suppose." Mrs. Reynolds sounded less than convinced. "Wish I had her here with me, though. You can't be comin' and goin' here every day. Here now, Miss Howard, she's done and sleepin'. Would you mind?"

Penelope's arms were stiff as she reached for the baby, and she worried she would drop the tiny thing. But the instant her hands touched the soft folds of the blanket, they remembered how to cradle a tiny life. How was that? Her arms hadn't ever cradled a tiny life. Only a cold shell.

"We're to name her Rose." The mother beamed at the child. "After Fred's mother."

The chair she sat in was a godsend. *Rose.* That was to have been her angel's name. It was the only name she'd picked, somehow knowing it was going to be a girl. "What a lovely name."

Mrs. Reynolds leaned back into her pillows. "You're a natural, Miss Howard. Many are glad you're goin' to that fancy ball. Past time for you to find a good man and settle. Have a few of your own."

Why did Lord Turner, of all people, suddenly come to mind? "We'll have to see, but it's kind of you to think so." She had no business contemplating anything of the sort. So he was clever with a few kind words. *Handsome faces seldom are.*

But the guilt he felt over his actions in the war, though misplaced, revealed him to be a man of honorable character. No wonder he behaved as he did. He felt he didn't have a right to medicine, all because he acted as anyone would in what must have been a moment of fear. Now she understood the emptiness and the tension. It was a mantle of shame he forced himself to wear. That was a cloak she understood. She had shed hers long ago. Was it possible she could help free him from his own?

But had she truly abandoned hers? Did she trail it along behind her?

No. That wasn't the same. That was reality. The consequences of her actions were a fact of life now. The child stirred in her sleep, and she rocked it gently. It was simple. She would never hold a child of her own.

It didn't take long for the mother to slip into a deep sleep. Penelope laid Rose in the cradle beside the bed and returned to the small kitchen. She had just settled to help Mrs. Reynolds along with her mending when the door to the cottage opened, and Sally walked in.

"Oh! Hullo, Miss Howard."

Penelope put her finger to her lips and showed the little girl her sleeping mother and sister. "They've just settled down," she whispered. Wait. The girls' school did not let out so early. "You shouldn't be here quite yet, should you?"

Sally climbed onto one of the kitchen chairs. "Miss Bromley is sick. She sent us all home. We're not to come back 'til Monday."

"Miss Bromley is ill? Is it very bad?" She'd just had dinner with them last night and seemed fine.

"She had to excuse herself two times."

Worry haloed Sally's eyes, so Penelope patted her cheek. "I don't want you to worry. I'll check in on her and make sure she's all right. Are you hungry?"

She fixed the child something to eat and gave her a quiet occupation until her mother awoke. The woman assured her now that Sally was there she would be fine for the time being.

What illness could Miss Bromley have caught so quickly? It couldn't have been from their dinner. She and Thomas were fine. But as she pulled up in front of the little cottage, she heard the unmistakable sound coming from the open window of someone being ill. She let herself in through the schoolroom, which had been added to the cottage.

"Miss Bromley?"

A sob was the only reply, and she soon discovered her lying on her side in her bed. Her back was to her. Her shoulders shook, and

Penelope rushed over. She laid a hand on her back. "Miss Bromley? Clara?" Clara moaned and curled up, inching farther away from her. Penelope wet a towel at the washbasin. She sat on the edge of the bed Clara was facing and tried to dab her forehead. The girl pushed her hand away with a grimace and rolled over. More sobs shook her body. Penelope laid the towel aside and wrapped her arm around her shoulder. Clara tried to pull away, but she refused to loosen her hold.

"Clara, what is it?" Her question evoked more sobs. While she waited, she rubbed Clara's back.

Clara finally rolled over and stared at the ceiling. "If I tell you, you'll hate me."

Penelope went cold. She was familiar with those words. She had used them herself, years ago. "I could never hate you or anyone."

She took a ragged breath and then another. "I told you I'm here because I must earn money for my family. The truth is my father sent me here to punish me and to get me away from Bristol." She spat out the last words. "My family is well off. Papa is in trade, and we hold a high position in Bristol society. I've been closeted and sheltered for as long as I can remember. I didn't go anywhere without Mama or a proper chaperone. Just before I was due to come out, I decided to slip away all by myself. To see what things were really like." Her voice turned wistful. "I met someone."

Penelope set her jaw. She knew what she would hear next.

"It was innocent at first. We would meet near the docks and just walk. He was so gallant and kind. But eventually, that was not enough. We both wanted more." She screwed her eyes shut. "We went to his rooms."

Penelope struggled to steady her voice. "Did he promise to marry you?"

"Yes. When Papa called me to his study, I thought he had come and asked for my hand. But I had been discovered slipping out unaccompanied. He was very angry, and I was terrified he had heard something more."

"Had he?"

"Yes. And no. He heard I was meeting someone, but nothing beyond that." She swiped her hand over her cheeks. "He said he would not have any scandal, and to oblige my eagerness for independence, he sent me here alone." Her next words were stretched and thin. "But he will find out soon enough. My time hasn't come for two months now."

"Oh, Clara," Penelope whispered. She walked to the window, but rather than trees and sky, she saw Papa and the twisted expression on his face when she told him of her child. And how it happened.

"You hate me now," Clara said.

She strode back to the bed. "No, I most certainly do not. I want to help you. Will you tell me who the father is?"

"Oh, just telling you has been too much." She covered her face with both hands, and her tears returned with deeper force. "Please, *please* don't ask me."

Penelope couldn't understand her vehemence. Why wouldn't she say? Then again, she was already so overwrought—she must try to calm her. Hysterics could not be good for the child.

Eventually, the tears abated, and she took a rough breath. "I *cannot* tell Papa. I have to get rid of it somehow."

Penelope gripped her shoulders and forced her to look at her. "No, *no*, Clara, you mustn't."

Her eyes darkened, and she wrenched herself free. "What else can I do?"

Penelope swayed and leaned back on her arm. How well she recalled such raw desperation. Uncle William had persuaded her to reconsider. She used his words now. "I will go with you when you tell your father. And whatever happens, I *will* help you."

"You don't understand. How can you?"

"I *do*." Penelope clenched her fists. Only one other time before had she spoken of it. She drew herself up onto the bed close to Clara, who was now staring at her with round eyes. She kept her voice quiet, mindful of the open window. "Five years ago, I met an army officer named Edmund Kern. He seemed everything a young man should be. Gallant. Kind. Handsome. But my father and uncle did not like him. I could not understand why." She swallowed away the tightness in her throat. "I was willful and young, and Edmund easily convinced me to elope. We would ask for forgiveness later, he said. But it was all a ruse. Once he had me away in the carriage …" Her mouth refused to form the rest of the words, and her voice would not allow her to utter them.

Silence laid a heavy cloak over the room. It seemed even the bird call and the whispers of the wind in the trees were muffled. Until Clara's voice rent it.

"And there was a child?"

"My uncle arranged for me to have her in a lying-in hospital in London." She slipped her voice down an octave just to get the final words out. "But she was stillborn."

They had wanted to wrap her in newsprint and throw her into the Thames. But she hadn't let them. She had stolen her away, and in the dead of night, her uncle had her buried under the oak tree at the Castle.

Clara's arms warmed the cold ache in her bones, and they clung to each other. Eventually, Penelope pulled away. "We must decide what is to be done."

The girl took her hand. "You must give me time. I want to write to the father."

"But you are so far along already."

"Please." Clara gripped her fingers tighter. "I promise not to do anything to the child."

Penelope relented, against her better judgment. If only she could take her to the cottage hospital and have her checked by Dr. Royston, but that was impossible. There would be too many questions. She knew little about midwifery, but her limited knowledge would have to do. "Then tell me how you've been feeling these past weeks. I want to make sure you and the child are well."

She stayed longer than was necessary, perhaps, but in the end, she had been able to ascertain that Clara's health was good and advise her on the morning sickness. She had some peppermint tea at Fairview she would bring over the next day. It should settle her stomach enough to enable her to teach by Monday.

Hunger churned her stomach as she walked up to Fairview's door. She had foolishly skipped luncheon. Afternoon tea would have to sustain her until dinner. The front door popped open as she approached it.

"Where in the blazes have you been?" Hannah stood in the hall and took her cloak, bonnet, and basket like a thief in the night. "I thought you were to be home by luncheon, and here it is nearly teatime."

"I had an unplanned visit to make." She started for the kitchen but paused at Hannah's next words.

"It's finished."

That smile on her face. It was far too broad and self-satisfied. "The dress?"

"What else? It's time you tried it on."

Penelope drew in a deep breath as Hannah took her by the arm and prodded her up the stairs. She reached out to open the door to the older woman's room, but Hannah laid her hand over the handle.

"I want you to know I had to take apart more than just the one dress. I hope I didn't tear apart one you were overly fond of."

That did alarm her, but not for the reason Hannah feared. At the rare expression of worry on the housekeeper's face, she sought to reassure her.

"It's all right. My memories of Mama lie here." She laid a hand over her heart. "And I think she would be pleased that her dresses were being used instead of gathering dust."

"She would indeed." The Cheshire cat grin returned as she turned the knob and let the door swing open. Penelope's jaw dropped as she saw the gown gracing the dress form in the center of the room.

"Oh. Hannah. What have you done?"

She should be sick with her head spinning at such a rate. First Clara, and now the dress. What would she do? She couldn't go to Hartsbury clothed in such finery. How could she possibly? And what was to be done about Clara? What would she tell Thomas if the father relented and married her?

A sharp tap of spoon against cup brought her back to the moment. "Do be careful, Thomas. This tea set was Mama's."

Yet he still set his cup down with a distinct tap. He thrust the plate of finger sandwiches at her. She stared at him.

"What?" he asked.

"What do you mean 'what'? Clearly something is bothering you." She waved away the sandwiches. "Has something else occurred with that tenant?"

"Which tenant?"

"The one in Somerset. I thought the matter was settled."

"It is." He took two sandwiches for himself but didn't eat them. "I'm just tired." She started to suggest he turn in early later this evening when he spoke again. "What about you? You weren't exactly all here when we sat down."

"Hannah finished the dress for the ball."

"Isn't that a good thing? It's only a few days away now."

"Yes, it's just—" How could she explain this to him? They were close, but there were things he couldn't understand due to the simple fact he was a man. "It's nothing."

He shrugged and picked up a sandwich. "We shouldn't be going in the first place."

"We can't back out now. It would look badly on Lord Turner and the Hall. Especially after all the fuss he made."

"And we can't have that, can we?" he muttered.

Penelope's brow knit together. He really was in a foul mood. She had meant to ask him about the tie pin, and like a coward, she had put it off for the past two evenings already. It had to be now, or she would never ask. She opened her mouth and blurted out a completely different question. "Have you been able to sketch lately?"

The words had barely left her lips when he whipped the napkin from his lap and threw it on the table. "No, I haven't."

He strode over to the window, and she joined him. She started to wrap her hand around the crook of his arm, but he pulled away. He hadn't been this way in a long time. Not since he'd come home from London years ago. "Please, Thomas. Tell me what's wrong. Let me help."

"Help." His voice sounded odd. "Yes, you are always eager to help." He ran his fingers through his hair and after a moment seemed almost normal. "I'm sorry, old girl. As I said, I'm tired. I rode and drove quite a lot over the past two days."

"Where?"

"I visited every farm and cottage the Hall owns for one reason or another today and yesterday." He rubbed a hand over his forehead. "And then, all the way to Highclere on Wednesday— which reminds me: Do you have my tie pin? Someone turned it in to the Castle, and Lord Carnarvon sent word that they had it. I put it in that basket Mrs. Lynch returned to you."

"Of course." Thank goodness. At least that was one worry she could remove from her ever-growing list. "I'm so sorry. I did find it and meant to give it back to you. I wondered how it had gotten into my basket."

Thomas' gaze cooled. "And what form did your wondering take? Did you think I lied about how I lost it?"

"No. I wasn't sure what to think."

Ice was warmer than his gaze. "I still have more to do today. I should get going."

"Thomas, wait."

She pulled him into a hug. "I'm sorry."

He said nothing, and his face was inscrutable as she watched him leave. That went well. There had been a perfectly reasonable explanation for the tie pin, yet she still managed to make him think she distrusted him.

She pressed her fingers to her eyes. This day had not gone at all as planned. Thank goodness it was nearly at an end. She needed a diversion. A drive perhaps. But she knew exactly where she would end up if she did that. She wouldn't go to the Castle. Not today. Going tomorrow would be hard enough. Instead, she forced her feet into the study. A book would do the trick. She rarely had time to read anymore.

But on her way to the bookshelf, the letter tray caught her eye. It was mostly estate correspondence for Thomas, but familiar stationery jutted out from beneath the rest. She fished it out and flipped it over to find the seal still intact. A breath escaped she hadn't realized she was holding. Thomas hadn't seen it then. He had almost opened last year's letter. She made for her room and, after locking her door, settled into her window seat.

Dearest Penelope,

I hope this yearly missive finds you well and happy. How have nearly five years passed so quickly? It seems only yesterday we parted ways. How are your brother and uncle? My parents are both well. At least, I am told they are. Sadly, we are still estranged. My sister is well too, though I do not see her as often as I would like since her marriage. She sends her best wishes.

How are you? I find that the passage of time has not muted the pain I felt when they took my child from my arms. They still ache to hold him. I thank the Lord we came to know each other during our confinement. I think I would have burst if I could not have spoken of this to another living soul.

We both lost our children in different ways, but the pain is the same isn't it? My child may as well be dead too. I do not know to this day who adopted him. You will be pleased to hear I have finally stopped trying to find out. You were right. It is not good for my soul to do so. I do pray he was placed with a good family. And I find that I still must mark the day by walking by the lying-in hospital. It is the closest thing I have to a memorial.

I have pleasant news to impart. I am engaged to be married. He is a good man, a solicitor. I met him while I searched for my son, so he knows about my past mistakes. He does not hold them against me, not in any way. I thank the Lord every day for him, for I know I do not deserve such a man.

I pray all well with you. I look forward to your reply.
Sincerely,
Edna Neale

So Edna was settled. At least one of them would have a happy ending. But who was she to say that? She may not be able to have children and, therefore, would never marry, but she had a happy ending, after a fashion. She had a roof over her head, a brother who loved her, and fulfilling work. The Lord had simply taken the dream she once had of a home and children of her own and exchanged it for another. She was blessed, even if she had some difficulties to deal with. Light and momentary troubles. He would help her work out Clara's difficulties, and who would remember what she wore to a ball in a year? And wasn't Thomas always having bouts of melancholy? She would apologize to him. For now, she should take advantage of his absence and write to Edna and congratulate her.

Laying her friend's letter on her bedside table—it wouldn't do for Thomas to happen upon it—she went down to the study.

Her mind may have spoken sense, but her heart refused to listen. As she wrote to Edna of Uncle William's passing and his new heir, she was forced to lay down her pen for a moment and purge Lord Turner's handsome face from her thoughts the only way she knew how. *Handsome faces seldom are.* Taking up the pen again, she concluded her letter, but then came another attack, worse than the first. *Admirable … I can't imagine a better person … you are very kind … a soothing manner … an amazing woman.*

Enough! There would be no more of this foolishness. Just as Edna marked the day of her son's birth by walking by the lying-in hospital, she would mark her daughter's by visiting her grave. And she would force her heart to realize that a future with Lord Turner—or any other man for that matter—was impossible.

CHAPTER 14

Thomas snapped the ledger shut. "I'm not sure what I'll be able to find for the man to do."

"There must be something." John leaned back in his chair. "What about his wife?"

"Mrs. Fletcher died a few years ago. The man's health has declined since his son's accident." Thomas drew forward. "And Peter needs a great deal of care."

"Then find someone to help care for him, and I will ask Parker if there is something Mr. Fletcher can do at the Hall."

"My sister is already seeing to that."

Of course she was. He should have known. "Good. In the meantime, don't demand his rent."

"Very well." Mr. Fletcher was already a month or so in arrears, but John didn't care. He couldn't evict the man over circumstances beyond his control.

He rubbed his eyes. As expected, the dreams had returned. They weren't as intense as they had been just after the war. But it was still unsettling to be woken in the predawn hours to the sensation of a man beating you to death with his own bloody limb. The limb you had just cut from his body.

"Are you all right?"

John dropped his hand and rose from his seat "I'm fine."

He glanced back at the mantel clock. It was still early in the day yet. So why had it seemed like their time going over estate matters had dragged on forever? As they walked through the library past the newest stack of medical books he'd prepared for Arthur, he rubbed his fingers against the palms of his hands. They passed into the hall, and John saw Thomas down the steps to his horse.

"Are you and your sister ready for the dance?" he asked as he watched Thomas mount.

"I suppose." The reply was lukewarm at best.

"I know it was unorthodox of me to insist you go, but you both deserve it."

"Of course, thank you." He smiled, but it didn't seem genuine.

John tried a different tack. "I heard they're inviting a number of young ladies."

Thomas arched a brow. "All for your benefit."

He shrugged. "I can only dance with one at a time. Besides, I have no intention of getting married."

"Hmm. Maybe I'll have a chance after all."

"Of course you will. And don't think I won't give you a raise if you pick one of them."

"Right." Thomas chuckled.

Gripping his hand, John bid him a good day, and he rode off.

He didn't go back inside right away. Instead, he looked up at the gray sky. Too bad it seemed like rain. Going for a ride might make sleep easier. His leg hadn't really bothered him since those first couple of days. And he hadn't visited the Castle yet. He wanted to see where Miss Howard had fallen to determine whether any other improvements could be made, aside from those that had been recommended.

Miss Howard.

He strode back to the stack of Arthur's books. He checked the titles once, twice, three times. But warm blue eyes taunted him, and he leaned against the desk, his arms straddling the stack of books.

Why had he said anything? He should have left. But her question cut so close to the matter, he couldn't have moved if he wanted to. And not just that. He'd never felt so free to speak with anyone. Even Maggie. Especially Maggie. Talking to her had always been an uphill battle. Half the time, their conversations had ended in a fight or hurt feelings. Miss Howard sensed what he felt and thought without him having to say a word.

With a violent shake of his head, he pushed away from the table. Enough of this stupid schoolyard crush. He had no business comparing her to the woman he'd almost married as if there were some chance with her. He would go for a ride; if it rained, it rained. Anything to purge these foolish thoughts from his mind.

George helped him change into riding clothes and, rather than call for his horse, decided to go to the stables and saddle Fortis himself.

"But my lord," Arthur said as John pulled a saddle from the tack room. "I can do that for you."

"I've saddled many a horse in my time. I know what I'm doing." He handed it to him so he could lay a blanket on the stallion's back. He paused. A little company would go a long way. He took the saddle back. "Go get a horse for yourself. I want you to come with me."

An older man stepped into the stable hallway. He had a round face and short, graying hair. Though shorter than him by a head, he carried an air of authority. "English horses and saddles are different than those American ones. Best let the lad do that."

John looked at the saddle. He was right. He handed the saddle to Arthur again.

"You must be Charlie Milford, the head groom. I'm sorry I haven't made it here before now to meet you and your staff." He thrust his hand toward him. "And please just shake my hand. All the bowing and scraping is getting under my skin."

The man took John's hand, his grip good and strong. "Good to meet you."

"Likewise. Can I borrow Arthur? I want to go to the Castle, and I'm not too sure how to get there."

"Certainly." He shouted an order to another groom who shot off to saddle another horse. "Heard you were unconventional."

He wasn't addressing him as sir, Lord Turner, or my lord. And he hadn't so much as dipped his head to him. Finally, an informal Englishman. "Sounds like you are too."

"Oh, I've a cousin in America. Been over there too, a few years back before all that war business. Got a sense of how you all do things over there. And I've heard a few things about you from Lionel Parker."

Arthur led Fortis out, and John mounted.

"Mr. Parker? My butler?" he asked as he settled into the saddle.

"The very same. We go down to the pub in Woodley for a pint now and again."

His straight-laced, poker-rod-backed butler kicking back in a public house with a man like Charlie Milford? That must be a sight to see.

Arthur rode up behind him, and John turned. "Ready?"

The young man nodded.

"I'll tell the boys they can act natural-like round you," Charlie said. He cocked an eye at Arthur. "Hear that? You don't have to go bowin' all the time 'less there's others round."

"Yes, sir, but if my mum ever caught wind of me doing that, it'd be my hide."

"It's all right, Mr. Milford." John gathered the reins. "I wouldn't want anyone in trouble with their mother."

Charlie's bark of laughter followed them as he and Arthur rode off.

The Castle was roughly a half an hour's ride from the Hall, which gave John the opportunity to quiz Arthur about the books he'd lent him as they rode. Arthur forgot his formality as he answered and asked questions of his own. The young man had a quick, logical mind, which would serve him well if he truly intended to go to medical school. John would follow William's example and help him. There were various paths Arthur could take to obtain his medical license in England, but he would need tutoring of some sort, and experience would be helpful as well.

John shifted in the saddle and clenched the reins a little tighter.

He'd speak to Dr. Royston and see if he would be willing to take Arthur on. They could borrow any books they needed from the library, and perhaps Arthur could work at the cottage hospital in some capacity and gain experience. Should he send him over to America first, then return here and then Edinburgh? No. Let Dr. Royston assess what would be the best path for him to take to get his medical degree and license. All John should do was provide the funds and materials to make that possible.

Arthur led him down a tree-lined path that steadily rose at a gentle angle, and before long, the Castle came into view. The path they were on ended at a small bridge which crossed the old moat. Another path crossed it, taking a circular route around the ruins.

Arthur stopped at the bridge and turned to him. "Would you like to go around them first, sir?"

Just past the bridge to the left were the remains of what was once a huge tower. It must have been magnificent in its day.

"No, let's go in."

They guided their horses over the bridge, and John surveyed the wide round grassy plain in front of him. "It was huge."

"Yes, sir." Arthur pointed to two of the three structures that interrupted the remains of the crumbled wall. "Those towers there were defensive towers." He gestured to the ruins to their left. "That was the great hall. You can see where Lord Renshaw had stairs built so people could climb up."

John swung down from Fortis, and Arthur followed suit. Noting a wooden hitching rail of sorts, he led his horse over.

"Another addition of my cousin's?" he asked as they wrapped the reins loosely around it.

"Yes, sir. We get tourists up here sometimes that take a picnic on the grounds." He cast a look up at the steel gray of the sky. "Won't be any here today, though. It looks ready to rain."

"Sorry about that. We might get a little wet on the way back."

"I don't mind, sir."

As they climbed up and around the great hall, Arthur told him bits and pieces of the history. They were taking in the view through what once had been a large window. "My mum doesn't like this place."

"Why not?"

Arthur shook his head. "She says it's haunted."

"Haunted?" John crossed his arms. "There's a story there."

"Well, it's said the second baron took a young wife. They were only married a month before he was called away to the Crusades. He never returned. She died bearin' his child, and they say she still wanders the great hall, walkin' in and round it, waiting for her lord to return. Lord Renshaw always said it was rubbish. But my mum swears she saw her here during the Harvest Dinner a few years back."

"The Harvest Dinner?"

"Yes, sir. Lord Renshaw would set up tents and take a meal with the farmers. All the Hall staff was invited too."

"That sounds fun. I'll speak to Parker and Mrs. Lynch about doing it again this year." He pointed out a large tree. "I'm surprised that tree's allowed to grow that close to the wall."

"Mum said Lord Renshaw was going to have it pulled down years and years ago but didn't for some reason. It's never bothered the wall."

"Let's take a look at it."

He strode across the meadow, Arthur trailing behind. A hearty English oak, by the looks of it. Laying his hand on the trunk, he walked around it and stumbled over something at the base. What was that? He knelt and pushed away the grass. A marker with an angel engraved on it.

"Is this what I think it is?"

Arthur shifted his weight. "It's an old grave, sir. The tree grew up around it, I'm told."

A large drop of rain hit John's head. More drops started coming down with the suddenness and velocity of cannon fire, and he and Arthur ran to the great hall. They were only damp by the time they reached its wide opening. John peered out at the horses. They seemed fine but were huddled together with heads down. He rubbed his bad leg. It ached from the run. He limped over to a dry spot. Better sit down and rest it.

"You didn't hurt your leg, did you, sir?" Arthur asked.

"No, it aches a little, but it'll be fine. I just need to rest for a few minutes before we start back."

"I think I should try to go back to the Hall and fetch a coach for you, sir. We won't be able to ride fast in this. It may take an hour or so to get back."

John rubbed his leg. "Maybe it will let up soon."

"I've lived here all my life, sir. This lot could go on for a while."

He was right. It used to rain like this in London. And his mother had told him how she'd be stuck inside for days. He relented, and Arthur made a dash for the horses. He returned a minute or so later with Fortis.

"I'll go faster with just one horse, my lord." He wiped water from his face. "With your permission, I'll ride Fortis back when I come with the coach."

"That's fine. Just be careful." John rose, took the reins from him, and pulled the horse inside.

He disappeared behind the rain. John pulled out his handkerchief and wiped down his horse. "Sorry I can't do better than that," he said when it was soaked through.

Fortis rumbled and nudged him.

Now where to sit? His leg still ached. An old fireplace lay farther inside and had a low ledge. Better than the ground he'd been sitting on. Within several minutes, the slight ache in his thigh disappeared, and he stood and walked on it. Much better now. The sprint to the cellar hadn't bothered it much, but had he attempted to stay astride Fortis in the rain for almost an hour, he would not have made it to the ball the day after tomorrow.

He ran a hand through his damp hair. Miss Abbott and every other eligible young lady would certainly be thrown at him. At least

Thomas would be there too. He considered the man his friend, his being his employee notwithstanding. He and Miss Howard were good people.

Her warm nature tried to thread its way around him, and he strode to the edge of the wide opening. The other side of the ruins and the tree that he and Arthur had been looking at earlier were just visible through the sheets of falling rain.

John tapped a fist against the stone. If the grave were as old as Arthur said, the marker would be more worn. The face of the childlike angel on the stone was still smooth for the most part, not pocked and marked by time and weather. And wouldn't it be marked with the name of the child that died? He'd been to enough graveyards to recognize a child's grave when he saw it. Arthur knew more than he let on.

Movement caught his attention. A form emerged from the square tower and moved to the tree. It stood there a moment then disappeared.

What on earth had that been? Or, rather, who? Mrs. Wilcox's ghost from the story Arthur told him? No. He was a reasonable man of science. It had to have been some trick of the wind and rain. He walked over to Fortis and rubbed his neck. There were no such things as ghosts.

Then he heard the faint crunch of gravel.

He peered into the dimmer part of the cellar. Had Arthur come back for some reason? He walked back to the doorway. Water and a small portion of light dripped in just on the other side of it from a hole somewhere above. He looked to the right as he stepped through. Nothing there. He turned to the left. Had he heard something?

A wet form walked straight into him, and he stumbled backward. He grasped a delicate pair of shoulders as he regained his footing and looked into the twin orbs of crystal blue staring up at him.

"Miss Howard!"

CHAPTER 15

She wore no bonnet. Had it blown off? The rain had molded her golden hair along the soft curves of her cheekbones. Her fiery hands splayed lightly across his chest, hands that could surely feel how his heart was responding to her being all but in his arms. And her lips—he stepped back and released her. No. That thought had not just crossed his mind.

"Lord Turner." Her voice was soft and raspy. She shivered and swayed slightly, catching herself by laying a hand against the stone wall next to her. "I ... I thought you and Mr. Wilcox had ridden off."

"You mean to tell me that was you out there at the tree?" He tore at the buttons of his coat and pulled it off.

"You saw me."

That was not a question. She averted her gaze as he maneuvered the coat over her shoulders. Something wasn't quite right. She wiped her wet cheek, and he tipped his head. Her eyes were red.

"You've been crying."

"The rain ran into my eyes." She dipped her face away and folded his coat around her. "Thank you." She walked over to Fortis and laid a hand on his neck. "So this is why I thought you both had left. You brought him in here."

Something had upset her. But what? "What were you doing out in the rain?"

A slight pause. "I got caught on the way to visit a friend."

He strode to the opening and peered out into the torrent. "Where are your horse and the cart, then?"

"I decided to walk." She smoothed Fortis's sleek coat. "If you don't mind my asking, why were you out in the rain today, my lord?"

Why was she trying to sidetrack him? "I hadn't been here yet, and I wanted to see what needed done to the square tower for myself. But you never really answered my question. Why were you standing out in the rain just now?"

"It's a silly reason."

"I thought we already established that you are not silly."

"That tree is special to me." She gathered his coat closer and sat on the edge of the fireplace. "When I was a child, Uncle William— Lord Renshaw—had a mind to have it cut down. He was worried it would damage the wall of the ruins. I begged him to let it be." Her face reddened. "I told him God Himself had decided it needed to be there, just for me. My uncle relented, and it has never bothered the wall. He used to say I was the tree's little angel. In time, we took to calling it the Angel Tree. I thought to come visit it today, and it began to rain."

"That explains the marker, then."

"Yes. My uncle had it placed there only a few years ago."

No wonder she'd been crying. She had come to remember William.

Fortis gave a rumble and yanked him back to the matter at hand. "Arthur has gone for a coach. It was easier for him to leave Fortis here with me. Your way home will be warm and dry."

"Thank you, my lord."

"Actually," he said as he sat down across from her on the far side of the fireplace, "I would like to thank you for looking for someone to help care for Peter Fletcher."

She tilted her head. "I am only doing my duty."

"You regularly go above and beyond that duty. It heartens me, knowing the tenants are under your care." He praised her; she turned a beautiful shade of pink, and he had the urge to praise her even more. He shouldn't do that to her, to either of them. But what was he supposed to do when someone did something that deserved a kind word? Say nothing?

"I just don't want to see them sent to the workhouse," she said.

"They won't be," he declared. "At least, not by me. I'm doing everything I can to find work for Mr. Fletcher."

She fingered a button on his coat. "Does it help?"

No use pretending he didn't know what she meant. He just had to pretend it didn't affect him as it did. "I hope it will."

The rain lightened some. The tree and the square tower were shimmery outlines, and thin trickles echoed from the rear of the cellar. Would she say anything else? Ask what he meant? No. She wouldn't. She would know he would not want to go into it. He was almost certain of it.

"Arthur Wilcox is a very considerate young man," she said. "Bright too. Too smart, I always thought, for the stables."

His heart surged when she broke the silence with this commonplace observation. He clamped a band around it. "Oh?"

"Yes. Mr. Gregory said he was one of the smartest he's ever taught at the boys' school. He even taught a time or two in his place."

John nodded. "Did he go on to any other school after that?"

"No. Although, Mr. Gregory did tutor him for a time. But his mother is eager for him and Joseph to do well at the Hall."

"Is there anything else beyond that for the boys and girls around here?"

"Most of the children do not aspire to anything beyond what our village schools offer. It is enough for them and their families to learn to read and write and, for the girls, how to sew and knit and keep a home."

"But to not want something more than that?" He grimaced. "That isn't what I call progress."

"It is progress, my lord. It was once scorned for the poorer class to read and write. Sir James even refused to hire servants who could."

"What changed his mind?"

"His daughter, Isabella Abbott, actually. I understand she insisted at a very young age that he stop the practice."

That wasn't in keeping with his first impression of her. "Good for her."

"I know Miss Abbott seems cold and distant, but I understand she is extremely intelligent. Her lady's maid is a former governess. I am sure you will enjoy getting to know her."

Even Miss Howard wanted him to marry. The thought deflated him. It shouldn't. "You should be aware that I have no intention of marrying her. Or anyone else for that matter."

A notch appeared between her brows. "But Ashford Hall needs an heir."

"It has an heir."

"But you will not live forever, sir."

John nudged the dirt with his toe. "I came here to take care of William's legacy. I will do that to the best of my ability and make sure it will remain that way once I leave this earth." He went on before she could object further. "Thank you for the tea you sent over."

She regarded him for a moment. "You're most welcome. I trust you are enjoying it."

"I am."

But that wasn't quite the truth. It was the exact blend she had served him in her parlor but, try as he might, he couldn't quite fix it the way she had. Every time he drank it, he found he'd added either too little milk and too much sugar or just the opposite. He'd never had a problem before.

"And I hope you enjoyed the basket that I sent over with Thomas," she continued.

Basket? "Your brother didn't bring over a basket today."

"I mean the basket I sent with him the day you arrived."

"I'm sorry, he never mentioned it."

"I see." She waved a hand. "That's quite all right. There wasn't anything in it the Hall didn't already have."

All the same, he would ask about it when he returned to the Hall.

The rain strengthened its efforts and slapped at the ground. The fresh, wet scent in the air doubled. Miss Howard shifted and released a deep sigh. Without thought, he spoke.

"Be still, sad heart! and cease repining;
Behind the clouds is the sun still shining;
Thy fate is the common fate of all,
Into each life some rain must fall,
Some days must be dark and dreary."

Good humor laced Miss Howard's reply. "I gather you are enjoying the library, my lord. But I can't recall who—"

"Longfellow."

"A fellow countryman. I should have known."

"Do you like to read?"

Her face grew wistful. "I do, but I do not have as much time as I used to."

"I can imagine." They must have a library at Fairview as well stocked as the Hall's. She'd read almost the same books as he had.

"My father was forward-thinking in that regard," she said. "He liked a good discussion after dinner and made sure we were well-read and well-educated. My mother protested at first."

"Why?"

"She said it wasn't good for my mind. She wanted me to keep to calmer or domestic readings, instead of *The Decline and Fall of the Roman Empire* or studying Latin."

"You know Latin?"

She laughed. "Why should you be so surprised at that?"

He raised his hands in defense. "I've just never met a woman who knew Latin."

"*Ecce signum*," she replied.

"Behold the proof." John chuckled, but she cocked her head at him, arms folded across her chest.

"Admit it," she said. "You agree with my mother just a little. Or you thought I would declare *Jane Eyre* my very favorite book, and no others would do."

"Is *Jane Eyre* a favorite?" He rested one arm on the ledge, leaning toward her.

Her jaw worked at hiding a smile. "I have to confess I do enjoy Miss Bronte's book a great deal. Probably more than I should. Have you read it?"

"No." But he knew exactly where it was in the Hall library.

"Perhaps you should," she teased.

She was far too perfect. In every way that mattered to him. And oh, how easily he could ruin her.

Gravel crunched as Arthur walked through the rear doorway. He saw Miss Howard and stopped.

"She was out for a walk and got caught in the rain," John said as he got to his feet. Now the Herculean task of offering her his hand without meeting her eyes. "Miss Howard, I promised you a warm and dry ride home."

CHAPTER 16

Penelope took his hand and allowed him to help her rise. His fingers burned into hers. Once she stood, he released her, but she would still feel their fire hours later. Arthur said something. The whirl of emotions was too intense to form a reply. She dared a glance at Lord Turner as he stepped aside for her to go first. The whirl threatened to turn into a storm.

Traitorous heart! She *could not* have feelings for this man. Why couldn't he be boorish or arrogant? Why did he have to believe her kindhearted and admirable and make an effort to always say so whenever they met? Why did his spirit have to match his face? Why did she so want to comfort and help him?

Even if he were to return her feelings, there could be no good ending for them. He needed an heir, and she could never provide him with one. She would just have to remedy that situation at the ball. In two days' time, he would be surrounded by the most eligible young ladies in and around Woodley. One of them would capture his fancy. One of them would be able to take care of his troubled heart.

Arthur led them down the damp passage until they came to another doorway. A short distance away sat Lord Turner's carriage. Arthur opened the umbrella he carried with him and escorted her over, and she was soon sitting inside. Before long, Lord Turner sat on the seat opposite her. Their knees would bump once they got going, and as he focused on settling into his seat, Penelope slid away from him to the opposite end of her bench so that he was catty-cornered from her. As a result, she drew near the window and caught sight of the Angel Tree. This was the first time it had rained on her angel's birthday. Perhaps God was helping her mourn her loss. At least she'd had a ready answer for Lord Turner when he asked about her tears. It was the truth. Just not all of it. The carriage lurched forward, and she watched the tree shrink from view. She had wanted more time. *Please, Lord. Give me strength until I have Mama's Bible in front of me.*

"Are you all right, Miss Howard?"

She forced brightness into her voice. "I am fine, my lord." She began to pull his coat off. "Thank you for the use of your coat."

"That can wait until we reach Fairview," he said. "After all, I promised you a dry and warm ride home."

He had. But the scent of his shaving soap—it was too intoxicating.

The ball. Speaking about that would distract her. "Are you looking forward to the ball, my lord?"

"I suppose." But he sounded less than interested. "I hope you and your brother are looking forward to it."

"We are." What ladies had she heard were to be invited? Before any came to mind, he sent the conversation in a different direction.

"Is your brother all right? He wasn't himself when I saw him today."

What should she say? Something had been troubling him, but she did not know what. Even if she did, she would hesitate to tell Lord Turner. Thomas needed his confidence.

Lord Turner leaned forward, his brown eyes warm with concern. "There isn't anything wrong with the Hall or a tenant? Something he may not have told me?"

"Oh no, my lord." That she did know for certain. "There was something about your property in Somerset, but it turned out to be nothing. He has just been tired lately."

"Is there anything I could do to help?"

"Actually there is." He should know about Thomas' artistic pursuits. He might be willing to help. "I hope you will agree with me when I say that my brother is good at managing the business needs of the Hall."

"I do. Without reservation. In fact, I find him to be excellent at his job, and I have told him as much."

"Thank you." Warmth singed her cheeks, and she was glad of the dim light. Schooling her heart, she continued, "But Thomas' talents do not lie merely in management. He is also a gifted artist."

"Really?" His mouth curled. "What does he do?"

"Sketches and paints. When he has the time."

Realization dawned on his face. "Miss Howard, I apologize for keeping him so busy. There have been many details to go over as I've tried to get a handle on everything."

"Please, do not apologize, sir. Of course you would have need of him. I only ask that you could, perhaps, spare him for a day or two."

"I'll do better than that." His eyes found hers. She nearly choked on her own breath. "I'll ask one of the bailiffs from one of my other properties to take over for a full week and order Thomas to enjoy himself."

Penelope's jaw dropped. "Thank you, Lord Turner. That is extraordinarily generous."

"Perhaps you should take time off as well. In fact, why don't you? You and Thomas could go somewhere together. I would even give you an extra week."

She hesitated. It was a tempting notion. But a fortnight? Who would see to the tenants and the cottagers in the village? Or the cottage hospital? Not to mention all the details at Fairview. It would be harvest time soon.

"I don't think the Hall or Fairview will fall apart," he said. Of course he knew what she'd been thinking. "There *are* people who can fill in for you."

"I know, my lord. It's just—"

"Where would you like to go?"

The firm lines of his face told her he did not care to hear the excuse she was trying to make. She gave a little sigh. Where could they go close by? "There is Southampton, or Brighton. Or the Royal Forest of Dean."

"All too close. I don't want you coming back in two days to check on things." He leaned back. "What about Ireland?"

Ireland? Years ago, before his trip to London, Thomas had dreamed about the two of them traveling there. He hadn't mentioned it since but she was certain he still wished for it. "Thomas would love that."

"Good. And don't even think of taking some sort of project with you related to the Hall. You told me earlier you don't get a chance to read very often. Take your Latin and Miss Bronte with you. If you need any more books, the library is at your disposal. I'll make the arrangements myself."

She raised her hands. "That won't be necessary. I can see to it."

"I insist. And I also insist on paying. You won't want for anything."

"Lord Turner that is too generous."

"As I said, I insist." Though he smiled as he spoke, the hint of steel was unmistakable.

She dropped her shoulders. "Thank you. May I ask one more favor?"

"Of course."

"Would *you* tell Thomas? I know he'll be grateful for the chance, but if he knew his sister was the reason—"

"I understand. It will be our secret."

An easy silence followed. Thomas would be so excited when he heard. The lines on his face would ease, and when he returned to Fairview, the concerns of the Hall would not weigh on him so heavily. And perhaps—*oh please, Lord God*—the time devoted exclusively to his art would allow the talent of his youth to return to his fingers. *Thank you, Lord, for this chance for him. And thank you for allowing me time away from here.*

No, that wasn't true. She flicked her gaze to Lord Turner. Her heart needed the time away from *him*.

Which families had been invited to the ball? Whose daughter would be most suitable for him? That the list was short to nonexistent was not helpful. Nor was the urge to put her name at the top. She clenched her jaw and shut her eyes. *Please, Father. Help my heart to stop being so foolish.*

The trip to Ireland would not come soon enough.

"You've been working too hard."

"My lord?"

"Weren't you dozing off just now?"

"No, I was praying." She twisted her hands under the coat. She'd spoken too quickly. She was not ashamed to say that she had been praying, but she couldn't admit her prayer had been about him.

But he didn't question her. Instead, he rubbed at a water stain on his trouser leg. "I'm glad your faith gives you strength."

The curious statement melted away her thoughts from just a moment ago. Didn't his faith do the same for him? "Thank you, sir."

Giving the stain a final swipe, he directed his attention to the window. He'd seemed like this earlier in the cellar, and she'd sensed not to push. But now something nudged her forward. "I don't know what I would do without the Lord's guidance or His grace."

He shifted his attention to her. "I can't imagine anyone needing grace less than you."

She studied her hands. "All have sinned, my lord. I am no exception."

"Very true, but I still find that hard to imagine."

"If my parents were here, they would be more than happy to inform you otherwise," she replied. Lord Turner's admiration resonated with the attitude her father had once held toward her. An attitude that could be far too damaging if left unchecked. "Pedestals can be dangerous things."

"I know," he replied. "And sometimes the fall from them can be permanent."

This fresh silence was no longer easy. It whispered in her ear and suggested that the war had damaged him far more than she realized. "I do not believe that. No one is beyond redemption."

"You don't know." His voice was so hollow it almost echoed. "You can't."

The coach came to a stop, and all at once he seemed himself again, but it was nothing more than a facade. "We're at Fairview. If anyone asks, I intend to say we encountered you walking near the Castle as we drove home."

"Thank you, my lord."

There was more she wanted to say, but he gestured toward his coat which she still wore. "I hope that helped keep you warm."

The door opened, and her chance was gone. Cleverly played on his part.

"Good day, my lord, and thank you again."

⁎⁎⁎

Mrs. Lynch stood at the door of the library. "You wished to see me, Lord Turner?"

John laid his novel aside. "Yes. Please come in."

She came forward and stood before his chair. She didn't like him. She respected his position, but the chill that hung in the air whenever he had to speak to her was almost tangible.

He rubbed his hands together before laying them in his lap. "I hope you can help me with a few things."

"I am at your disposal, sir."

Why did that thought make him uncomfortable? He plowed on. Best to get their meeting over as quickly as possible. "First, do you know what became of the basket Mr. Howard brought with him my first day here?"

"Cook unpacked it, put the contents in the house stores, and the basket was returned to Miss Howard."

"Do you recall what was in it?"

"I wasn't present at the time, sir. But I do recall Cook saying it was jams and cheese and bread." A slight scowl crossed her face and was gone the next instant.

"I can imagine the bread is probably gone."

"Yes, sir. I had the scullery maid feed the rest to the birds."

He allowed a slight edge to his voice. "If the jam and cheese are still around, I would like them sent up on a tray."

"Very well, sir."

"Secondly, Mr. Howard and his sister are planning a vacation."

"A vacation?" Her voice was a tad sharper.

He paused and searched for the English term. "A holiday. I wonder if you would see to the tenants while she is gone. I'm sure Mrs. Trull, Fairview's housekeeper, would be happy to assist you if you want."

"I'm sure I can manage." Her knuckles were bone white as she clenched them. "Is there anything else?"

"One more thing." Thank goodness. John resisted the urge to blow on his hands. "I want to continue holding the Harvest Festival just as Lord Renshaw did. Arthur Wilcox told me it's always very popular. Can you and Mr. Parker see to that?"

"Of course, sir. When will Mr. Howard and Miss Howard be leaving? It's just that Miss Howard also helped organize the event. If she is to be gone soon, I will need to know a few things from her."

"I'm not sure. The arrangements have yet to be made. But soon. I'll ask her to meet with you before she leaves."

She looked anything but pleased at the prospect. "Very well. While I'm here, my lord, I have a concern. I've noticed Arthur Wilcox in here quite a bit during his free time. I don't mean to pry, but the maids have found him in here by himself at times. Their virtue is in my care, and I don't want any harm to come to them."

If she didn't mean to pry, why ask? "Mr. Wilcox has my permission to come in here to read whenever he has the opportunity. He's helping me with a project. I've spent a great deal of time with him, and I assure you your fears are completely ungrounded." He picked up his book. "That will be all, thank you."

The fire felt considerably warmer once she shut the door behind her. He didn't like her any more than she liked him. Her efficiency at her job was the only thing that stood between her and unemployment for what she just implied about Arthur. Maybe he should let her go anyway.

He got up and walked to the window. August had slipped into September, and the days were growing shorter. A bare hint of color rested on the horizon as he looked out over Ashford Hall's sweeping front lawn. He had no doubts about Arthur's character, but something bothered the groom about the marker beneath— what had Miss Howard called it—the Angel Tree? If it was what Miss Howard claimed it to be, why had he been uneasy about it? Come to think of it, why were their stories different? Arthur knew too much about the ruins to be wrong, so why would Miss Howard lie? Or perhaps she had not told whole truth?

Did the rest of the story have something to do with the fact there was a child buried under that tree? How could it be connected to Miss Howard? The expression on her face as they drove away spoke of more than just grief over William. Something about it upset her more deeply than that. And he did not like that idea. Not one bit.

An infant sibling? Or a cousin? Parker had mentioned Lady Renshaw had been unable to have children. He did not say that she and William hadn't tried. A child of theirs would be buried with them in the church cemetery. He'd been there already, to pay his respects to Lord and Lady Renshaw. Mr. Gregory had graciously shown him the marker. Only their names were listed. Two things were certain. Something about the tree troubled Miss Howard, and Arthur Wilcox knew something about it.

A growl raked across his throat. He started for the bell pull next to the fireplace, his heart beating for the first time in almost a year with purpose. Whatever it was, he would force the facts out of the lad and fix everything.

A bare inch from the pull, he snatched his hand back. What was he doing? Fix everything? What happened whenever he tried to fix everything?

Resting both hands against the mantle, he bowed his head. He would destroy her and her deep and gentle faith. He refused to be responsible for wiping away that look he'd often seen on her face as she listened to Mr. Gregory speak or when she prayed. He would be more damned than he was already.

No one is beyond redemption. He had no doubt she believed it but, as he'd said, she didn't know. Maggie's sister, Beth, had died because he'd been drunk. A monster had taken Beth's virtue, another monster had tried to take the child born of that crime, and now the monster who killed her sat before a warm fire with a book at his elbow, trying to convince himself he could be forgiven.

He picked up *Jane Eyre* and returned it to its place on the shelf. He would begin what preparations he could for the Howards' trip in the morning. The sooner she got away from him, the better.

CHAPTER 17

After giving his coat and hat to the footman, John emerged from the dressing room at Hartsbury Manor and reluctantly walked toward his hosts who stood at the doorway of the ballroom. Mrs. Baines gave him a critical look up and down, taking in his tailcoat, silk tie, and vest. Her pinched face told him she had found nothing amiss. George had planned his attire tonight with the care and attention of a general preparing for battle. He would be elated it passed the most exacting of inspections.

"Good evening, Mrs. Baines."

She tipped her head. "Good evening, Lord Turner. You recall my brother, Sir James Abbott?"

"Of course."

"Do go in, Lord Turner," he said. "My daughter is inside arranging the evening's dancing."

Clusters of people stood around the ballroom, and he tugged on his vest. He didn't know any of them, but then that was the purpose of the evening. He had already gotten to know his tenants, and now it was time to get to know his neighbors.

Miss Abbott approached with the grace of an ice queen with her periwinkle dress and her ash brown hair swept up in a braided bun.

"How do you do, Lord Turner?" Her voice was as morning frost.

"I'm well, thank you, Miss Abbott." He glanced around the room. "Although I'm afraid I don't seem to know anyone here aside from you, your father, and your aunt."

"Then allow me to remedy that." She took his arm and guided

him toward a group of people. "Do you intend to dance this evening?"

"Yes. But I hope you will forgive me if I decide to sit out the second half," he replied. "An old injury."

"Of course."

Had William foreseen this when he insisted on the dancing lessons? It wouldn't surprise him. What had been an irritation at the time had now become a blessing. Now he could make it through the evening without looking like a bumbling American.

She introduced him to a fair number of people. Not all of them were snobs. Most were welcoming, although some were a tad cool in the face of his American accent. Unless, of course, he asked their daughters to dance. As they walked away from yet another effusive mother, he tugged at his cuffs. It was one dance, but they acted as if he'd all but proposed to them.

"Do not worry, Lord Turner," Miss Abbott said. "Only one more mother-daughter hurdle. Then I think etiquette will be satisfied."

"Pardon me?"

"I quite understand why these balls are so tiresome for people like you and me." She arched a brow. "Not enough people of substance or intelligence to suit either of us. What a pity the concept of the salon is out of fashion."

"Er, yes, a pity." Miss Howard had been right. Miss Abbott had a sharp mind. Too sharp for her own good.

After she obtained one last name for his dance card, she guided him over to a side room. Several small tables dotted the space as well as a long table which held a punch bowl and other small finger food. "I must see to more guests, Lord Turner. I hope you will excuse me."

"Of course, but before you leave, would you do me the honor of dancing with me this evening, Miss Abbott?" He couldn't help but notice the card hanging from her wrist was not as filled as it should be.

She seemed to glow as she added his name to her card. He would be walking a very fine line tonight. She was a nice enough lady, but marriage was out of the question.

He got a cup of punch and then noticed Dr. Royston approaching. He stiffened but managed to greet him civilly enough.

"I know. You weren't expecting to see me here," Dr. Royston said. "Why would Sir James and his sister invite the village doctor to their grand event? Services to the Crown. By rights, I should be referred to as Sir Henry Royston, but I prefer the title of doctor."

John caught the inference. Then he changed the subject. "Are you familiar with some tenants of mine? The Wilcoxes?"

The doctor nodded. "I am, indeed. You want to speak to me about Arthur Wilcox, don't you?"

"Yes," John said. "Has he spoken to you already?"

"No, but I know about his hopes to become a doctor. Lord Renshaw mentioned Arthur's aptitude for medicine before he passed. He hoped you would see it as well and encourage it." He drained his glass and set it aside. "He would be pleased."

"To be honest, I think you would be the best person to see to his education." John looked out over the crowd. "While I have every intention of funding Mr. Wilcox's education, I think he would be better off working at the hospital with you."

When the doctor didn't reply, he glanced over to find a deep frown creasing his face. "I assume that, once again, Hall matters keep you far too busy to take care of it yourself?"

John ignored the disapproving timber of the man's voice. "Yes."

Dr. Royston exhaled. "Very well. I will have to consult the board, but as you are the patron, I don't see any reason why it would not be possible. I will send word when I have seen to the arrangements."

"Thank you." John finished his drink and glanced around for a servant to hand his glass to.

"I understand you toured the cottage hospital." Dr. Royston spoke before he could make his escape.

"Yes. It's a fine establishment."

"Thank you. Lord Renshaw gave generously to make it so. But you didn't get to see all of it. Only one ward."

"I saw enough." A servant finally happened along, and he set his glass on the offered tray. "If you'll excuse me."

"Actually, I wonder if you could give me just another minute of your time." As the doctor continued, John clasped his hands behind him. "I got a very peculiar package in the post yesterday morning."

"Oh?"

"Yes, from the States. A Dr. John Hodgen, the Dean of the St. Louis Medical College in Missouri, sent me some extensive notes on the use of a splint he devised for fractures of the femur." The doctor's voice rose a notch. "Do you know Dr. Hodgen?"

"No." He had never actually met him, but his suspension splint was the reason he could walk around on two good legs instead of being in Peter Fletcher's unfortunate position. With the search for work for Mr. Fletcher stalled, sending him a telegram in Dr. Royston's name was the only thing that had finally allowed him to sleep more peacefully.

"Nor do I. Yet it was very curious of him to send them, considering one of my more recent cases." If Dr. Royston expected him to admit to anything, he would be disappointed.

Someone approached from behind. Miss Abbott spoke. "Lord Turner, the Howards have arrived."

Just in time. John turned to greet Thomas and his sister. His agent was dressed much the same as he, but he was unprepared for the sight of Penelope Howard.

Sage green brocade began bell-like at her feet and then rose to hug her slender waist. The sleeves, edged in creamy lace, wreathed only her upper arms, leaving her shoulders bare and taking his breath away. Honey gold hair hung in masses of ringlets lifted high on her head; one of them hung lower than the rest and brushed her collarbone. Her cheeks grew a violent shade of red as she drew her gaze elsewhere.

Thomas cleared his throat.

He'd been staring. And her brother had noticed. But he took John's hand when he offered it.

"It's, uh, good to see you both. I hope you came ready to dance. There are quite a number of young ladies here."

"Yes, I know. Miss Abbott already has names on my card." He nodded toward his sister. "And it looks like the old girl there won't be gracing the walls tonight."

Miss Abbott had led Miss Howard toward a group consisting mostly of gentlemen, and she accepted a dance from one of them. It was just nerves that caused John's hands to clench, and the fire in his chest must have something to do with the punch he just consumed.

"Good to see you, Mr. Howard," Dr. Royston said. "And it's good to see your sister out and about again. Let's hope she can find someone to settle down with."

"Pen?" Thomas scoffed. "She's married to the Hall and Woodley."

"She may not be after tonight," the doctor replied.

The cluster of gentlemen around her had doubled, but John did not join them. No good would come if he were to hold her in his arms, even if it was no more than the length of a waltz. The wall clock told him it was nearly time for the dancing to start. He excused himself to find his first partner for the evening. The first dance was the quadrille, and as groups of four partners formed on the dance floor, Miss Howard and her partner stood directly across from him and his.

A gentleman's daughter, the diminutive young lady looked up at him curiously. "Isn't that Miss Penelope Howard? The sister of your estate agent?"

Such a surprised tone, as if Miss Howard being here were inappropriate. Had she heard? She must have since she avoided her pointed stare.

"Yes, what about it?"

The careful balance of polite iciness in his voice pressed her lips together for the entire dance, which made the sensations aroused by the brief encounters with Miss Howard required by the dance impossible to ignore. For the remainder of that half of the evening, he managed not to be caught near her again. But even so, she and her partner would occasionally brush by him and his partner during the odd waltz.

He soon escorted Miss Abbott to the dance floor. A good number of murmurs and ice-cold expressions from some of the more eager mothers followed them. Her aunt, however, smiled like a cat that had got into the cream.

"I believe we are going to be the talk of the evening, sir," Miss Abbott said as the music began.

"I hope I haven't given you or anyone here the wrong impression." How could he say he was just being polite without offending her?

Her reply was blunt and to the point. "You do not have to worry. I am in no way expecting you to propose this evening or any other."

"That is … reassuring."

"But make no mistake, I am glad you asked me to dance. I have a request of you that my aunt would not wish me to make."

"Oh?"

"I have long heard of the Ashford Hall library." Her gray-blue eyes grew sharp with intensity. "I understand you have a whole section devoted to scholarly study. I would like your permission to come explore it. With my lady's maid, of course."

"I would be happy to have you come by. You're welcome any time."

A hint of warmth melted her features. "Then would tomorrow suit? I know tonight will be late, but I could come in the afternoon."

He agreed. The waltz ended, and he escorted her back to her aunt who sat in one of the many chairs arranged along the side of the dance floor.

"Thank you, Lord Turner, for the dance and your kind permission," she said.

"Permission?" Mrs. Baines' protuberant eyes went from her niece to him.

"Lord Turner has graciously granted me permission to come explore Ashford Hall's library, Aunt." Anyone would have thought he had just proposed to her.

Her aunt blanched.

"Isabella, what am I to do with you?"

But Miss Abbott sat down in her seat, unaffected by her aunt's displeasure. Sensing that she wished to speak to her niece without him present, John excused himself.

When supper was announced, he escorted his last partner into the dining room where a buffet was laid out and people stood, talking as they ate. After taking a light meal, he escorted her back to the ballroom and then returned to the dining room. His leg had held up fine, but if it were to remain so, he should sit out the second half of the dancing. Where was Thomas? A little male company would be nice before duty required him to mingle. He found him standing off to one side of the dining room with a glass of champagne.

"Hullo, John." He raised his glass and took a generous sip. "Enjoying yourself?"

"Perhaps you shouldn't drink the rest of that." Too many bitter memories came roaring back at the mild slur in his agent's voice.

"This? It's only my first glass." He set it down on a nearby table.

Of champagne, maybe. There weren't any spirits in the punch so far as he could tell. Unless Thomas had brought a flask. A little food would steady him. "Have you eaten yet?"

"I will in a moment. Here comes my plate now."

Miss Howard approached with two laden plates, pausing a moment when she saw John. She handed her brother his food.

"Good evening, Lord Turner." She had danced for the entire first portion of the ball and still looked as fresh as a new spring day.

"You look very well this evening, Miss Howard."

"Thank you."

Why had he said that? The color that rose in her cheeks only heightened her beauty.

Thomas snorted. "You act as if that's the first time you've noticed, John." His voice rose on the last few words. A few people turned their heads before resuming their conversations.

"Thomas," Miss Howard hissed.

His next words were quieter. "Sorry, old girl. I guess I should stick to the punch."

"A good idea," John replied.

Mrs. Baines approached. "Oh, Miss Howard, there you are. Lord Turner, Mr. Howard."

"This has been a lovely ball, Mrs. Baines," Miss Howard said. "Thank you so much again for inviting us."

Mrs. Baines' next words seemed to creak they were so stiff. "You are most welcome. But I wanted to tell you that I finally realized where I had seen such lovely brocade before. This was your mother's dress, was it not?"

John didn't miss the raised eyebrows of the ladies nearby, and judging from the fresh wash of crimson in her cheeks, neither had Miss Howard. "Yes."

"I knew it." Triumph colored her voice. "This is the same dress she wore to the ball Lord Renshaw held when she first came to Woodley to visit Lady Renshaw, is it not?"

"Not exactly. This was fashioned out of two of Mama's dresses."

"Oh, you're right, of course. There was no lace on this particular gown, and those rosettes that lined the front of it are gone now." Mrs. Baines bent slightly to examine the skirt. "You can't even see where they were. You are a clever seamstress, my dear."

"Actually," Thomas said, "our housekeeper and cook, Mrs. Trull, did the work. The old girl is far too busy to tend to it herself."

Miss Howard laid a hand on her chest, and Mrs. Baines' eyes narrowed. "Well, I shouldn't be very surprised. After all, all of Ashford Hall and Woodley are under her *express* care."

"Yes, they are." John raised his chin. Now he just had to master the urge to throw something. "And we're all better off for her efforts."

Miss Howard drew in a sharp breath. "If you would excuse me." Setting down her untouched plate, she quit the room.

Mrs. Baines set her cane as she eyed Miss Howard's retreat. "You place a great deal of trust in her, Lord Turner."

"I do. I have no reason not to." He glanced at Thomas. How could her own brother be so focused on a plate of food?

"You don't wonder why a woman of her beauty and reputation has not married?"

"No. That's her business."

She ignored the edge in his voice. "You might want to make it yours, Lord Turner. She represents both you and Ashford Hall." She nodded before stepping away into the crowd.

John's nails bit into his palms. "How could you just stand there?"

Thomas swallowed what was in his mouth. "John, Mrs. Baines has had it in for our family since Uncle William married Aunt Amelia and not her. Don't take it so personally."

"I do, and so should you. Especially when she takes aim at your sister."

Thomas waved a hand. "She's tough. She can take it."

If they had been any place else other than Hartsbury's dining room ... "You should have said something."

"I didn't have to. You did just fine on your own."

Better leave before he punched the man. John followed the path Miss Howard had taken. After making his way through those entering and exiting the dining room, he stepped into the entry hall and back into the ballroom. The large banks of double doors which ran along the back were wide open to allow fresh air to circulate among the dancers. Across the mass of dancers, he saw a bit of green brocade slip through them. It took an age to edge his way across the room, but it wouldn't do for anyone to think he was deliberately following her and make the wrong assumptions.

When he made it over to the doors, he found himself on a large terrace. Gas lamps were lit, and a few pairs of ladies were taking a turn in the small gardens at the bottom of the stone steps. The terrace was edged by a stone balustrade which curved around the edges of the house. Not seeing her down in the garden or on the terrace, he walked to the right and around the corner of the house. There she was, tucked away out of view of the doors, her back to him. He stopped. The moonlight glowed in her hair. She seemed relaxed enough, standing in front of the balustrade, staring out into the dark. Perhaps she was all right.

He shifted away, but then her hand rose and wiped each cheek. Without thinking, he strode over to her. Before he could speak, she turned and threw herself at his chest. His arms came around her without a moment's hesitation. Warning bells screamed in his mind, but he quickly silenced them. Nothing had ever felt so natural or so right. One hand rested on her waist, and the other gently rubbed her back.

She drew in a rough breath, and he tightened his hold, closing his eyes and resting his cheek on her soft curls. Letting out a shaky sigh, she pulled back just enough to stare at his vest. He'd give half his inheritance to be the moonlight playing across her face.

"I'm sorry, I know it shouldn't matter what she says," she whispered. "And I know you didn't mean to embarrass me, Thomas—"

"Penelope."

She looked up with a gasp. In another moment, she'd step out of his arms.

She didn't.

Instead, her eyes locked on to his. She relaxed against him, and fiery warmth grew beneath his hands. Where on earth his racing heart was going didn't matter. Hers was right alongside it. Her gaze dropped to his lips the same moment his slid to hers. His eyes slipped shut as their foreheads touched, and there was nothing else except the delicious thrill of her breath against his cheek.

He wasn't sure which of them trembled when their lips brushed. One thought dominated his mind. He hadn't felt anything softer or tasted anything finer. He lowered his mouth for another sip.

"Miss Howard?"

CHAPTER 18

M iss Abbott!

Penelope stumbled back, scanning the walkway behind them. It was empty. Had she seen them and run off?

"Miss Howard?"

No, she was still looking for her and would find her in another minute. She faced Lord Turner, but he was leaning heavily against the stone balustrade, his head lowered.

What should she say? Anything? Everything? If she had thought for one moment it had been him rather than her brother—

The same thing would have happened.

Hadn't her heart hoped Lord Turner would come to her aid? Almost counted on it? Oh, why hadn't Miss Abbott waited a second, a minute, an *eternity* longer before calling out for her?

No. It wasn't right. She should apologize for her brazenness.

But he spoke first. "I'm sorry."

His voice was deep and throaty. Penelope took a small step toward him. "No, my lord, I—"

"Miss Howard?" Miss Abbott called again, much louder this time.

Penelope walked away. She would apologize later. Just as soon as her head got her heart under tight control.

She met Miss Abbott just before she came around the corner of the house. She seemed irritated. Had she seen them?

"Your brother just told me how my aunt spoke to you," she said. "I must apologize."

Penelope relaxed. "It's quite all right. I was just ... getting a bit of fresh air."

"Of course." She stepped back as if to leave, then paused.

"Is something wrong, Miss Abbott?"

She tipped her chin up. "Would you take a turn with me? There is something I wish to ask you."

"Certainly." She gestured toward the terrace and, as soon as Miss Abbott's back was turned, stole a glance behind her. Lord Turner hadn't moved. She paused another fraction of a second then followed Miss Abbott.

Miss Abbott locked arms with her, and they walked along the edge of the terrace several moments before she finally spoke. "My aunt—and my father for that matter—are very determined that I should marry."

"Yes." Penelope's heart twisted. Miss Abbott's relatives were determined she marry Lord Turner. "I am sure they only want what is best for you."

"I have not yet had anyone ask for my hand. But it is only a matter of time before they can persuade someone to do so."

"Persuade? I think you are being hard on yourself, Miss Abbott."

They came to the steps which led to the lawn and stopped. "I don't think I am. I know I am not as graceful or tactful as most ladies my age, and I find most of the local marriageable men boorish, immensely stupid, or both. Lord Turner, I have found, is the sole exception."

"He is a very fine man." The words sounded far steadier than her heart.

"He is, but he has given me the distinct impression he has no desire to marry. And as I have no wish to be a baroness, there is little else to be said concerning him." Her eyes narrowed. "But my aunt and my father will eventually find somebody for me to wed, and I pride myself that I am logical enough to see the sense in the arrangement, despite the fact I would rather not enter into such an agreement. As I said before, I lack many, if not all, the qualities a lady of my breeding and social standing should have." She looked down at her clasped hands. "I wonder if I might come with you sometime when you see to Lord Turner's tenants. Hartsbury and its tenants will one day be mine, and I want to be prepared, you see."

"Surely, your aunt is the more appropriate person to prepare you for your inheritance."

"I rarely go with her." Though her face remained impassive, a flood of color filled her cheeks. "My presence sets most of the tenants on edge for the reasons I have already mentioned." She took a deep breath. "I have admired you for some time. I never understood why my aunt harbors such disapproval of you when you do so much good for the Hall and everyone in Woodley. You have a kind heart, and my objective in coming with you is to study you. I hope I can adopt some of that same kindness into my character."

She almost laughed. Miss Abbott made the whole thing sound like it was some sort of scientific study. Did she realize that true kindness was a matter of the heart, that empathy was as important as action?

Miss Abbott waited for her answer with a sort of calm detachment. She hadn't a clue.

"I would be happy to have you along whenever you have the opportunity," she said. "I usually go once a week, on Tuesdays."

Her brow arched. "Once a week? My aunt goes but twice a month."

"It was my mother's custom." Penelope linked arms with her once more and guided her toward the ballroom doors. "She found it made for a closer relationship between the Hall and its tenants."

As they entered the ballroom, Mrs. Baines eyed them with a narrow gaze from across the room. Penelope asked, "Will your aunt be offended?"

Miss Abbott gave her an unladylike shrug. "Perhaps, but do not let it concern you." Releasing Penelope's arm, she faced her. "Thank you."

She thrust out her hand. She wanted to shake hands? Penelope clasped the tips of her fingers, then watched her edge the dance floor to rejoin her aunt. What a curious woman. Penelope couldn't help but like her, despite her frigid regard of the world.

Several feet away, Lord Turner was talking to a group of gentlemen. She moved away before he noticed her. It had been ridiculous to run off like that. And shameless to pretend that Thomas would come after her when she knew all along it would be Lord Turner. Yet *he* had apologized. Why? She had kissed him, not the other way around.

But he'd said her name. Her Christian name.

She darted to a corner and pressed a hand to her roiling stomach. It meant nothing. It *had* to mean nothing. What about her plans for tonight? Yes, of course. She fumbled for her dance card and gazed at the back of it. She had made note of everyone he'd danced with this evening. Who had he seemed to favor?

None of them. He'd been kind and polite, the perfect gentleman, but the fact of the matter was *she* had been the only one he had seemed to take an interest in.

There was no other way to explain the fire in his chestnut eyes, the wild pace of his heart beneath her hand, the way he'd drawn her to him—*stop!* She clenched her hands. She had to stop now. The refreshment room. That's what she needed. A glass of punch would steady her. Then she would have Thomas take her home, where she would climb back on her shelf, and her infuriatingly beautiful dress would be relegated to the depths of her wardrobe.

Thomas was already in the refreshment room, laughing, rather loudly, with a group of ladies. His hand grazed the waist of the woman next to him—Miss Whitaker, a confirmed flirt—who rewarded him with an expression of mock disapproval.

"Thomas?"

He grinned at her. "Well, if it isn't my sister. Did Lord Turner find you?"

Catching the hint of spirits on his breath, she ignored his question. "I was just speaking to Miss Abbott. Thank you for sending her."

"It was she who was looking for you. I merely told her where you were and why." He slid his eyes in Miss Whitaker's direction and winked.

Penelope took his arm. "I'm tired and wish to go home."

"Couldn't Lord Turner take you?" Miss Whitaker's voice danced mischievously. "It was his coach that brought you, I noticed."

"Lord Turner was very kind to send a *separate* coach for our use this evening." The flirt quickly stiffened at the edge in Penelope's reply. "One that we are now ready to leave in. Thomas?"

She squeezed his arm. To her relief, he said his goodnights and escorted her to the door. Through some sort of good fortune, Mrs. Baines was not to be found, and they made their farewells to Sir James.

In the carriage, as they made their way down Hartsbury's drive, Thomas lounged back in the corner of his seat and raised one foot to rest on the edge of hers across from him.

She flipped her skirts away from his boot. "You're drunk."

"A bit tipsy, perhaps, old girl. I didn't drink that much." He shrugged. "I was enjoying myself."

"As you enjoyed yourself in London? That hardly ended well. I thought you had given up all that."

Bright moonlight shone through the coach window and caught the cold points of blue in his eyes. "According to you, perhaps I haven't." He pulled a flask from his breast pocket and took a sip. He grimaced when a sip was all he got. "All out."

Penelope set her jaw and looked out the window. But his eyes were still on her, a sensation difficult to ignore.

"You know, you didn't answer my question back there? Did he find you?"

"It hardly matters now."

"You mean to tell me after looking at you the way he did nearly all evening, good old John didn't come looking for you?" She gave him a warning glance. He ignored her. "That's a surprise, especially after defending you so eloquently to Mrs. Baines."

A warm thrill shot through her chest, but it froze at her brother's next words. "I've only seen one other man stare at you for that long, and that was years ago. Whatever happened to old Edmund Kern?"

An iron rod replaced her spine. "He was stationed to a post in India."

"I never understood why our father *and* Uncle Will disapproved of him." He snorted. "Then again, our father was the master of disapproval, wasn't he? I don't think the man was happy unless he was *unhappy* about something. Even you seemed to lose some of your shine in his eyes toward the end."

"Enough!" she snapped. "Whatever you thought of Papa, he was an honorable man who wanted the best for both of us. Perhaps he did you a grievous wrong by—"

"*Perhaps?* He eroded away my skill to almost nothing!"

"What else could he do? What did you expect from him in light of the circumstances?"

"Mercy!" She jumped at his wounded growl. "He was my father, and I needed his mercy and his forgiveness."

"He said he forgave you. That … that last day."

"The words of a dying man fearful for his own soul." Thomas turned his attention to his window.

Her throat tightened at the lines of pain on his face. "He did love you, you know."

Without shifting his gaze, he shook his head. "No. He loved *you*. He *never* loved me."

They rode the rest of the way home in silence.

Once they reached Fairview, Fanny opened the door for them. Thomas stumbled as he walked in. Fanny looked at Penelope.

"Go to bed, Fanny. I will take care of Mr. Howard."

"Yes, miss."

Penelope helped her brother mount the stairs and opened the door to his room for him. He tossed his top hat aside and yanked off his coat then his tails. Falling into bed, he was asleep by the time she had carefully laid his things over a chair and placed his hat on his dressing table. He didn't budge when she removed his boots. She opened the curtains. He liked to sleep with them open so the morning light would wake him.

Moonlight fell on his side table next to his bed. She stepped over to it and watched his back rise and fall for a moment as he lay there, face down. He kept the key to his attic studio in the drawer. That look Miss Whitaker had given him. She grasped the drawer pull. It slid out an inch, squeaking a little. The next instant, his hand clenched hers, and she gasped.

Thomas propped himself up on one elbow. "Don't."

She let go of the pull, and he released her hand as she moved away and quit the room, the door slamming shut behind her.

CHAPTER 19

John stood at the door of the Hall, hands clenched behind him, as he watched Miss Abbott and Mrs. Baines exit their carriage. Where was Miss Abbott's lady's maid? She had said she would be accompanying her this afternoon, not her aunt.

A hawk flew overhead. He envied it.

He swallowed the yawn that threatened to escape his throat. Despite arriving home last night at a reasonable time, sleep had eluded him. He'd sent George off to bed and prowled Ashford Hall's corridors and stairs. Penelope—Miss Howard—dogged his every step. Her scent of lavender and roses clung to him, and their brief kiss replayed in his mind. It was as if he were back in Philadelphia, trying once again to stay sober and failing miserably. One taste, and he wanted more.

He'd finally had enough when he found himself in the library reaching for *Jane Eyre*. After coming close to chucking the book out the window, he forced himself to bed where sleep eventually took him.

Maybe Miss Abbott or her aunt would ask to borrow the book. But Miss Abbott was immediately drawn to the scholarly section of the library while the elder regarded the rooms with a pinched, downturned mouth and cool eyes.

"I imagine you are wondering why I'm here, Lord Turner," she said.

"I admit, I'm curious," he said politely.

"Well then, perhaps we could speak together in your morning room. Where it is less dust"—she paused—"more private. I am sure my niece's reputation is safe within the walls of your library."

She lowered her chin. "Or any library for that matter. If I recall, we can reach the morning room through Lord Renshaw's study."

He led her to the room and paused to shut the doors. Mrs. Baines stepped deeper into the room to take note of the covered furniture.

"Mrs. Lynch hasn't opened this room yet? At Hartsbury, she was such a model of efficiency."

That explained nearly everything about Mrs. Lynch. "I didn't know she had worked for your brother."

"She rose to the position of head housemaid before she decided to come here. We were most sorry to see her go. But then we couldn't blame her. She had risen as far as she could with us. I wouldn't trade Mrs. Fisher even for her." With the end of her cane, she attempted to flip up the corner of a sheet that covered a small chair but stopped when dust billowed off it. "You really should let her at least air out this room, sir."

"I don't need this room, so there's no point in bothering her with it." He clasped his hands behind his back. "But we're not in here to talk about my housekeeper."

Mrs. Baines planted her cane in front of her and propped her hands on the head. "First, there is this matter of Arthur Wilcox. My brother is on the board, and he told me of your request to Dr. Royston. You wish your *groom* to study medicine? Why? Will it improve your breeding stock?"

John worked his jaw before replying. "No. Mr. Wilcox has told me he wants to become a doctor. As he is a very intelligent young man, I see no reason why he shouldn't."

"I see," she replied, although her whole bearing indicated she really didn't. She waved a dismissive hand. "That really isn't my most pressing concern. I'm sure you must still be wondering about the remarks I made last night regarding Miss Penelope Howard."

"No. I'm not." Knowing now of her petty dislike of the Howards, they had occupied his thoughts for less than a minute.

"You know, of course, that Miss Howard is Lord Renshaw's

niece by marriage." He nodded, and she went on. "Did you know he arranged for her training as a nurse?"

"No, but it doesn't surprise me. William was a benevolent and generous man."

She sniffed lightly at his use of Lord Renshaw's Christian name. "Yes, well, Miss Howard is a Nightingale nurse."

"Of which I am also aware." He squeezed the bridge of his nose. "I really don't see where you are going with this, Mrs. Baines."

Her voice flattened. "Fine. I shall get to the point. She began her training five years ago at the age of twenty." She stared at him as if this piece of news should speak volumes.

"And?"

"Lord Turner, surely you know Miss Nightingale's school will not take anyone under the age of twenty-five. And she left here for that institution very suddenly."

"What are you suggesting?" He heard his voice as if it came from the bottom of a well.

She did not heed its depth. "Only that you might want to look into it. She is your representative to your tenants, however unorthodox that role may be. Her reputation should be beyond reproach."

He crossed his arms over his chest. "It is beyond reproach. Unless you can prove otherwise?"

She pulled in her chin. Finally, he had the upper hand.

"No," she said. "I can only offer you my suspicions."

"Which are nothing more than circumstantial." He strode over to the doors and pulled one open. "And I would appreciate it if you kept them to yourself."

Mrs. Baines swept past him. A noise distracted him from following. The other door that led to the entry hall was ajar, but he saw no one through the slender crack. He shrugged. It must have blown open somehow.

He entered the library just as Mrs. Baines passed her niece, who sat surrounded by books at the long oak table.

"Isabella, we're leaving," she said.

Miss Abbott looked up with wide, keenly disappointed eyes. Almost too disappointed. "But Aunt Dorothea, I haven't finished."

Her aunt merely continued her retreat from the room. Miss Abbott bit her lip and rose, gathering up the books she had pulled. John joined her and helped. Her alabaster face was an abnormal shade of pink.

"I wanted to write down the names of the books I hoped you would allow me to borrow." She spoke to him but glanced up at the window as she did so.

John caught a familiar figure step behind the bush outside. "That's all right, Miss Abbott. Just take what you want. I have a list I can check and figure out what you've borrowed."

"Isabella!" Mrs. Baines cackled from the grand foyer.

The sight of the cool and collected Miss Isabella Abbott flustered and hurried was one he would not soon forget. Thanking him, she held the books to her chest, gave the window a final look, dipped him a quick curtsy, and dashed out of the room. John only just made it to the front door to see them off. He strode back into the library and threw open the window that had so enraptured her.

Arthur stared back, his face whiter than a snowy day. "I know what you're going to say, my lord. But I swear I had no idea she was in the library or who she was."

"Come in through the side door like you usually do." He gestured toward the small door that led outside, situated at the end of the room, then closed the window and met him at the table. A frightened rabbit stared back at him.

"I'm not angry," he said before pulling a little of the humor from his voice. "But I would like to know what happened."

Arthur's shoulders dropped. "Mr. Milford was done with us for the day, like usual. So I thought I would see if you had any more books for me and return the ones I finished. I almost didn't come in because I saw you and Miss Abbott through the window. But then you left, and I thought I was in the clear." He pointed at the shelves next to the door. "She was just over there, where I wouldn't have seen her, trying to reach for a book. I didn't think, my lord, truly I didn't. I ... I reached up and got it for her."

"Being helpful isn't a crime."

"No, sir, but I've heard Mrs. Lynch isn't pleased about me coming to the library. One of the maids told me."

"Don't worry about Mrs. Lynch. *I* trust you, and that's what matters." He softened his voice. "Go on."

As he picked up the thread of his story, he turned red. "She looked at me, and I looked at her, and for a minute we didn't say anything. Then I saw what book she had—that Latin book you gave me—and I introduced myself and told her it was very useful. She didn't believe me until I started in on my Latin verbs, then she spoke them too. But then we heard you coming, and she shoved me out the door. I went to the window." His face fell. "I didn't realize she was who she was until I saw Mrs. Baines. What will she think of me when she finds out who *I* am?"

"You might be surprised," John said. "She left here with some books, but she didn't get a chance to write down which ones she was taking. Do you have the time to help me figure out which ones they were?"

Between the two of them, they soon formed a list. John went to his study and wrote a quick note to Miss Abbott. He folded it and the list together and handed the packet to Arthur.

"Shall I give this to Percy to take to Hartsbury, my lord?" he asked. Percy was the hall boy who, among other things, ran messages for the Hall.

John shook his head. "I would prefer you take this to Hartsbury since you know how important the contents are. And be sure to tell them I told you to put this into Miss Abbott's own hands."

Arthur's eyes widened. "But she'll know who I am. *What* I am."

"Better to find out what kind of woman she is sooner rather than later." Maggie flashed through his mind. "Trust me."

Arthur paused then waved the note. "You're right, my lord. Thank you." He strode to the side door and out of the library toward the stables.

John watched him go before turning back to the oak table to reshelve the books. One thing was clear: the lad was a goner. He reminded John of another young man he knew a long time ago. Himself. He'd been the exact same way the first time he'd seen Maggie Harding.

What had he done to her? She'd been a good woman. She understood his need to work with the poor in an effort to absolve himself, and God knows she tried tirelessly to get him to stop drinking. But when all was said and done, they wanted different things. The war had made paupers out of her and her younger sister, Beth. She longed to re-enter society. But he didn't see himself worthy of that. And they fought. And he drank. And in the end, Beth had paid for it.

The night of one of their fights, Beth had slipped away for some fresh air and, not being familiar with that part of the city ...

Bile rose in his throat. Both he and Maggie had tried to convince her to keep the child. But she couldn't bear the thought. She'd tried to get rid of it, and when that hadn't worked, Maggie brought her to him. But he'd been drinking. He should have sent for Robert. Why hadn't he?

Because he'd been a fool.

Was he even a bigger fool for coming here? He raised his fist to his mouth. Somehow the faint scent of lavender and roses lingered on his hand. If he didn't get Penelope Howard away from him, and soon, he would be.

CHAPTER 20

Lord Turner did not attend church Sunday morning. Mr. Gregory had skillfully expounded on the topic of redemption, and Penelope turned the message over in her mind as she and Thomas rode home. Would it have eased his soul? But then it was something of a relief, him not being there. Their encounter at the ball was still fresh in her thoughts. If only she could erase it from her memory.

Thomas cleared his throat. She roused herself. Had he said something? "I'm sorry. What did you say?"

"I asked if you knew why Miss Bromley wasn't at church this morning."

"I'm not certain." They were driving along the road her cottage was on. She should look in. In all likelihood, her morning sickness had taken a turn. "Why don't you let me off at the end of her lane? I'll check on her and walk home. The day is very fine."

"All right, but if she's ill, convince her to come to Fairview where you and Hannah can care for her."

"That is very kind of you. But I'm sure she will want to remain on her own."

He gave her a reproving snort and snapped the reins. "Make sure you convince her."

Her heart weighted her down as she walked up the short lane to Clara's cottage. His feelings hadn't changed, even after Clara had muted her own the last time she had dinner with them. What if he had to be told? If he did, he, of all people, should understand.

As she suspected, Clara's morning sickness was to blame.

"I ran out of tea," she said as Penelope settled her in a chair in front of the fireplace. "I meant to ask you for more, but I forgot."

"I'll bring some later today. Is there anything else you need at the moment? I would stay, but I must get back for luncheon. You know Thomas. He doesn't like to wait."

Clara swallowed. "Yes, I know. But if you could wait one moment longer, I have news."

Penelope sat in the chair opposite her. "The father?"

"He's coming to discuss everything."

Every muscle in her body cried out in relief. *Praise God.* "I am so glad. When? I can arrange to be here if you know the day and time."

"It will be when his duties permit." She clenched her hands. "But I must meet with him alone."

Alone? Surely she had not heard right. "What do you mean? You cannot meet with him alone. It isn't proper."

The girl lifted her chin. "How? We've been alone together before."

"Precisely. And you were fortunate no one discovered your dalliance. How can you be willing to risk your reputation once again?"

"What does it matter if we are to be married?"

"Has he given you any promise of that?"

"No, but why else would he come here?"

Penelope rose and swiped a hand across her forehead. "You cannot be so naïve, Clara. Did it ever occur to you that he might refuse to marry you?"

Stony silence followed. It was almost a full minute before Clara replied. "Did it ever occur to you to not step into that carriage?"

Penelope faltered. What was there to say to that? She gathered her Bible and reticule and let herself out.

Clara's words followed her home, biting at her heels with every step. She had often asked herself that question. But what did the answer matter now? Things were as they were and nothing could change them. In the end, she was still a child of God. Yet, even after such a reasonable argument, the words still stung and weighed her down.

"You've been quiet," Thomas remarked as they sat in the study after luncheon. He flipped shut his volume on sheep husbandry. "You're sure Miss Bromley's illness is nothing serious."

"Yes, I'm sure. She'll have no problem teaching tomorrow." She stared down at the book she'd been reading. Or pretending to read. She needed to convince Clara to let her be there when the father called. The first step was to try to heal the breach between them. Tomorrow she would be busy with seeking out someone to help at the Fletchers, and the next day, Miss Abbott would be accompanying her on her visits. Perhaps she could send a note with the tea.

Fanny stood in the doorway. "I'm sorry, Mister Thomas, Miss Penelope. This just came from the Hall."

She handed Thomas a note. Penelope returned to her reverie. The father was coming when his duties permitted. And he was from Bristol. So he could not be coming for a day at least—

Paper appeared before her eyes. Thomas stood over her, with the note. "Apparently, this is for you."

The depth of his voice startled her. Was the missive from Clara? Had she written too openly of her condition? She unfolded the note with shaky hands. They relaxed the next instant. It was from Mrs. Lynch wanting to know about any details she could give regarding the Harvest Dinner before she and Thomas went on holiday. But why should that bother him? Surely Lord Turner had told him already.

"A holiday?" he asked evenly.

Evidently not.

"Well, yes. What's wrong with that?"

"May I ask why?"

"I told Lord Turner of your artistic pursuits, and knowing how hard you have been working, he offered to send us to Ireland for a fortnight." His whole form tensed, so she quickly continued, "I remembered how you always wanted to paint there. I had hoped you'd be pleased."

"It's harvest time, Penelope," he said. "I would have thought you would know what a busy time that is, not only for me but for the whole estate. And with him reinstating the Harvest Dinner, it will be busier still."

She gaped at him. "But Lord Turner is getting a bailiff from one of the other properties to see to your duties. Thomas, think. Two weeks of nothing but painting and sketching. Your old talent might return." She snapped her mouth shut. She'd said too much. He lowered his head and backed away. "Oh Thomas, I'm so sorry."

"So I am nothing more than a dishonest, talentless estate agent." Despite her pleas to remain, he left the room.

The headache that had kept John home from church finally subsided as he strolled around the Hall's garden after lunch. Should he stay at the Hall? It might be better for everyone concerned if he lived in London. He was sending Miss Howard away for what? A two-week reprieve? She would return, and they would be thrown together in some way, shape, or form. And somehow history would repeat itself.

He wandered toward a fountain. Water trickled and danced from an urn held by a weatherworn cherub.

Atop a pedestal.

Pedestals can be dangerous things.

Miss Howard's words were truer than she realized. He'd fallen from his own, from Maggie's, and worse, he'd fallen from God's. Because what else was salvation but that? The Lord had raised him up and seated him with Christ, just as the Bible said. And what had he done? Jumped off. Willingly. Permanently. There was no hope of climbing back up. How could he when he was still falling? He grasped a wrought iron gate for support. He was falling into a pit with no bottom and no hope.

When he finally looked up, he realized he was holding onto the gate which, according to Parker, led to William's favorite part of the garden. No. He pushed himself away. He couldn't walk there. It would only add to the weight that now bore down on him and increase the speed of his eternal fall.

As he rounded a tall hedge, Thomas strode toward him, eyes narrowed. He hadn't seen him since their encounter at the Ball. Considering his current mood, the man was not the most welcome of sights.

"Hall business will have to wait for another time." He strode past him, but Thomas did an about-face and matched his quick pace.

"I'm not here on Hall business," he said.

The venom in his voice caused John to come to a halt. "Then what do you want?"

Thomas stopped as well and folded his arms across his chest. "I understand a trip to Ireland is in my future."

"How did you find out?"

"My sister told me."

Miss Howard told him? After being so adamant that *he* tell him? "And what if it was?"

Thomas let loose a bark of humorless laughter. "My little sister. Always looking out for me."

"Which is more than she can say for you." The memory of him standing by, blithely eating a plate of food while Mrs. Baines picked Miss Howard apart flew across his mind, and his hands curled into fists.

"And why should you care so much, *Lord* Turner?" Thomas sneered. "Don't think I missed how you stared at her at the ball and how readily you went after her. What I can't fathom is, why send her away when you so obviously have feelings for her?"

John refused to take the bait. "And I can't fathom why you treat her so poorly. You act as if she's your servant instead of your sister."

"Thank you for your generous offer." He spat out the words. "But considering the upcoming Harvest Dinner and our regular duties, a trip is out of the question."

Thomas strode back the way he came.

Two days later, Arthur stepped through the doors to John's study. "You wanted to see me, sir?"

John leaned back in his chair and sighed. Arthur had come just in time. The estate books he'd been going over had come perilously close to being chucked out the nearest window. He really had no business taking on the monotonous task without Thomas. But he'd been left with little choice. He arched his back, rubbed his neck, and then started shifting the mess before him. "Yes, Arthur. Please sit down."

Some papers slipped off, and Arthur picked them up. "Is Mr. Howard here, my lord? You usually go over these with him."

John took the papers and set them aside. Where was the letter Dr. Royston sent? "No. Mr. Howard is busy today, so he sent these for me to look over." He tensed as anger reignited in his chest. He tamped it down. He had good news for Arthur. No sense in letting Thomas spoil it.

He found the letter and held it as he spoke. "You've been tearing through the medical books in the library."

"Yes, your lordship. I hope I haven't taken any you might want."

"No. But it's clear that you have a genuine interest in it. How would you feel if I were to sponsor your medical education?"

Arthur sat up straight and grasped the arms of the chair. "Really, my lord?"

"Yes. But I warn you, it's not easy. You will have to work very hard."

He set his jaw. "I will. I'm no stranger to hard work."

"Good." John took the chair opposite him and handed him

the letter. Arthur's fingers flew to open it. John knew what it said. Dr. Royston had made all the necessary arrangements, and Arthur would start at the beginning of next week. He would room with the doctor and assist him when he was not studying.

Arthur's shoulders dropped. Not the reaction John expected.

"What is it?"

"Nothing, my lord," he said as he folded the letter. "I just thought you and I would be taking this on."

He'd anticipated this reaction. "Dr. Royston is the better choice than I am. Besides, depending on the route you want to take, tutoring will be necessary to bring you up to speed in certain subjects."

Arthur shifted in his seat, repositioning his legs. "Why can't I work under your lordship?"

John waved at his desk. "The estate takes up a great deal of my time."

He rose and began to straighten it. He closed ledgers with quick snaps and set them in a stack.

Arthur didn't move. "But tutoring me here would make more sense. Dr. Royston doesn't have a library like this."

John forced his voice past the ball of guilt that clogged his throat. "The library will be at your disposal. If you need anything, you can come take whatever you like, whenever you like."

"Why—"

The sounds of yelling and horse's hooves drifted in through the front windows, interrupting their conversation.

They strode to the front portion of the library. A small pony cart tore up the drive with Miss Abbott at the reins, her face a chalk-white mask of fear. Arthur knocked over a chair in his haste to get out the door, and John followed close behind. Why was she driving Fairview's cart? It slid as it came to a halt, the horse nearly sitting down.

"What's wrong?" John bellowed as Arthur grabbed the horse's bridle.

"Miss ... Miss Howard." Miss Abbott all but fell into Arthur's arms as he helped her down.

No! John flew to the back of the cart. But the sight that met his eyes was not what he expected.

It was worse.

Miss Howard held a little girl across her lap, blood staining her plain cotton dress as the bone from the child's broken shin protruded through the skin. The girl was wailing, and Miss Howard stroked her hair as she tried to soothe her. Despite the chaos, she was the picture of calm. "We were visiting her father's farm when she fell. You must help her."

The wood bit into his fingers as John gripped the side of the cart. Help? How could he help when all he could see were ghosts of wounded men before his eyes? And Beth Harding among them. And the blood. Acrid, metallic—he screwed his eyes shut and then opened them. The memories disappeared, and the little girl's wails turned to whimpers as Miss Howard hushed her.

"Arthur!"

The young man dropped Miss Abbott's hand and joined him. "Sir?"

"Your first patient," he said.

"What?" Miss Howard stared at him.

Arthur was no less surprised. "But sir—"

John grabbed him by the shirt and pushed him toward the cart. "Don't leave her in pain. Do it."

Their eyes met for a brief instant. He should be ashamed of himself. Arthur had no experience with this. He'd only read about it. John had done it countless times. For less than a second, he considered it. No. He couldn't.

With a jerk, Arthur pulled himself from John's grasp and climbed into the cart. A detached calmness came over him. Good. He wasn't panicked. Miss Abbott watched, frozen to her spot.

"Arth—Mr. Wilcox?"

Arthur knelt beside the whimpering child. "Izzy, go round to the stables."

As Miss Abbott picked up her skirts and ran off, Parker darted down the steps toward them. John instructed him to fetch some strips of cloth and two lengths of straight wood. The butler sent Joseph off to fetch them.

"Does Arthur need assistance, my lord?" he asked.

John shook his head and walked over to the side of the cart. "What bone is that?"

"The tibia," Arthur replied.

"You remember what to do?"

He set his jaw, then gave the little girl a small smile. "Hullo there, Sally."

"What'r you goin' to do, Arthur?" she sniffed.

"I have to pull on your leg, just a bit." He flexed his fingers.

"Get on with it," John muttered.

At the same moment, the little girl began to cry. "Arthur, please don't!" Arthur gave Miss Howard a warning look, and she bent over the little girl, blocking her face from her legs. "It will all be over in a moment, darling."

Without warning, Arthur yanked on the leg. She gave a blood-curdling squeal and was quiet.

Miss Howard checked her. "She's just unconscious."

John rested his head against the side of the cart. Well done, Arthur.

When Joseph handed Arthur the cloth and wood, John said, "Be sure to—"

"I know." There was a depth to Arthur's voice. And why not? Parker watched John with a set jaw.

Charlie Milford jogged up with Miss Abbott close behind. "What's going on? This young lady came back to the stables, cryin' of broken bones and looking whiter than death."

"Arthur has just set his first broken leg," John said.

Charlie looked at his groom with a raised brow. "Good for you, lad."

"Thank you, sir." Arthur climbed from the cart. "Go fetch the best-sprung carriage the Hall has, Mr. Milford. This girl needs to get to the cottage hospital as smoothly as possible."

"It's coming round now."

Sure enough, a carriage came around the corner of the house. Arthur, with Joseph steadying the splinted leg, lifted little Sally from the bed of the cart and carried her over to the carriage that halted next to it.

"I'll accompany the child on the journey," Miss Abbott said. A bit of color had returned to her cheeks.

"Isabella, are you sure?" Miss Howard asked, accepting Parker's aid out of the wagon.

"Yes, I'll be fine now that the ... blood ... is covered up." She walked over to the carriage and gave Arthur a quick look of admiration. It softened her face and gave her a loveliness that he wasn't aware she possessed.

Color rose in Arthur's face as she climbed in, and he and Joseph gently positioned the child next to her.

Arthur shut the door. "I'll go with them. It will give me a chance to see where I'll be staying and find out what I should take with me when I go."

"Where would you stay but here?" Charlie stared at his groom as if he didn't quite recognize him.

"I meant to tell you later today, Mr. Milford," John replied. "Arthur plans to become a doctor. I've arranged for him to study with Dr. Royston. This will be his last week with you."

"So that's why you've been havin' all those books in your room." He walked up to Arthur and shook his hand.

"I'm sorry if this leaves you short-handed," John said.

But Charlie shook his head. "Couldn't be happier. Always thought he was too smart for the stables."

"Arthur," Joseph squeaked, "what will mum say?"

"I sincerely hope your mother will be one of the proudest women in the county," Parker replied. He added his good wishes, then he and Joseph walked back into the Hall.

"They should get going. Sally needs attention," Miss Howard said, her voice unusually quiet.

Arthur climbed up on the seat next to the driver. "I'll see Miss Abbott home before I return."

John raked a hand through his hair, then over his face. He could hardly blame the lack of respect in Arthur's voice. What if the break had been more complicated or Arthur had pulled it at the wrong angle? John had turned away from medicine to prevent himself from hurting people, and now that very avoidance could have hurt a child instead.

Miss Howard said something to Charlie about the cart, but he didn't stay to hear it. He rushed up the stairs two at a time. He started toward the library, but an angry voice stopped him.

"What on earth were you thinking?" Miss Howard swept over the threshold. Her hair was tousled, and her eyes were blue sparks. "Arthur has no experience setting bones. Did you not see how terrified he was? How he hated to cause Sally pain? Why wouldn't you set it?"

"Why did you even bring her here to begin with?" He could hardly believe she had done it. He had thought she was different, not like Maggie. While his heart told him she was truer than that, he plowed on. Perhaps if he growled and raged at her, she would see just what kind of monster he was and leave him alone. "You should have gone straight to the cottage hospital."

"Going there would have taken twice as long." Her voice echoed throughout the hall. She took a step toward him. "Ashford Hall made the most sense because you are a doctor—"

"I *was* a doctor!"

She strode up to him until she was inches away. Raising her head, she locked her eyes to his. "I don't believe that."

Her scent of lavender and roses toyed with him, dissolving his anger. And her declaration …

"The war does not have to keep you from your calling." Her

voice grew soft and beautifully, dangerously warm.

Her fingers curled around his. Their heat threatened to seep through to his heart. He should tell her everything. She would understand.

Would she understand how he killed Beth? And even if she did, would he deserve her mercy?

"Yes, it does. It's better that way." John jerked free and backed away. He needed to get away from her. Much farther than the few feet between them now. "Why did you tell Thomas about the trip?"

She swayed at the rapid change in subject. "That was an accident. He opened a message meant for me."

Regret shone on her face. He clenched his hands as he focused on a seam in the floor. "Why doesn't he want to go?"

"I don't know. He wouldn't tell me."

"I could make him go," he offered.

"No. That would not be wise."

"Why?"

She shook her head. "It's not for me to say."

He whirled around. First that blasted tree, now this. What was she refusing to tell him now? He stopped, both hands frozen in his hair. Did one have something to do with the other? Surely Thomas wasn't wrapped up in the reason a child was buried beneath that tree. His arms swung to his sides as he turned to ask her, but she was gone. He strode to the door and watched her drive away from the house.

CHAPTER 21

The next morning, Penelope set out early enough to walk to Clara's cottage before her students arrived. She could have sent someone to take the tea to her. Maybe she should have. But Clara's determination to meet with the father of her child alone drove her to take the task upon herself. Clara had not thought this through. She didn't realize what else was at stake aside from her reputation. With the school being funded from her uncle's annuity, there was the reputation of the Hall to consider. But what about her? She didn't have a spotless reputation, yet the honor of the Hall rested on her shoulders more heavily than Clara's. The ugly gash she'd made in the fabric of her own life had mended, but poorly. What business did she have saying anything to Clara? Hadn't she made enough mistakes just over the past few weeks? First her suspicions about her brother and then her scheming over their trip—Thomas still wasn't speaking to her.

Then there was Lord Turner.

First the ball, then their argument. She still didn't understand everything he'd said. How was it good that he allowed the war to keep him from being a doctor? He was such a good man, a kind man. The first man in years who touched a part of her soul that—

She stopped. There would be no going forward with that thought. She would send a note of apology, then stay away from him. Far away. Though how she would manage that, she hadn't a clue.

She walked up to Clara's door and knocked. Clara opened it with a cool countenance. "Good morning, Miss Howard."

"Good morning, Clara." She waited to be let in, but the girl did not move an inch. She offered the tin of tea she'd bought. "I promised to bring you this. I'm sorry I could not come until today."

"You shouldn't have troubled. I am very capable of taking myself to Woodley to purchase tea."

"Of course you are." But she was puzzled. Since when did Mr. Brown stock peppermint tea in his shop? Yet even as she had the thought, a breeze carried a whiff of mint from inside the cottage. Whatever brand he carried, it was an inferior one. She withdrew the tin. "How are you feeling?"

"Well, as you can see. Please excuse me, Miss Howard. My students will be arriving soon."

Penelope caught her before she shut the door. "Clara, please. Reconsider. I could wait in the schoolroom if you like."

"I've made my decision. Unlike yours, mine will turn out for the best." The door slammed shut.

Penelope raised her chin and strode away from the cottage. Clara was young and impulsive; she really hadn't meant what she'd said. Being with child made every woman a tad sharp. But the sting of her words had dealt their blow. And the truth of them cut deep.

John reined Fortis in from a canter to a walk and looked around to see where he'd finally ended up. He could just see the Castle in the distance. He rubbed his bad leg. Time for a break and that was as good a place as any. If there was a corner or an inch of the estate he hadn't yet seen, that wasn't the case now. He'd been riding over it for the better part of the day. With any luck, the ruins would be deserted despite the crisp cheerfulness of the day with its blue sky and lazy sheep's wool clouds. How could such beauty exist in the same moment as the turmoil that raged in his heart?

He had been foolish to come here.

All he'd wanted was a safe haven, a place to ride out the rest of his days in peace and quiet with no danger of hurting anyone else ever again.

Instead, his fall from grace was picking up speed.

Fortis ambled over the bridge that spanned the Castle's moat. An empty expanse of green and ancient stones greeted them. It should have seemed peaceful, but the breeze that played in his hair as he tied Fortis to the makeshift hitching post was a gale and the sunshine as blinding as heavy rain. His gaze was drawn to the shade of the oak tree. No. He didn't need to wonder after that again. The great hall. It would hold his interest. He wandered in and around it as he ate an apple he'd taken from the Hall's orchards. But in the end, the ache in his leg drew him back outside. It needed rest. The tree with its enormous trunk invited him to sit beneath its fading green branches. He sighed. Resting in its shade would do no harm.

His riding coat served as a blanket as he sat at the base of the tree on the opposite side of the angel marker. He didn't care what George would say about his coat later. He only wanted to stretch out his leg and ease its ache.

Drawing up his good leg, he rested one arm on his knee. He made a study of the grass, then the wall, then Woodley, and then the patchwork fields beyond. In whichever direction London lay, it would be best for all involved if he shut up the Hall and went there. Things were well in hand here, and if he stayed, he would only manage to make things worse. The storms he'd run from had followed him. Best to leave before the maelstrom became a hurricane. He hadn't had Ashford House shut up entirely. He would go there until he knew where he would be going next. George would go with him, but Parker would have to stay, as would Mrs. Lynch. There were many details to be sorted out and a mountain of ramifications to avoid thinking about. One in particular.

The look in Penelope Howard's eyes when she heard the news.

He got to his feet, putting weight on his leg. Most of the ache was gone. He leaned down and picked up his coat. It was time to head back if he meant to go through with his plans.

Lavender and roses. There was a thread of it mixed with the breeze. On the other side of the tree, Penelope knelt in front of the angel marker. She had pushed back the long grass surrounding, tore out some in small clumps. There was a fierce yet almost sad look in her eye as she stared at the marker.

She rose to her feet as he approached, stray blades of grass clinging to her skirt. "Lord Turner."

"Miss Howard."

Questions about what she was doing and why faded away. They didn't matter now. He was leaving. And the thought of not seeing her again, of her soothing presence in his life gone for good, was too much. He could barely breathe for the weighty ache in his chest.

He took a step away. "I was just leaving."

"My lord." Her voice halted him. "I must apologize for my anger the other day. I was too harsh."

Dear God, what kind of angel was she, apologizing to *him*?

"No, Miss Howard. The fault was mine. I had no business forcing Arthur to set that break. You had every right to be harsh." Guilt doubled the weight in his chest.

"Why?"

He floundered for a response. The reasons were there on his tongue. But he held them back. "Why?"

"Yes. Why?" She stepped up to him until she was just a few handbreadths away. "What did you mean when you said it was better that way? It's not just the war, is it? Whatever the reason is, it cannot be that bad."

He could immerse his soul in the compassion that welled in her azure eyes.

Monster.

Butcher.

He swallowed. "There are things in my past … things you shouldn't ever have to know about me." She opened her mouth, but he rushed on. "Trust me when I say my hands have hurt more than they've helped."

She grasped his arm. "God's grace covers all such mistakes, my lord."

His breath caught in his throat, in part at the possibility behind that thought, but more so at the deep tremor that raced through him at her touch. His voice grew thick. "Not mine."

"Everyone's." Her voice thinned and tightened. "Yours ... and mine."

Hers? What could this woman have possibly done to need grace? She was grace itself. And kindness. And light. Impossibly perfect, and he was utterly unworthy of her.

He should leave. He needed to leave. But the tears on her cheek willed him to raise his hand and wipe them away with the pad of his thumb. The instant his fingers touched her, they demanded his hand cup her face and his thumb trace a path from her cheek to the soft, delicate skin where her jaw met her slender neck.

She trembled beneath his touch, and he threw down his coat and drew her to him, unable to deny himself any longer.

He drank in her soft sweet lips; he drowned himself in her, a doomed man. No matter how far he went or where, he would always take a piece of this woman's soul with him.

A silken, throaty gasp rose from her as his lips traced the line of her jaw to the edge of her neck. He wove his fingers into her hair and, for the briefest moment, he pulled away to plumb the depth of her eyes. With a soft, almost desperate, whimper she pulled him back to her, deepening their connection, her hands driving an intoxicating path from gently caressing his face to digging themselves into the folds of his shirt. At that moment, he dared to believe in the grace she spoke of, that it was possible for him to cease his endless falling and right himself once more. With her by his side.

With that single thought, his mind caught up with his heart.

Everything she ever dreamed was in his kiss. His lips spoke more eloquently against hers than any praise he'd ever given her. She groaned as he feathered them from her mouth to her neck, and the next thing she knew, he had raised his head, searching her eyes. *No, don't stop. Not yet.* She pulled his head down to meld his lips with her own and all but drank the faint taste of harvest apple from his perfectly proportioned mouth. Her fingers caressed his face. Her head spun with the scent of his shaving soap, and she allowed her hands to travel to his shirt. She buried them in the soft linen and felt his heart match the untamed beating of her own.

The next moment her hands and lips were empty.

He stumbled away from her with a wild look of horror. Reality took hold, and she realized what she'd allowed. Shaking, she backed into the tree. She reached behind her and clung to it for support.

"I'm sorry," he murmured. He reached down and fumbled for his coat.

A part of her longed to rush to him and force him to stop apologizing. But sanity all too quickly returned to her thoughts and heart.

"No," she heard herself say. "I don't know what I was thinking, my lord. Perhaps it would be best if we forget this ever happened." She winced. Did those words sound as ridiculous aloud as they did in her heart?

"Yes," came his soft reply, and she glanced up to see him striding—almost running—toward Fortis. Tears filled her eyes, and the sight of him thundering away from the ruins quickly turned into a kaleidoscope-like mosaic.

She had to rally. The verse in Mama's Bible. What was it? She couldn't recall. She rushed to the angel marker. The sight of that would surely still her heart. But her heart pounded along with the sound of the horse's hooves as he galloped away. She slumped into the tree and slid down it with a deep sob. Dusk had fallen by the time her tears were spent. When she returned to Fairview, she refused both dinner and questions and went straight to her room.

CHAPTER 22

Pink just edged the sky as Penelope descended the stairs and walked down the hall to Fairview's little dining room. She caught the scent of toast and heard the clink of a teacup. She hadn't risen early enough. Thomas sat at the small table in front of the fire. He raised a brow at her, his cup half raised. "You look awful."

So he was speaking to her again. "I'm fine." She sat down across from him and poured herself a cup of tea. "I'm not feeling particularly well. It will pass."

"And yet still up at this early hour." He took up his fork and stabbed at a piece of his egg. "What a trooper."

She resisted the urge to slam her cup down on the saucer. "Yes, what a tough old girl I am."

His gaze flicked upward. At any other time, his cool regard would have pained her. But not today.

"I sprain my wrist, and you do nothing. I claim to not feel well, and you don't even urge me to return to bed. Why am I always your tough old girl and never your sister?" She leaned her head against one hand, covering her eyes. Thomas grasped her other hand, and she peered at him through her fingers.

"You're both." He gave her hand a squeeze. "I know you, Pen. You could be at death's door and still feel the need to power on no matter what I said." He let go and felt her forehead. "You're not fevered. So what's bothering you?"

She leaned back in her seat. How did it seem that he was the brother she had once known and yet not at the same time? No, her jumbled thoughts had more to do with weariness and yesterday's events than anything else. "First of all, let me tell you again how sorry I am for the Ireland trip."

His countenance stiffened, but he gave a bare nod. Good. Apology accepted. She took a sip of tea and spread jam on a piece of toast.

"And?" he asked after a moment.

"And what?"

He motioned with his fork. "You said 'first of all.' I can only assume there was a 'second of all' to what is troubling you."

There was, but she could not say what it was. Even thinking about what happened at the ruins could not be permitted. What else had happened yesterday? "I'm afraid Clara and I had a bit of a row."

"What? Why?"

Again, something she could not tell him. "Something silly. I'm sure we will work it out."

"She is better, I hope."

"Yes, as I said before, it was nothing serious." If things worked out the way Clara hoped, he would be disappointed. But it would serve her right if it didn't work out. That was un-Christian of her. But then again, the hardest lessons were the ones best learnt. Didn't she know that by now?

They concluded the rest of their breakfast with civility, though things were still not quite the same. Thomas set off on foot for the Hall while she took the cart.

As she drove down the lane away from Fairview, shaving soap and harvest apple assaulted her senses. She drew in a sharp, deep breath. There. That loosened the tightening of her chest and stilled her racing heart. She had too much to do today to dawdle on foolish giddiness and pipe dreams.

A call to Miss Oliver was in order. Penelope had, as promised, visited the spinster the day after she had waylaid the matron outside the cottage hospital. As suspected, her complaint was the result of a poorly cooked meal. Penelope had persuaded her not to dismiss her maid and promised to give Prudence a cooking lesson.

The two lived at the edge of Woodley. It was a newer part of the village and a little farther out. The new well was just a few yards from Miss Oliver's cottage. That those living in the small cluster of cottages had asked for the well was understandable. Walking back and forth to the village green to use the pump consumed time, and some did not possess even a handcart to haul water. The well was dug, but the pump had not yet come from the manufacturer in Cardiff. A temporary stone well house had been erected with a rope and bucket.

Penelope pulled up to the gate. How odd. The windows were shut tight. Miss Oliver liked to have her windows open when the weather was fine, as it was today.

She climbed from the cart, walked up the little path to the door, and knocked. No answer. She stepped to the window and stood on her tiptoes to peer in, but the curtains were pulled. She knocked harder, but still no answer. Should she force the door? No, that would be excessive. Perhaps she had gone out. But then, why didn't Prudence answer? Had she taken her maid with her or dismissed her? Heaven forbid she'd fallen or taken ill.

She would call by the cottage hospital on her way back to Fairview, but first, she must visit Hartsbury Manor. Her visit to thank them once more for their hospitality was long overdue. By the time she reached the drive, the reins had cut creases in her fingers, and the little she'd eaten for breakfast roiled in her stomach. A groom took charge of the horse and cart. Stone gargoyles stood watch on either side of the immense double doors, with a knocker to match. The footman who answered looked at her as if she were coming to beg for bread. She lifted her chin, gave her name, and requested to see Mrs. Baines and her niece. The servant led her past the ballroom doors. Moonlight and toffee-brown eyes seeking hers … She forced her gaze onto the livery of the footman in front of her.

"Miss Penelope Howard."

She strode into the room to find Isabella Abbott sitting alone at her desk surrounded by books. A pair of wire-rimmed glasses perched at the end of her nose, and she took them off as she rose to greet her.

"Miss Howard." She paused. "Excuse me. Penelope. It is good to see you."

As usual, her manner indicated just the opposite, but having now spent more time with her, Penelope knew she should not take it personally. But then at the sight of her workspace, perhaps she should?

"I hope I haven't disturbed you," she said as she sat down on the sofa Isabella indicated. "You look as if you were in the middle of something."

"I am, but it can certainly wait." The footman had not yet left, and she asked him to bring them tea before sitting down next to her. "I'm sure you were expecting my aunt to be with me. I know you will be relieved when I say she has just gone out on some errands and is unlikely to be back soon."

"I see."

Isabella's shoulders slumped. "And I see I have blundered once again. I'm afraid I will never be the woman my father and aunt wish me to be."

"Do not be so hard on yourself." Penelope laid a hand on hers. "God has blessed you with a great deal of intelligence. You will learn."

She shot up out of her seat and walked to the window. "You do not understand. I am not made for this life. I was made for another."

What passionate words to come from Isabella Abbott. And her normally pale cheeks were stained crimson. "What life were you made for?"

"I'm sorry. I am not making myself clear." Emotion buffeted her face, and her cheeks grew even redder. She picked up a book from her desk then returned to the couch. "I have always prided myself that I am not an overly emotional person. Emotions get in the way of clear thinking and speaking." She handed the tome to Penelope as her voice slipped to a breathy whisper. "What I meant was that I was made for *another*."

Still not grasping her meaning, Penelope took the book and opened it. It fell open to the letter that lay between its pages. She glanced at Isabella who nodded. The note was in Latin, but that did not surprise her as much as to whom it was addressed. Arthur Wilcox.

The day of Sally's injury. The way they had looked at one another, Arthur's intimate use of Isabella's Christian name—it all came rushing back bold as brass.

"We met in the Hall library the day after the ball," she said. Her eyes were as soft as a dove's wing, and she looked as feminine as Penelope had ever seen her. "I never met a young man who knew Latin. Especially one in his station."

"So you know he is a groom at Ashford Hall?"

Isabella's eyes flashed. "He *was* a groom. He is going to become a doctor."

"How?"

"Lord Turner is sponsoring him. He has arranged for him to work at the cottage hospital and is going to obtain a tutor to help him enter university."

"I had not heard."

"It is a recent development." Isabella's cool countenance refreshed itself. "Although, I find myself surprised Lord Turner is not undertaking the task himself. Arthur was quite disappointed."

"Do not be too hard on him. He has his reasons. Things are complicated."

Questions floated in the air, and Penelope spoke again before Isabella could voice them. "I should be going. I have other errands to run, and I must stop by the hospital."

"Would you be willing to deliver something for me?" She laid her hand on the book. "When you see Arthur, place that in his hands. He told me he would be moving to Dr. Royston's home next to the hospital sometime today."

Penelope squeezed her hand. "Of course." She gripped the tome. Edmund and she had communicated similarly. "Isabella, are you sincere in this? Is Arthur?"

"I am prepared to do whatever it takes to be with him. I have not known him long, but I do know my own heart in this. And I am certain of his." Cool steel returned to her eyes despite the warmth in her voice. "I hope I can trust your discretion until I find the right time to tell Papa and Aunt Dorothea."

Lord, let them be wiser than I was. "If I do not see him, I will keep this safe and hidden until I do."

"Thank you."

Her horse shouldn't be able to pull the cart for the weight of the secrets Penelope held in her heart. Clara's, Isabella's, Thomas'. Her own. The road blurred, and she pulled the cart off to the side where a short, tree-lined lane led to a field that had lain fallow for the season.

Oh, her own.

She leaned back in the seat, casting her eyes up at the cruel blue sky. Despite wrapping her arms around her middle, emptiness bit them while memories of her angel filled her heart. She lowered her head. Would she have time to visit the ruins today? And if she did, would she find him there again?

She pressed her lips together. The pressure of his hand that drew her to him. The scent of shaving soap. The tang of harvest apple on his lips—

No.

She backed up the cart and guided it again to the road. Snapping the reins, she arrived at the hospital in short order, and as she climbed down, she hoped the heat in her face was not noticeable. *Forgive me, Father, for entertaining such reckless hope.*

Enough of her foolish dreaming. Miss Oliver took precedence. She entered the hospital and searched for either Dr. Royston or Matron Talbot.

She found both in the matron's office. They greeted her, and the doctor helped her into one of the chairs in front of the matron's desk, then resumed his seat in the other.

"What brings you here today, Nurse Howard?" The matron offered her tea which she declined.

"I was in Woodley running errands, and I thought to stop by Miss Oliver's cottage," she replied. "But it is shut up, and there doesn't seem to be a soul around." Dr. Royston raised a brow at Matron Talbot, who looked down at her hands. Penelope's mouth went a little dry. "Is she here?"

"She was," the matron said. "I'm afraid I became cross with her."

"Why?"

"Miss Oliver came several days ago complaining yet again about cholera," Dr. Royston replied. "I wasn't here at the time."

"Again? But I visited her the day after she came here the first time. It turned out to be indigestion, as we suspected."

"Yes, she mentioned that." Miss Talbot sighed. "You know how the woman gets under my skin. I'm afraid I was quite firm. In truth, I was rather harsh."

"But what does that have to do with where she might be?"

"She made it quite plain she was going to go where she would not be a bother, her and Prudence," the matron replied. "When I went to apologize, I found the house exactly as you say. We can only assume she went to her sister's in Southampton."

Penelope leaned back in her seat and sighed. She understood how difficult Miss Oliver could be, but the matron should have exercised a little more patience. She was a spinster, after all.

Dr. Royston patted her hand. "You know she's done this before, Miss Howard. She'll return when she's cooled off and forgiven us."

"She will, of course, have a new ailment to complain of," Miss Talbot added. "But then again, I suppose she wouldn't be the Felicity Oliver we all know and love if she didn't." Regret stained her expression. "I will sincerely apologize when she returns, I promise."

"I know you will, Matron." She should be relieved, but why did something still not feel right about the whole thing? Then again, nothing had been quite right lately. She raised a hand to her eyes.

"Are you all right, Miss Howard?"

She lowered it. "I'm tired, that is all."

"I would tell you to go rest if I thought you would listen."

"You sound just like my brother."

The three of them chuckled as they rose from their seats and headed toward the door. Another nurse approached them as they exited. "Matron, the water you sent for is here."

"Thank you, Nurse Campbell." She directed the man carrying a stoneware jug to the kitchen. "For Mrs. Travers."

"From the new well? She must be pleased."

"She was. A little too pleased. She won't hear of drinking from the village pump now." She started in the direction the lad had gone. "I had better make sure he can get in the door. I'm not sure anyone is back there at present."

As she strode off, calling after him, the doctor retrieved his watch and checked the time. "And I fear I had better go check Mrs. Travers. I'm told she had a bit of a fever; otherwise, she would have been sent home today."

"Yes, I am surprised to hear that she was still here," Penelope replied. "But if you have a moment, might I ask where Arthur Wilcox is?"

"I cannot say. He is not due to be here for a few days yet."

The sound of a coach pulling up drew them to the window.

"Well, well," the doctor said. "I wonder what Lord Turner could be doing here?"

Penelope's heart skidded to a halt. Arthur climbed out unaccompanied. Thank goodness. Her heart could resume beating.

He entered and approached them. "Miss Howard, Dr. Royston. Sir, I know I'm a few days early, and I hope you don't mind, but I'm that eager to start."

"Lord Turner has freed you from his service?"

"Yes, sir. I'm no longer needed at the Hall."

"Very well." He motioned toward the coach. "I assume you've brought your things with you?"

"Yes, sir."

"Good. Let me pen a note to my housekeeper, and I will send you over. Once you have settled your things, come straight back here." He started for his office. "Oh, as it happens, Miss Howard was looking for you just now."

"I'm very happy for you, Arthur." He would make such a fine doctor.

"Thank you, Miss Howard. I hope I'll make Lord—the Hall—proud."

His voice held a bitter edge she hoped to soothe. "I know you're angry, but there are things which concern Lord Turner that you don't understand."

"Such as?"

"I cannot say." How could she explain it to him when she didn't fully understand herself?

"Dr. Royston said you wanted to speak to me?"

She opened her reticule. "A mutual friend has asked me to give this to you."

"Izzy." He almost snatched the book from her hand. He realized his mistake and floundered. "I can explain. It's just a book she means to lend me."

"You both may trust me. But I must ask. What are your intentions?"

"The best." His voice and face were keen and steadfast. "I love her. I know that's quick to say, but I do. I only want what's best for her."

"Of course you do. I'm sorry." He was nothing like Edmund.

"It's all right. I understand." And he did. Even five years ago when he had come with her uncle to fetch her from that awful inn, he had understood. Acting as a messenger between him and

Isabella was the least she could do in light of the service he had rendered her the night she returned with her child. It was Arthur who had buried the small box under the Angel Tree.

Dr. Royston's footsteps echoed from around the corner. Arthur slid the book into his coat pocket as he approached.

The doctor handed Arthur a note. "Give that to Mrs. Richards. She will make sure your things get settled. But I am curious. Why did Lord Turner agree to let you go so soon?"

Arthur glanced at Penelope as he answered. "He's leaving Woodley, sir."

"What?" Surely she had not heard him right.

"I see." Dr. Royston asked the next question on her tongue, although his surprise was considerably less. "And has he said where he intends to go?"

"London first, according to Mrs. Lynch. After that, he's not decided."

"And when does he intend to leave?"

"Before the end of next week. He told Mr. Parker to admit me if I need anything from the library. He and Mrs. Lynch and a few of the others will remain on."

"Well, I guess that is the most we can hope for," Dr. Royston said. "I hope you will excuse us, Miss Howard, we have a great deal of work to do."

"Of course," she replied and took her leave.

Once in her cart, she snapped the reins, and the horse pulled ahead. How could Lord Turner come and act as if he were going to stay only to leave? Why?

Did she really have to ask? The foolishness with Sally, all her prodding and questions—had her desire to help only hindered? Yes. And whatever had been content to nibble away at his soul must be consuming it whole.

How she regretted her actions. But wasn't it for the best? If he stayed, it would only make their situation worse. But his departure would tear a hole in her heart which might take a lifetime to heal.

CHAPTER 23

John didn't need to look up from his desk to know who was standing in front of it. "Yes, Parker?"

"Mr. Fletcher is here to see you, sir."

John glanced up. The man's face was in keeping with the stoniness of his voice, a quality that had been there since he announced his departure to the staff. All the servants seemed cooler, even George, and he was going with him. The only one who seemed pleased was Mrs. Lynch. No surprise there. He took a deep breath and laid down his pen. "Show him in."

He gave him a curt nod and started to walk back through the library.

"Parker."

He stepped back. "Sir?"

John sighed. A statue stood before him, staring at a point somewhere behind his desk. He rose. "I'm sorry to be leaving so soon after I got here. I know it's unorthodox, but you knew that about me when I arrived." He extended his hand. "I hope you understand."

Parker's mouth pursed. "No, sir. I do not understand nor can I accept your apology."

"Excuse me?"

"I can tolerate the unusual, the revolutionary even, to a degree." He met John's eyes with a marble-like stare. "This is simply unacceptable. You have been entrusted with Ashford Hall, and you are now abandoning it."

"I'm not abandoning it." He rounded the desk to stand toe to toe with Parker. "I'm simply leaving it in more capable hands than mine."

"Mr. Howard and I are not the masters of the Hall. *You* are. *You* are its caretaker."

"You can't mean to tell me there aren't others who do the exact same thing?"

"No, I cannot say that. But I can assure you their legacies are not the better for it." He showed Mr. Fletcher into the room, then left. Parker didn't understand, couldn't see the future as he saw it. A disaster would unfold if he stayed. A situation much worse than an abandoned legacy.

Mr. Fletcher shifted his weight from foot to foot, bringing John back to the matter at hand. "I'm sorry, Mr. Fletcher. Please have a seat."

The man settled onto the edge of the offered chair. The fabric of his trousers had thinned considerably at the knees, and the cuffs of his jacket had seen better, cleaner days.

John leaned forward. "What can I do for you? Has Mr. Howard been able to find you work at Fairview?"

The man shook his silver head. "No, sir. He told me, though, that you were thinkin' of askin' round here."

"Yes, I'm hoping Mr. Milford might need some help since Arthur Wilcox has left." He stopped. Mr. Fletcher frowned at him. "Is that a problem?"

"O' course it's a problem, sir." His gravelly voice inched up a notch. "I can't be workin' with horses and such. I'm too old. And look at ma hands." He laid his cap on the desk and held them up.

John's brows constricted. Rheumatism. The malady had sapped whatever strength they once possessed.

"Then I'll find some other job. For you and your son." He rose from his seat, resting his hands on the edge of his desk. Think. There must be something. He had to fix this. He *had* to.

"Lord Turner, with all due respect, what kind o' jobs round here for a wrung-out old man and a one-legged cripple?"

Cripple. How many times had he heard that word in the recovery hospital? The other patients had stoned him with the word. He gave his desk a helpless glare. "How can you think that? How can you have no hope?"

"Hope doesn't change what's true, sir." How could the man sound so calm? "That's what we are."

"No!" He pounded his desk, jumbling the papers and books strewn across it. Mr. Fletcher said nothing. He picked up his cap and rose from his seat.

"Where are you going? We still have to figure out what to do."

"I know what Peter and I will do, sir. That's what I come to tell ya. My sister lives up in Gloucestershire, in the Forest of Dean. She and her family don't have much, but they're takin' us in."

He started to leave, but John darted around his desk to block his exit. "No. No, I won't allow you to become a burden to her. Not when I can help."

"But you can't." He put his hand in his pocket and thrust a small pouch into his hands. "Beggin' your pardon sir, I almost forgot to give this to you."

"What's this?"

"The rent I owe you. Thank ya for being patient. I sold what was mine that we wouldn' be needin'."

John stared at the bag in his hands. His shoulders slumped, and he leaned back against his desk. "I'm so sorry."

He heard the reply as if through a fog. "For what, sir? For the cart slippin' and takin' ma Peter's leg? For ma old age? None o' that's your fault."

He shook his head. The man had no idea. The bag he'd given him jangled faintly as he laid it on his desk. His thirty pieces of silver. Mr. Fletcher gripped his shoulder. How could the man look at him that way? With so much peace?

"You were in the war, sir?"

John's heart gave a start. "What?"

"You were a doctor, in your war in America."

"Yes." He flexed his hands.

The old man sighed. "Have a young cousin over there. He

fought. Got wounded too."

John stiffened. Any moment this man would tell him about how a surgeon had cut off an arm or a leg. His face grew hot.

"He come out of it all right." All the air rushed back into John's lungs. "But he told me 'bout those hospitals." He paused, and John looked at him. "It couldn' been easy seein' ma boy."

The peace that lay in Mr. Fletcher's face mesmerized him. He longed for it like a dog begging for a scrap of food. And it caused him to shake his head. "No." His voice clotted and stuck in his throat. "It wasn't."

"He's angry, so he is. Says the same thing you just did about my sister takin' us on. That he's a burden. Got short with the doctor too, for takin' his leg. But I tell him, 'Pete, you're alive. You're still here with me. And that's not a burden. Would be more a burden if the Lord had taken ya. And He knew that. So He used the doctor to keep a good part of you here with me to spare me sorrow upon sorrow as the Good Book says.'" The old man's eyes blazed with the strength of the sun. "I'll take my boy alive and angry any day over dead cold and in the grave." He squeezed John's shoulder. "You just think on that, sir."

John stared into his heart for a long time afterwards.

"Thank you for the books, sir."

Stone had more to do with Arthur Wilcox's face than warm flesh. It seemed to be John's day for dealing with statues. First at the Hall and now here at the cottage hospital. Arthur's anger had only strengthened. Who could blame him?

"I know you'll do well. Parker knows to let you in whenever you need something."

"Yes, sir. You've told me." His eyes flicked toward the door. "Excuse me. I have work to do before I leave for the day."

"Ah, Lord Turner."

John forced a pleasant expression to his face. "Good evening, Dr. Royston."

The doctor approached them and noticed the books in Arthur's hands. He took them and studied the spines. "Good, you've brought them."

"Those are the rest of the books I have on miasma," John replied.

"Thank you. Our young protégé needs to have the facts reinforced." He thrust them back into Arthur's hands. "He seems to have developed an idea that certain afflictions have more to do with what is ingested."

Say something, Arthur. Defend yourself. Wrong or no, he should still try to defend his theory. Catching his attention, John tilted his head, eyebrows raised.

Arthur shuffled the books. "I'll read through these and send them back to the Hall when I'm done."

"Don't back down, Arthur," John said. "If you don't defend your theory, how will you defend a diagnosis?"

"A valid point, Lord Turner," Dr. Royston replied. "Why don't you join us for dinner? Young Arthur can give us his arguments, and we can educate him."

John hesitated. Staying would only compound Arthur's anger. But he agreed anyway. Perhaps that anger would provide some fuel for his argument.

The doctor was pleased. "Good. If you will give us a moment, I want Arthur to take note of my instructions to the night nurse over a particular patient."

"Is everything all right?" John asked.

"Yes." He waved his hand. "Some unusual symptoms. Nothing to concern *you*, Lord Turner."

The two walked off. He wasn't sure which was worse, Arthur's glowering or Dr. Royston's arrogance. It would not be an enjoyable dinner. He could always leave a message that he had been called away.

In the end, he waited. Arthur was wrong, but the notion he suggested was interesting. At the very least he owed it to him to hear him out.

It wasn't a new premise. After Dr. Pasteur's success in proving a living organism had been causing casks of wine to go bad, many doctors were questioning the established theory that bad air caused diseases such as cholera and the Black Death. He agreed with the miasma stance, but it wasn't surprising that Arthur's youth and exuberance would lead him to give ear to such a revolutionary theory.

Over the course of the meal that evening, it was clear that his interest was more firmly rooted than John thought wise. Arthur had done his homework and made his case so passionately, he hardly took a bite at dinner. But Dr. Royston's sharp mind shouldn't be taken lightly. He questioned and poked holes in everything Arthur put forth.

"But sir, how do you explain that Dr. Pasteur discovered outside contaminates were causing the wine samples to go bad or that he discovered an organism was making silkworms die?" Arthur stood before both of them in the study as they took their tea. He waved off John's offer of a cup.

"That has nothing to do with *people* getting sick," Dr. Royston snapped. "Ensuring the rich have their wine and the survival of worms to spin their fine clothing means very little."

"But it has everything to do with something other than a bad smell causing disease," Arthur shot back. He grabbed a book from the desk the doctor had lent him for his use. It was a volume of the back issues of *The Medical Times and Gazette* for 1854. One of Ashford Hall's tomes. "If you want evidence of people getting sick, Dr. John Snow all but proved that the water from the Broad Street pump in London was the cause of the cholera outbreak that year."

"That's preposterous and was thought so by the other leading minds of the day." Dr. Royston set his tea cup aside with a rattle. "I fail to see how you have made your point."

"Arthur, I've read that letter to the editor." Let Dr. Royston rail away. John would remain calm and reasonable. "Dr. Snow admits at the very start he found little organic impurity in the water."

"But when they removed the pump handle people stopped dying."

"They also made vast improvements to the streets by scrubbing them with chloride of lime, ridding the street of its stench." Dr. Royston rose from his seat. "Which was more than likely the solution to the problem than any of this pump handle removal." He took the book from Arthur, closing it with a snap. "Hippocrates, Vitruvius, Galen, Fracastoro, Andry—all these brilliant minds have proved the validity of miasma over hundreds of years. In future, you will confine your reading of disease to works that have a basis in fact."

He handed the book to John. "If you would be so good as to remove that from my home." Then he rummaged through the other books on Arthur's desk. "Of course. *On the Mode of Communication of Cholera* by Dr. John Snow. This one as well, Lord Turner."

Arthur flashed a pleading gaze at John. He should throw him a bone. Something. They would part more amicably. But how could he in all honesty support his wild theory? He laid the books on the table next to his chair. Perhaps this would convince him. "Arthur, I am familiar with a man who was in one of the worst prison camps during the War Between the States. Andersonville."

"Ah, yes, Lord Turner. I've heard of it." Dr. Royston resumed his seat and indicated that Arthur should sit as well, but he remained as he was.

John cleared his throat and continued, "Mr. Kirby told me about the stream that flowed through the camp where the prisoners were kept. It reeked and disease was rampant, especially during the hot months. And more than simply cholera—consumption, malaria, dropsy."

Arthur stilled and considered this for a moment. "Is the stream where the men relieved themselves, sir?"

"Yes, therefore the stench."

"If you'll forgive me, sir, therefore infected drinking water. Did they drink from the stream too?" John hesitated, and Arthur jumped on it. "There! Dr. Snow claims that the sewage running into the Thames seeped into the groundwater."

"Enough," Dr. Royston barked. "Lord Turner, while I appreciate your effort, it would seem you are only dragging him further astray. It appears it would be best if you left his education to me as you first insisted."

Outside, the last bits of light painted the horizon in red, purple, and orange, a sight that was lost on John as he stared out the coach window. One of the books fell onto the floor of the coach. It remained there. He shouldn't have gone. What right did he have? He wasn't a doctor—

He used the doctor to keep a good part of you here with me ...

Again the words reverberated in his heart, beat against it as they had since Mr. Fletcher left. He'd done his best to ignore them, but now in the silence of the carriage, he couldn't any longer.

Could it be that absolution was so close? Was what he saw as sin really a service to God? He leaned his head back against the seat and stared. Something crumbled in his soul, and the tiniest sliver of light slipped through.

His leg twitched. Why did he still have it? For all he did, why could he still walk and those soldiers couldn't? Why had he chosen to be selfish? And there was Maggie and Beth to consider. What about what he'd done to them? How could God contend with that? He couldn't, could He? What was it? That God's soul could not contend with man's? And there was a price to be paid for everyone's sins. He had to accept that price. Even if he had been meant to spare those men's lives, that didn't absolve him from his cowardice. Or his failure to—

Grace. My grace is sufficient ...

He started. Who had said that? The carriage was empty. He leaned forward and rested his forehead in his hands. It couldn't be so simple. It couldn't be that freeing. It couldn't be that he felt his descent slowing. His sins were too damning. Weren't they?

He leaned back and looked out the window. In the lingering dusk, he caught sight of the path that led to the ruins.

Penelope.

She'd spoken of grace too. With tears in her eyes. Tears that he'd wiped away. Soul-stirring warmth grew in his chest. She would understand. The thought still tortured him. Why? Because it was true? Or because he so wanted it to be true? His eyes slipped shut, and the scent of lavender and roses filled the carriage. His fingers curled as they recalled the silkiness of her hair, and his tongue ran along the inside edge of his lips as he remembered her soft sweetness.

With a start, his eyes snapped open. No. No more. He shouldn't be torturing himself with notions of grace and the thought of caring for a woman like Penelope Howard. The wages of sin was death. Thoughts like those had to die. By the end of the week, he would leave Woodley, the Hall, and hope behind him.

CHAPTER 24

*A*nd *we know that all things work together for good to them that love God, to them who are called according to his purpose.*

The verse echoed in Penelope's heart. What a blessing Mr. Gregory had made it the focus of yesterday's sermon. It cut through her jumbled feelings and returned her heart to order. For the most part. Lord Turner's imminent departure still weighed on her, but the knowledge that somehow the Lord would set everything to rights buoyed her and gave her strength to carry on.

The weather was so fine when she stepped out Fairview's door she decided to walk her first few visits before taking the cart. The lane leading to Clara's cottage came into view. She should try to talk sense to the girl once more. Did she want to? No, not after her last two attempts. But she needed to if for no other reason than to try to heal the breach between them. Clara sat on the bench just outside her little garden, but the instant she saw Penelope, she rose and rushed to her. Her expression spoke of remorse. Had the father rejected her again? They grasped hands.

"Penelope, I am sorry," she said breathlessly. "I was so cruel."

"Please, it is all right," Penelope replied. "You've been worried and ill."

"That is no excuse." She regarded the ground for a moment. "And I hope you won't be too angry when I tell you I've met with the father just as I planned."

Tension filtered to her hands, and she squeezed Clara's. "What did he say?"

Joy shone in her face. "He is going to procure a special license."

"Oh, Clara!" She gave her a quick embrace. "That is wonderful news."

"But how shall I explain things to Mr. Gregory?" Clara asked as they parted. "I promised to remain for at least a year."

"Do not worry about that. I will help you talk to him, and if need be, I can take on your duties until someone else can be found."

"But you are so busy already."

"I don't mind. I will manage." Yes, it would be good for her to be busier. Once Lord Turner departed, she would need the distraction.

Cheerful laughter like holiday bells drifted in on the breeze, and soon Clara's pupils appeared along the path.

"You are feeling well today?" Penelope asked before they were in earshot.

Clara's hand drifted to her midsection. "I am more than well today."

After helping her settle her charges, Penelope continued on her rounds. The news of Lord Turner's departure weighed on the hearts of many. She did her best to put a positive light on it. Parker would be staying on at the Hall, and she and her brother would remain. But most were still disappointed. She could hardly blame them. But as Mr. Gregory had said, the Lord settles matters better than mortal man. She wasn't sure how, but He would. She would trust in that.

Her route home for luncheon took her back by Clara's. There was proof of His divine hand. Things had seemed so precarious for her young friend. But He had settled it by working on the heart of the child's father as she prayed He would. The blessings of answered prayer.

Upon arriving at Fairview, she walked back to the stables and asked for the cart to be made ready. She'd drive the rest of her rounds after a quick lunch.

"You seem more cheerful." Hannah was in the kitchen preparing their food when she walked in. "Seems like I haven't seen you smile in an age."

"I am feeling better today, more rested, thank you, Hannah." Penelope had managed to put off both her and Thomas by claiming fatigue as the source of her melancholy, a malady neither would question. And thankfully, they hadn't.

Her hands slowed as she pulled at the ribbons of her bonnet. Hannah was laying out the meal on the kitchen worktable. "What's this? We're eating in here?"

"It's just you, me, and Fanny today."

"What about Thomas?"

"Left in a rush this morning not long after you. Mumbled something about having to return to Somerset." Would he ever be able to settle things with that tenant? He really should get Lord Turner involved. What was the point of that? He soon would be too far away to do anything useful.

Hannah handed her a letter. "Came for you this morning."

Good. She could use the distraction. She read the front and opened it as she sat down at the worktable. It was a response from Miss Oliver's sister in Southampton. She had written to her after hearing of the old woman's run-in with Matron Talbot. Had she got there safely?

Dear Miss Howard,

I am so very glad to receive your letter. My sister wrote to me almost a fortnight ago to say she would be coming to stay, and I have not heard from her since. I am at a loss as to what to do since I have no direction for anyone else in Woodley. Has she been taken ill? Any news you could send me would be—

"Oh no," Penelope gasped.

Hannah stepped over. "What is it?"

"I have to go." She crumpled the letter in one hand and snatched up her bonnet and reticule in the other. There was no other place Miss Oliver would go, was there? She strode down the hall to the front door.

Hannah followed close behind. "Miss Penny, what is it? What has happened?"

"I must get to Woodley immediately." Where was the cart? Of course. It wouldn't have been brought out this soon. She headed to the stables. She would help ready it herself if she had to.

At the stables, she found Bessie between the shafts while a lad fiddled with the harness. She stuffed the letter in her reticule and climbed in.

Hannah grabbed her arm. "Here now, you can't go running off with no proper explanation—"

"I haven't any time to explain. I'll send word as soon as I can." She snapped the reins the instant the stable boy finished and raced down the drive with as much speed as she dared. As she neared Woodley, she altered her course. The cottage hospital. She would stop there first and fetch Arthur. He could help her get into Miss Oliver's house. Perhaps she had left a clue as to where she had gone. That was the only explanation. She couldn't have been ill all this time without anyone else knowing about it. Unless … No— that did not bear thinking about.

Penelope pulled up in front of the hospital. She rushed through the doors and stopped. Something was wrong. The front hall was strangely quiet. She took a few more steps. Matron Talbot's office was empty, the door hanging open. At that moment, Arthur appeared from the direction of the men's ward, jacketless, shirt sleeves rolled to his elbows, and only a few buttons of his vest fastened. His tie was as haggard and sagging as his eyes which widened when he saw her.

"Miss Howard. How can you be here so soon? Dr. Royston only just sent someone to fetch you."

Before she could reply, the doctor appeared. He looked as worn as Arthur, but he wore his coat and hat, and his medical bag was in hand. "She's here already?"

"I need to borrow Arthur." Penelope held up the letter. "I've had word that Miss Oliver is not with her sister. My brother is away, and I need help getting into her cottage." The two men looked at one another. "What is the matter?"

"Miss Oliver's neighbor found her this morning," Arthur said. "There was a smell coming from her cottage."

She raised a cold hand to her mouth. No. It couldn't be. Why hadn't she forced her way in before?

Doctor Royston's face was grave and dark as he regarded his feet. "We should have listened to her."

"Cholera? But how? How did she get it?"

"I don't know." He rubbed a hand over his eyes. "I can understand how the smell from her corpse could have permeated the air. Many of those who have fallen ill were her near neighbors."

"What about Prudence, her maid? Can she tell us anything?"

"She's gone," Arthur replied. "No note or anything. She must have gotten scared and run away." He looked at the doctor. "Sir, what about the bottle of water we found?"

Doctor Royston raised his hand, and the sharpness of his gaze cut his sentence short. "Enough. I will not hear anything else on the subject. Surely you can understand how the smell from her corpse could have permeated the air. And now it has spread here. There is too much to do to waste time on useless theories."

Arthur set his jaw.

Penelope's gaze slid from Arthur back to the doctor. "Spread here?"

"The matron and Nurse Campbell fell ill yesterday evening," Dr. Royston replied. That explained their haggard appearances. Those were the only two nurses the hospital employed. "Most everyone in the men's ward has fallen ill, and those who were Miss Oliver's near neighbors have been sending word for me to come since early this morning." Dr. Royston looked at his watch. "That is why I sent for you. Someone needs to help Arthur until I can return."

"Of course. Have you sent for anyone else? What about Mr. Martin?" Woodley's elderly apothecary was known to help them on occasion.

"He is one of those I have to go see, and I haven't had time to send word elsewhere." He met her eye. "There is only one doctor who could get here quickly enough to help us, and we both know he will not come."

"I will do all I can," she replied.

"Thank you," the doctor called over his shoulder as he strode out the door.

Penelope turned to Arthur. "How many more in the women's ward are ill?"

"To be honest, nearly everyone is." Arthur grasped her by the elbow. "Mrs. Travers passed away late last night."

Penelope bowed her head. A moment for grief was all that could be afforded. She laid a hand on her forehead. Who had she attended the last time she filled in for Nurse Campbell? Her hand dropped along with her stomach. "What about Sally?"

"She's fine except for a mild fever. We sent her home."

"Good." She drew in a deep breath. Cholera. It had been a long time since her training days, but she still recalled with unfortunate clarity what to expect. "What were you about to suggest to Dr. Royston that made him so angry? Where was the water from?"

"Nothing. It doesn't matter." His flat tone drove away any further questions.

"Then I will go to the women's ward in a moment. I should send word to Fairview and have Hannah send my uniform." As she walked into the matron's office, she pulled off her cloak and hat. She sat down at her desk. "I will also send word to Hartsbury to see if they can send any of their servants to help us."

Arthur rooted himself at the doorway. "I was able to send word to them."

"Through Miss Abbott?"

"She's sending who she can."

"And the Hall?"

"You heard the doctor. He won't come."

"He is still the patron of this hospital and needs to be notified."

She slapped another sheet of paper in front of her. "And he will certainly be able to at least send someone to help." She paused and softened her brisk tone. "I still have hope for him, Arthur."

"I don't." He backed away from the door. "I'll fetch Dr. Royston's groom to take those for you." His footsteps echoed in the hall. She stared at the blank sheet of paper in front of her. Arthur might be right. Lord Turner was leaving in just a few days. And she hadn't heard from or seen him since that day at the ruins. Her face warmed. She would write only to Fairview for help. Hannah could come and perhaps a few of the stable boys. A simple notification would suffice for Ashford Hall.

But despite her practical thoughts, her hand chose to listen to her heart. The note Dr. Royston's groom left at the Hall was less than formal.

The hours and minutes seemed to have a mind of their own, coming and going as slowly or as quickly as they wished and never in any semblance of order. Penelope looked out the window as she pulled it shut. Was it evening or morning?

"I hate to shut up all this bad air, but I can feel a chill coming on." She had already done as much in the women's ward.

Arthur said nothing. He merely slipped a sheet over yet another patient and looked at her with haggard eyes. It was the apothecary. Dr. Royston had him brought in only hours ago. Some of the younger patients were holding on, but the older ones like Mr. Martin were slipping into Death's grasp far too easily.

"Help has arrived from Hartsbury," she said as she walked over to him. "You should go rest." She'd had cots set up in both the doctor's and the matron's offices some time ago, but neither of them had made use of them.

"So should you." Arthur rose. "You look worse than me."

She shook her head. She did feel off, but that was inconsequential.

Dr. Royston had sent only the worst cases to the hospital, and their twelve beds were full. She looked at the sheet that clad Mr. Martin. It had been full.

Arthur followed her gaze and then snatched up the empty bottle of castor oil on the bedside table. "I've been giving this to him and everyone else in here exactly as Dr. Royston told me." His knuckles whitened as they gripped the bottle. "What good has it done?"

She shook her head. "I wish I could tell you. But he has much more experience than either of us. We must trust that he knows best." She covered her nose. Thick, rancid sickness coated the room now the windows were closed. "I'll send for someone to clear the buckets. And when Mr. Gregory returns, I will tell him about Mr. Martin."

Arthur set the bottle back down and glanced at the buckets next to each bed. "All of them are just expelling liquid aren't they?" he asked so softly she almost didn't hear him.

"Yes, but—"

The door to the ward opened, and Mrs. Richards, Dr. Royston's housekeeper, walked in. Her lips curled at the smell, and she raised a handkerchief to her nose. They guided her into the front hall.

"What is it, Mrs. Richards?" Penelope asked.

The housekeeper took two great gulps of fresher air. "It's the doctor. He's sick. Mr. Gregory just brought him."

"No vomiting or"—Arthur paused as he attempted to be delicate—"anything else?"

"No, I mean, I don't think so. He's only just arrived. But he's burning with fever."

"Then it's not cholera." Fever wasn't a symptom. Penelope looked at Arthur in partial relief.

"But now we have no doctor." He buttoned his vest and rolled down his sleeves. "You'd better take me to him, Mrs. Richards."

As they left, Thomas walked in with two more of their laborers. Thank the Lord, more help. She guided them to the men's ward to empty the buckets, warning them of the smell.

Lord, please don't let the bad air sicken them as well.

When she returned, Clara stood in the hall, her arm linked with Thomas'.

Penelope rushed to her. "Are you well? Why are you here?"

"Mr. Howard brought me. I came to help," she said.

Why did Clara look up at Thomas with fear in her eyes as she took off her cloak? But of course, she was afraid. Anyone of her age and inexperience would be. What had Thomas been thinking?

Penelope stilled the girl's hands. "Thomas."

"She insisted."

"You must take her home this instant."

"Why?"

"Because she shouldn't be here in her condition."

Clara's eyes flew to hers.

He glanced at Clara, then back to her. "Her condition?"

Quick, say something, anything. "Can't you see she's not feeling well? We have enough to deal with here."

He shrugged. "Hannah is here, isn't she?"

Penelope raised a hand to her eyes. He was acting so oddly, and she had no time to sort out why. "Please take her home." She pulled Clara's cloak snug about her shoulders. "Thomas will make sure you are safe. Go home and rest."

"She's right, Miss Bromley," Thomas said. "I'm sorry, old girl. I shouldn't have brought her."

His expression was contrite as he took hold of Clara's arm and guided her toward the door. She glanced back at Penelope, and he patted her hand. "Don't worry, you are quite safe with me."

A headache pricked behind Penelope's eyes. The soft gleam of moonlight slipped through the door as it shut behind them. It was nightfall then. Turning, she swayed a little. Steady there. She allowed herself a second to lean against the wood-paneled wall before she pushed on to the men's ward to supervise those she'd sent in a few minutes earlier.

CHAPTER 25

Miss Howard's note hung from John's hand as he stared into the fireplace. He'd sent what supplies he could, but nothing else. His own people were too busy preparing for his departure and, according to Mrs. Lynch, could not be spared if he still meant to leave tomorrow. Tomorrow? Or was it today? He'd stayed up so late staring at Miss Howard's soft, elegant handwriting that he didn't know what time it was.

She had not asked him to come. She had simply notified him of the epidemic and then penned the following:

My grace is sufficient for thee: for my strength is made perfect in weakness.

Unlike Mr. Fletcher's words, they didn't reverberate against his heart. They clanged and pummeled it and burned themselves into the walls of his mind until they were almost all he could see.

My grace is sufficient …

My grace is sufficient …

My grace is sufficient …

He shot up from his chair, crumpling the note in his hand.

"What do you want from me?" The prayer came out in a savage growl. "I've already fallen from Your grace. Do you want me to go even faster?"

And not only that but give Miss Howard a front-row seat as well?

He grabbed fistfuls of hair. A grim laugh slipped past his lips. Maybe he should. Because the look that he would see in her eyes when he failed would kill him or drive him mad. At this point, either was preferable.

Near the back of the library, a door opened with a bang. John shot around the corner to find Arthur raising the wick on a lamp. He strode to the shelves, using the pool of light to rifle through books, pulling down the bound back issues of *The Lancet* one by one. After flipping through a few pages and not finding what he wanted, he tossed them to the floor.

"Where is it?" he muttered.

"What are you doing?" John asked, striding forward.

"More than you are at the moment." Arthur opened another volume and checked the date. "I know I saw a treatment in one of these."

"For cholera? There are dozens of treatments."

"And none of them work." Arthur threw yet another book on the floor and pulled another one. He opened it and seeing the date thumbed to a section a third of the way in. A gleam lit his eye, and he snapped it shut, holding it up in front of John's face. "I've found it."

John tore it from his hands. "There is no one answer, Arthur. No sure treatment."

"And how would you know?" Arthur yanked the book back. "When was the last time you even looked at these, let alone read any of them? All you do is sit in that chair of yours and bore yourself to death with running the Hall." Arthur grabbed him by the edge of his vest. "Do you have any idea what Miss Howard and I have been dealing with?"

John pushed him away. "Of course I do. I've seen cholera before."

"Then you know without a doctor to help us, things are only going to get worse."

"What do you mean?"

"I mean Dr. Royston is ill. He can't even rise from his bed. Miss Howard and I are practically on our own. You are the only doctor within fifty miles of Woodley."

John launched himself at Arthur and grabbed him by the collar.

"And you left her there alone to fend for herself?"

Arthur shoved him away. "No, *you* did." He picked up the book and backed toward the door. "I would give my last breath to help the woman I love. Not supplies."

He turned on his heel and kicked books out of the way as he left. The windows shook as he slammed the door.

John ran to the bell pull in the front of the library, giving it more than one vicious yank. He then strode into the front hall, not waiting to think over what he was about to do. All that mattered was helping her. Where was everyone?

"Parker! George!"

The next instant, both of them strode into the hall, tying their robes as they came. Parker took one look at John's face and quickened his pace.

"My lord?"

"Rouse Mrs. Lynch and have her wake two of the oldest, most experienced housemaids, then call for a coach and have them meet me out front in ten minutes. My trip has been postponed. I'm needed at the cottage hospital." He made for the stairs and motioned for George to follow. He would need to change into older clothes. And fetch his medical bag.

"Very good, sir." There was a smile in Parker's voice as he spoke. "Shall I send a telegram to Mr. Worth, the surgeon? If he cannot come, perhaps he will be able to send someone else who can help."

John agreed and climbed the stairs two at a time.

Three-quarters of an hour later, medical bag in hand, he led Mrs. Lynch and the two housemaids into the hospital's front hall. He continued on around the corner and passed the women's ward until he came to the doctor's office. Arthur sat behind the oak desk, poring over the book he'd taken from the library. His head shot up, and his eyes grew as John turned the book toward him and began reading.

"The article by Dr. Latta. Good thinking, Arthur." He pulled out another book from his bag. "But you missed this volume by

Dr. Girdwood. It's more recent." Arthur took it and began to read while John set down his bag and shrugged out of his coat. "We'll need water from the village pump."

"I'll send someone right away." The feminine voice came from behind him.

John turned. Miss Howard. Penelope. All he wanted to do was stand there and take her in, ask her how she was, and embrace her in a wordless apology for staying away. Instead, he motioned for his housekeeper and maids to follow her.

"Thank you, Nurse Howard." He did take note of how pale she looked. "I'm sure you know where Mrs. Lynch, Maud, and Janet will be most needed."

Did she sway slightly as she led the other women away? He caught Arthur's eye. "When was the last time she slept? Or ate?"

"Too long," he replied, rising from his chair. "Mrs. Trull went back to Fairview to rest, and she tried to get her to go too, but she refused."

John tapped a fist against his leg. If she kept this up, she would collapse.

Arthur spoke again.

"There's a cot in the matron's office, sir. Now that Mrs. Lynch and the others are here, you may be able to convince her to take a break."

If he couldn't convince her, he had every intention of forcing her. "See what instruments and supplies we have on hand, then have someone go for water."

John walked out into the hall just as Miss Howard was exiting the women's ward with a bucket. What did she think she was doing? A footman from Hartsbury started past, and John ordered him to take the bucket from her. He then took her by the arm.

"But I told Mrs. Lynch I would return," she protested.

"Then she'll be waiting a few hours," he replied. They came to the open door of the matron's office, and he stabbed his finger at the cot. "Rest. Now."

Rather than come up with another argument, she raised a hand to her eyes and seemed to almost wilt. Her other hand gripped his forearm for support.

"I am so very tired. I don't even know how long we've been at this." She swayed, and John swept her up in his arms. Why hadn't he come sooner? Fool. He settled her into the cot. She grasped his hand as he rose. He squeezed her fingers.

"Rest," he whispered. Then, in spite of himself, he knelt and brushed a kiss across her forehead. Her eyes slipped shut, and he forced himself to move away.

When he returned to the hall, he almost ran into Mrs. Lynch just outside the door. "I was in search of Miss Howard, my lord. She told us she would return with instructions."

He pulled the door shut behind him. "*Nurse* Howard is resting. I will be there as soon as I check on Mr. Wilcox."

"Very good, sir." She walked back to the women's ward. He had the uneasy feeling she had spied on him but brushed the idea away. There were too many other things to worry about. Arthur would need his help administering the treatment he'd found. He might have revolutionary ideas about the spread of sickness, but John was almost certain he was on to something.

"Lord Turner." Who shook his shoulder? It wasn't George. He opened the windows to wake him. Never shook him. He lifted his head. Dr. Royston's office? Of course, the epidemic. How could he have fallen asleep? He started to rise, but someone pushed him back down and placed a cup of tea in front of him. Miss Howard moved away from the desk to open a nearby window. It was dawn. Dawn? It had been dark when he came in here.

"How long was I asleep?"

"Several hours," she replied. "I wanted to let you sleep longer, but more cases have come in." She sat in the chair in front of the desk. "I don't understand. Why are people still becoming ill?"

"I don't know." It had been almost two days now since they started the venous saline treatment. The water injections had made a significant difference, and nearly every patient who had been in the hospital when he first arrived had been sent home to recover. But more had taken their place. "I've sent word that everyone should keep their windows open and their surroundings clean. It should be working."

"What about Arthur's theory?"

"How can the same water that's curing people be making them ill?" He stood and walked over to the washstand and splashed his face. He shook the towel he used to dry off. "We'd all be ill if that were the case."

He slapped the cloth down and braced his hands against the stand. This was his fault. He'd come too late. If he had been here sooner, he and Arthur might have found the treatment days sooner. Fewer people would have been laid out behind the hospital if it weren't for his inaction. And they might have been closer to finding the true cause behind this outbreak.

"Your coming made a difference, my lord."

John's heart almost parted from his body. How well she read him. How perfect she was for him. Over the past two days, they had worked seamlessly, side by side, she knowing what he needed before he asked for it. As she did now. Except he didn't deserve it. "I should have come sooner."

"But you came. Thank you, Doctor."

"Don't call me that." He swung around. She stood too close to him. He walked around her toward the door.

"That is what you are." The jagged edge to her voice brought him to a halt. "You have more than proved that over these past days."

"I've only proved that I'm a fool." He strode out the door and didn't stop until he was outside.

The sharp morning air bit at him. If only it would swallow

him whole. He should send her home. Thanks to Mr. Worth, two nurses would arrive today. Parker and Mrs. Lynch were taking turns going back and forth between here and the Hall. Fairview was close enough for her to go with one of them.

A rider came tearing up the road toward the hospital. He pulled up in a shower of dust and pebbles and jumped down to hand John a note. His jaw tightened as he read it.

Isabella Abbott had cholera.

CHAPTER 26

John checked Miss Abbott's pulse, then laid her arm back across her waist. She didn't wake. He turned to her aunt and father who stood near the door of her room. "She's all right for now. But she'll need to have the water injections if she's going to recover."

For once, Dorothea Baines seemed at a loss as she crept toward the bed. "I cannot imagine how she could have contracted it." She looked at her brother. He said nothing; his face looked as if it might shatter at any moment. Mrs. Baines gathered herself and seemed to regain a semblance of her acerbic spirit. "What do you need from us, Lord Turner?"

"Ideally, you should let me take her to the hospital where I can look after her myself."

"That will not be necessary," she replied. "She will be treated here."

"Fine. I will send a nurse to sit with her and administer the injections. She will have everything that's needed and instructions on how your cook is to prepare the water."

"We would also appreciate it if you would send her maid back to us," she said. "I cannot imagine why she sent her over."

He'd argue if he had the energy. Miss Phillips had been worth her weight in gold. She wasn't given to hysterics and had a soothing way with the patients. He'd even been tempted to teach her how to administer the injections. Maybe he should. She would be the best choice to care for Miss Abbott.

Arthur burst into the room, followed by a footman. "Where did she last get a drink of water?"

"I'm sorry, Sir James," the footman said. "I tried to stop him.

He charged in the instant I opened the door."

"We will discuss that later. Leave us." Mrs. Baines directed her ire at Arthur. "What do you mean barging in here? What does water have to do with anything?"

"Nothing," John said. "Please excuse him. He should be at the hospital." He grasped Arthur's arm.

Arthur shook him off. "Why didn't you tell me?"

"Because I knew you would insist on coming, and I needed you to stay put."

Arthur stepped around him to the end of the bed and stared at Miss Abbott. He rubbed his forehead. "What has she had to drink? From where?"

"I told you that can't possibly be the cause," John said. "We're successfully treating people with water."

He met John's glare. "It's not the same water."

"Water is water."

Mrs. Baines cleared her throat. "My niece takes her water from Hartsbury's private pump. We all do. And as you can see, only she is ill."

John took hold of Arthur. "Come on. We'll discuss this on the way back."

He jerked free. "I'm staying. I'm going to give her the treatment myself."

"You'll do no such thing." Fury sparked in Mrs. Baines's eyes. "Leave here at once."

"Arthur." Miss Abbott raised her hand an inch or so before it flopped back across her waist.

Her aunt flew to her side. "You're going to be fine, Isabella."

She tried to take her niece's hand, but Isabella pulled free from her grasp. "Arthur …" Her eyes opened and closed. She took a few deep breaths.

Arthur approached, but her aunt blocked his way.

John ran a hand through his hair. What was Arthur thinking? If his outlandish theories didn't finish his career, Mrs. Baines and

Sir James would ruin it.

Sir James stepped forward and pulled his sister out of the way. "Let him pass, Dorothea."

Arthur sat down on the edge of the bed and took her hand in both of his. "Izzy."

She opened her eyes and smiled. "You're here."

"Yes, I've come. When did you last take a drink of water? Where?"

She tried to swallow. "The well ... where we ... leave our book. When ... you sent word you ... needed help ... I was thirsty."

Arthur raised her hand and kissed it before leaning forward and placing another kiss on her forehead.

Good thing Sir James still had a hold of his sister's arm. Mrs. Baines looked ready to pounce like a lioness protecting her cub.

Arthur urged Miss Abbott to rest and rose. He deliberately bumped into John's shoulder as he strode from the room.

"I apologize for his behavior," John said to Sir James. "I'll send Miss Abbott's maid and everything that is needed over at once."

Before they could respond, he left the room and went after Arthur, but he was already riding away from Hartsbury as John stepped out of the house.

Dr. Royston grunted and crossed his arms over his chest. "I have to admit, I'm impressed."

John leaned back in the chair next to the doctor's bed. "I wish this treatment were more effective, but the mortality rate has decreased dramatically. If we could figure out what's causing it, we might stand a chance."

"The instructions you've sent will work," the doctor said. "We must give it time."

"It's been two days now, and I have to wonder."

Dr. Royston grimaced. "Don't tell me you're even considering that ridiculous water theory?"

"Of course not, but there has to be something we've overlooked."

"Hmpf. You need to get Arthur Wilcox under control. Where is he now?"

"I understand he went back to the Hall." John had gone to the hospital first to arrange for Miss Abbott's care before coming next door to check on Dr. Royston. When he asked after Arthur, he was told the young man had just left, mentioning that he needed something at the Hall.

"Perhaps he should remain there after this is all over," the doctor said.

"No. Whatever his ideas are, I've seen him work. He'll make a fine doctor."

"If his ridiculous ideas don't kill someone first." The older man slid down in his bed a little. The fever had left him exhausted.

John rose. "I'll let you rest."

"Thank you. But bear in mind, I still have my reservations about that lad."

John returned to the hospital. He wanted to sink into the cot in the doctor's office, but there was something else he needed to do first. Parker walked out from the men's ward and took John's coat as he shrugged out of it. By the looks of him, he hadn't been there long. He still wore both vest and tie.

"Has Mrs. Lynch left for the Hall yet?" John asked.

"No, my lord, but she is just about to."

John told him to have her wait and went in search of Miss Howard, finding her alone in the kitchen, preparing a pot of water for the injections. He'd been gone for almost two hours. Had she rested as he'd told her to before he left? Probably not. As he stepped over to her, she raised her head.

"How is Miss Abbott?" she asked as she stirred the water.

"She's young and strong. I think she'll survive." Judging by the way she and Arthur had looked at one another, she had a lot to live for.

Miss Howard measured out the muriate of soda and added it. She glanced up at him. Her eyes were more gray than blue, but they still held trust. And they shouldn't.

"It's time you went home," he said.

She shook her head. "I can't. There's too much to do."

"The nurses from Mr. Worth will be here later today. Mrs. Lynch is leaving for the Hall shortly. She'll take you to Fairview."

She gave the water a final stir and pulled it off the stove to the worktable behind her. "I'll let them know there is more saline cooling." She turned and stumbled.

John caught her by the shoulders. "You're going home."

"Is that an order from my doctor?"

He shook her and spoke through gritted teeth. "I told you not to call me that. I don't deserve it."

"Yes. You do." Her chin trembled, and she steadied it before continuing, "I've watched you and worked with you. You rode in exactly when you were needed and fought bravely. I've never worked with a better doctor."

"I'm no knight in shining armor, Penelope."

"You are to me."

No. No, he wouldn't do this to her. He wouldn't have her thinking as Maggie had—that he was something he wasn't and could never be. "I am far from perfect."

"I know that."

"No. You don't." He released her, and she slouched against the worktable. "You have no idea what I've done."

"It doesn't matter. You are not beyond redemption." She stumbled over and reached out to him. "Please, please let me help you."

He batted her hands away. It was time she saw him as a monster. "No. I've had enough of your help. Is that all you can do? Nose around in other people's business? Leave me alone. I don't want your help. I don't need your help." He grasped her arm and all but shoved her to the door. "Go home. And don't come back."

She felt nothing. A woman sat across from her. Mrs. Lynch? Yes. That's who it was. The Hall's housekeeper. Lord Turner's housekeeper. Had he really told her not to come back? Worse, had he told her he didn't need her help? She rested her head in her hands. It was too much.

"Are you all right?" This couldn't be Mrs. Lynch. The voice sounded too kind. But they were the only occupants of the coach.

Penelope took a moment before answering. "I'm quite tired."

"Of course you are." The housekeeper moved to sit beside her. "You've been working very hard. I've watched you. And I'm afraid I misjudged you in the past. I'm sorry."

"Thank you. I mean, that is quite all right." She rubbed her forehead. "I'm so sorry, I'm not really making any sense."

Her throat closed. Her world had gone all topsy-turvy. Mrs. Lynch was being kind and Lord Turner cruel. His harsh words echoed in her ears. *Leave me alone. I don't want your help.* Had she been wrong about him all along? Was he really no different than Edmund Kern?

"My dear, you've gone so pale. Are you sure you're not ill?"

Penelope closed her eyes and swallowed hard. "I'm fine. I'll be fine."

Would she? After hearing such words from him, would she ever be fine again?

The coach stopped in front of Fairview.

"Penelope—may I call you that? Let me get out and help you down."

"Yes, that might be wise."

The door to Fairview opened, and Fanny rushed out. "Are you all right, Miss Penny?"

"She's exhausted," Mrs. Lynch replied. She supported Penelope with an arm around her shoulders. "Where is Mrs. Trull?"

"She's visitin' for Miss Penny."

"Then you will have to help me get her to bed."

The stairs seemed to take forever to climb. Once in her room, it seemed Fanny was taking far too long loosening her stays. All she wanted was her bed and the oblivion of sleep. Perhaps she was dreaming. She had to be dreaming.

She pulled away from her maid's hands and stumbled to her bed, nearly upsetting her bedside table.

"Oh, but Miss Penny, I've not finished." Fanny's words floated somewhere above her head as did Mrs. Lynch's reply.

"Leave that and cover her up. I'll tidy her bedside table."

Penelope mumbled her thanks before blackness took her.

CHAPTER 27

John slumped back in the chair behind Dr. Royston's desk. Two hours. In that time, two more had died, people were still getting sick, and Penelope Howard had gone home. He still tasted the acid from the words he had spoken to her. But it had to be done. For both their sakes. As soon as Dr. Royston was up and about, he would leave the hospital and then Woodley.

In the meantime, he needed help. He'd sent George to fetch Arthur. They should be arriving soon. Aside from Arthur's help, John needed to speak with him. Arthur was putting his future in jeopardy by continuing to cling to his water-borne disease theory. He leaned his head back. Just a few minutes' sleep.

George burst through the door. "My lord, you need to come, right now!"

"What is it?" John grabbed his coat and followed his valet.

"It's Arthur." They rushed through the front hall and out the door. "He's about to do something monumentally stupid."

A horse was ready and waiting for each of them.

"What?" John asked as they mounted.

"He's going to blow up the new well west of the village." George led the way. They had been riding hard for roughly ten minutes when an explosion caused their horses to rear. John and George struggled to stay in their saddles.

"Blast it! He's gone and done it!" John shouted.

They calmed their mounts and urged them on. Soon, they rode into a dust cloud, and John coughed as grit coated his throat. A small group of people turned as they approached. John and George dismounted, and the crowd parted as the two of them rushed forward.

Arthur and Charlie Milford stood next to a pile of rocks. The smile Arthur gave his old boss disappeared as John walked up.

"What do you think you're doing?" he asked.

"What should have been done days ago," Arthur replied.

"It was that new stuff of Mr. Nobel's," Charlie interjected. "The gardener at the Hall uses it for gettin' rid o' stumps. I think we might have used a bit much though, Arthur. But it did the trick."

John glared at them. "You've destroyed property, and people could have gotten hurt."

"People were already getting hurt because of this blasted well." Arthur stepped forward, hands clenched.

Charlie laid a hand on his shoulder and, far from his normal, jovial behavior, narrowed his eyes at John. "Now, now, Lord Turner, we warned 'em off. And it seems to me destroyin' property is a small price to pay to keep people from dyin'."

"But there's no way of knowing if this is the solution or not." He waved at the dust that settled around them. "If it did have something to do with this well, you might have made it worse. Who knows what gases you may have released into the air?"

"No more people will get sick after this," Arthur stated.

"But where will we get water now?" someone from the crowd called out.

There were murmurs of assent. Had Arthur thought of that? Some of these people had no way to get to the pump in the village green.

"I will make sure you all have a way to get to the village pump until other arrangements can be made to re-dig the well."

There was a scuffle of gravel behind him. Charlie held fast to Arthur's arm. But he couldn't hold back the murderous glare the young man shot him.

John dispersed the crowd, then confronted both of them. "I should have you both arrested, but I have enough to deal with now. Arthur, don't come back to the hospital." He flicked his gaze to Charlie. "You and I will discuss this later."

Charlie gave him a curt bow of the head. "Yes, *my lord.*"

Now both of them were angry with him. Fair enough. He was as angry with them, if not more.

He and George headed back to the hospital. When they arrived, he thought he might sink to the ground when he got off his horse. The ride had not been kind to his leg. He leaned against the animal for a moment, then pushed away and followed George inside, sending him off to help Parker, and went to the doctor's office.

Miss Phillips, Miss Abbott's maid, waited for him. "Lord Turner?"

"What can I do for you?" he asked. "Is Miss Abbott doing well?"

"Yes, my lord. She is responding to the treatment. I was looking for Mr. Wilcox. Is he here? I have something of importance for him from Miss Abbott."

The letter she held was thick. Miss Abbott must not be doing too badly if she had the strength to pen a love letter.

"I'm afraid he isn't here," he said. He held out his hand. "I will make sure he gets it."

She hesitated. "I was told to deliver this into his hand, sir."

"As I said, I will make sure he gets this. I'll give it to him when I return to the Hall. That is where he is. For now."

Thanking him, she gave a quick curtsy and left. John walked back to the doctor's office and, tossing the missive on the desk, collapsed onto the cot and finally slept.

⁂

"Lord Turner."

John opened his eyes and blinked at Parker standing over him.

The butler stepped to one side as he sat up on the edge of the cot. "I trust you are now more rested."

He nodded. He did feel better, physically at least. Pushing more recent events aside, he stood and rubbed the stubble on his face. "Why does this feel longer than it did an hour ago?" He hadn't slept any longer than that, he was certain.

"My lord, you slept the rest of the day and all through the night. It is now mid-morning."

John stared at him. "That can't be. What about the patients? Who else has passed? How many new cases do we have?"

"Everyone is quite well, sir," he replied. "No one else has died, and word is, as of this morning, no more people have become ill."

That no one else had succumbed was good news, but he had expected to hear that the number of sick had tripled, considering the dust and grit rising into the air due to the blast.

Parker continued, "Mr. Wilcox was here not long after you fell asleep." He frowned. "He gathered a number of things."

The letter Miss Phillips had given him. He walked toward the desk. "There was a letter here for him. Did he get it?" When Parker didn't answer, he asked, "What?"

"He read it but did not take it with him. Rather, he left it and asked that you read it at your leisure." He raised his chin as he spoke. "Mr. Wilcox opened it right here at the desk, my lord. The look he gave you when he was finished was most disrespectful, and I made sure he understood my displeasure."

John rubbed his chin as he moved to stand behind the desk. The pages of the letter lay strewn across it. He gathered them and read the contents. The more he read, the more blood he felt leave his face and extremities. He was almost shaking as he laid down the last page.

Parker stared at him, concern etched on his face. "My lord, are you all right? What does it say?"

"It says that I'm a fool."

All John could do was wait.

With Dr. Royston now recovered and the epidemic under control, John and his servants had returned to Ashford Hall. Parker explained to him they all needed to rest before they could resume his plans to leave. It was altogether possible the man was trying to put him off and give him a day or so to reconsider leaving Woodley. In light of how hard his staff had worked, he had consented.

In the meantime, he would wait.

Sleep came in bits and pieces. Otherwise, he wandered. The evening of the third day found him haunting the gardens. The sun set in a flaming ball of red as he made his way back to the Hall. As darkness shrouded him, he ambled to the side door that led into the library. Arthur's door. He opened it. The oil lamp the young man had lit the night he'd returned looking for answers still sat on a side table. Someone had long since extinguished the flame.

A dim light came from his study. His dinner. He'd requested a tray be sent there last night. The kitchen staff had probably concluded he'd want to eat in there again. He'd ring the bell and tell them to take it away. He wasn't hungry. Sighing, he started toward the front of the library.

"You look exhausted."

At the sound of the familiar voice, he stopped short. "Robert!"

His old friend leaned against his desk. The curl of his mouth suggested he was no longer angry with him. The quick yet hearty bear hug confirmed it.

John pulled away. It seemed odd to smile. "What are you doing here?"

Robert's brow rose. "I might ask you the same thing. Do all English lords wander into their grand homes through a side door?"

If smiling felt strange, a chuckle, however short, felt even more so. "No. I was just out for a walk."

"In the dark?"

"It was light when I started," John said. "You never answered my question."

Robert clasped his shoulder. "I was invited to a medical

conference in Vienna. Sarah convinced me to leave early so we could stop and see you."

"You brought Sarah? Where is she?"

"London. She wasn't feeling up to a train ride after our voyage over."

"Rough crossing?"

"In a way. Sarah was sicker than she usually is at the beginning of a sea voyage." He bounced on the balls of his feet a little as he spoke. "She's due next summer."

"That's wonderful. I'm sorry to not see her, but I'm glad she stayed behind." He winced. "We've had sickness here."

"Yes, your butler, Parker, told me." His mouth twitched. "About time you got back on the horse."

"Oh, yes. Back on and fell right off again." John walked to the other side of his desk.

His friend sighed. "Dare I ask what that means?"

"It means, as usual, I have made a mess of things."

"Again, huh? What now?"

"First I refused to help, causing more people to die than should have. And when I did finally decide to help, my arrogance nearly cost more lives because I refused to see the answer right under my nose." He told him about Arthur finding first a treatment, then the cause of the epidemic. "He even has proof. Look at this."

He swept up Arthur's letter from his desk and handed it to Robert. Other papers flew about in his wake, but he'd straighten them later. He lowered himself into his chair.

Robert ambled as he read. After a few minutes, he came to a stop next to John's desk. "This is good work. So it came here in the bottle of water found in this Miss Oliver's home?"

"Yes. They found packaging. It had been shipped from her sister in Southampton. Apparently, her sister thought the water from her street pump would be good for her."

"Mr. Wilcox has an interesting hand."

"That's not his handwriting. It was written by a woman, a

Miss Isabella Abbott. She also sketched the picture you see there."
He described Miss Abbott and her situation, refraining from
mentioning her relationship with Arthur.

"Yes. She's saying it's the same organism a Filippo Pacini found
in the intestinal tract of a cholera victim. Fascinating."

"Apparently she has a microscope," John said. "Before she fell
ill, she was able to compare the water samples she was given from
the bottle, the well, and the village pump. She found the organism
in the bottle and the well but not the pump."

"And did you do as Dr. Snow did? Cut off access to the well?"

"No. I wouldn't listen. Arthur took matters into his own hands
and did it himself. And I threatened to have him arrested. I told
you I made a mess of things." He'd sent a letter Hartsbury, but it
had come back unopened. And Arthur could not be located.

Robert handed the papers back to him. "What are you going
to do now?"

"Leave. The arrangements are all made. I would have been in
London already if it weren't for all this. I'm giving the household
staff another day or two of rest, and then I'm shutting up the
house."

He dropped the letter onto his desk. A paper flew off and
landed at Robert's feet.

"So you're running away? Again?" Robert picked up the paper
and glanced at it.

"I need to go someplace where no one knows who I am."

"And where no one knows you're a doctor." Robert worked his
jaw. He waved the paper he held. "Who is this Penelope Howard?
She seems to understand what you need better than you do."

John stood. Miss Howard's note. Someone must have tidied
the library and placed it on his desk. He reached for it, but Robert
pulled it away from his grasp.

"*My grace is sufficient for thee: for my strength is made perfect in
weakness,*" he quoted.

John lunged forward and tried to take it again, without success.

"Don't start on me, Robert. There's not enough grace in the world sufficient for what I've done."

"John, you're human. We all are. Or don't you think I've made mistakes too? Mistakes I'm not proud of."

"That's different, Robert. You're—"

"I'm weak." He took a step back and spread his arms out. "I'm not ashamed to admit it. Because that's when God is strongest, when His *grace* is at its strongest. When I make mistakes. Especially the ones I can't fix." He held the note out to him.

John snatched it back. The smallest glimpse of her elegant hand was enough to make him catch his breath. And it was impossible not to imagine the tenderness on her face as she wrote it. He laid it face down on his desk, refusing to meet his friend's eye.

"She means something to you doesn't she?" Robert crossed his arms. "The woman who wrote that? I've never seen you react like this. Even over Maggie."

John stared at the back of her note. "Yes."

"Then she's one in a million. Like Sarah. And you'd be a fool to leave her." He strode to the door but paused. "If you decide to be a fool, we're staying at the Westminster Palace Hotel in London. Be sure to come see Sarah. But don't count on seeing me. I'll more than likely be out."

CHAPTER 28

"Are you sure you're feeling up to going out?" Hannah sat on Penelope's bed as she stood in front of her mirror doing her hair.

Penelope looked at her through the glass then regarded her own reflection. It had been four days since she had come home from the hospital. Exhaustion no longer lined her face, and the circles under her eyes had disappeared. Physically, she felt well rested.

Her heart was another matter altogether.

Self-control was paper thin. It was taking everything she had. She needed to get away, for an hour or so at least, and release her pent-up emotions.

She lifted her chin as she finished securing her chignon.

"I'll be fine, Hannah. A walk and fresh air will do me good."

"Yes. A walk will certainly help what's ailin' your heart."

Penelope's hands froze. How could she know? "What do you mean?"

"I don't know. Wish I did. I've known you since you were a babe, and I can tell when somethin's wrong. You act like you were bein' held together with spider silk."

Penelope took a deep breath. "I'm going to visit Clara Bromley."

She walked down the stairs to the hooks where her cloak and hat hung. "I shouldn't be gone long."

"I'm prayin' for you."

Hannah's voice was softer, gentler than she'd ever heard. She reached out and gave the woman a quick embrace.

"Thank you," she whispered. She pulled away and cleared her throat. "On second thought, I might be a while. I think I might stay and help Clara with her students."

As she made her way down the lane that led from Fairview to the main road, she pressed a hand to her chest. The tears that she had held back for days fell freely. She stopped and looked up. God would work this out for good. Somehow. Even if it wasn't in the way she wanted.

He was still leaving.

Thomas had said as much yesterday. If leaving meant God would help him find the path to grace, then so be it. John Turner's soul was more important than the yearnings of her heart. It no longer made sense to deny she loved him. He wasn't like Edmund. No matter what he'd said. He'd only pushed her away to protect her, and she loved him all the more for it. A love that plumbed to a depth that almost scared her, it was so strong.

She had never felt this way for Edmund.

Leaves crunched under her boots as she moved on, and an autumn breeze fingered her cloak. Her courtship with Edmund played through her mind. She had seen what she'd wanted to see in him. Not the lecher that he was. If her uncle had succeeded in making him marry her, would she have been happy? More than likely not. He would have placed himself above her needs, and she would have found herself in a loveless marriage. And that would have been far worse than her situation now.

The breeze had dried her earlier tears, but she had to reach for her handkerchief to dry the ones that now slipped down her cheeks. She couldn't allow Clara to see her sad.

She managed to compose herself and was soon walking up the little lane to Clara's cottage. She knocked on the door. No answer. The windows were open. Penelope angled herself toward them but didn't quite look in.

"Clara? Are you there?" She wrinkled her nose at the scent of mint. Had her morning sickness returned? If so why was she still drinking that horrible tea she had obtained at Mr. Brown's? She'd had Thomas take her their blend.

She knocked again, and when Clara still didn't answer, she peered in the window. Clara lay on the floor, a small bottle lying empty nearby and the contents of the room in utter chaos.

Sleep was still somewhat elusive. John rose early, ate little, and once again took to wandering the Hall. Sometime mid-morning, Parker approached as he stared out a window in one of the upper floor rooms.

"Yes, Parker?"

"The staff is more than sufficiently rested, my lord. Are you ready to leave? We can have everything ready by early this afternoon."

"Charlie Milford hasn't left us, has he?"

The pause before Parker's answer marked his surprise over the question. "No, my lord. Mr. Milford is still here. He's in the stables, I believe."

"Good." He started down the hall toward the stairs, then stopped. He hadn't answered his question. "I'm sorry, Parker. I don't want to leave."

The butler raised a brow at him.

"Not today, I mean. Not yet. I—"

"John." Parker's straight back and cool gaze were undermined by the softness of his voice. "Take your time."

He nodded and made his way down the stairs and out the front door.

Indecision worked at him. One minute he was ready to turn his back on the Hall and all that William had entrusted to him, and the next he wanted to stay. Stay and see if it was possible to live again. Stay and see if *she* were possible, even after everything he'd said. *My grace is sufficient* ... Every time the hope of that verse rose in his heart, he pulled it back down. How could he hope? What right did he have? Was he really still falling for eternity or had he stopped? And if he had stopped, how could he pick himself up again? What foothold could he use? How could he stay there?

A stillness lingered around his soul.

When he reached the stables, a boy directed him to a stall where Charlie groomed Fortis. The horse rumbled at his approach, and Charlie's face hardened.

"Good morning, *my lord*." Charlie faced him, gave him a bow of the head, and resumed grooming.

John winced. "Mr. Milford?"

"What can we do for you today, *your lordship*?" He gave Fortis's hindquarters a swift sweep of the brush.

"Charlie."

The man paused, but the horse's sleek coat held his attention.

"I'm sorry. You and Arthur were right. Your actions saved many lives."

"That's all right. But you did your own share savin' lives as well. Arthur couldn't have done it without ya."

The stillness intensified. He could almost hear it. "I did?"

The groom cocked his head at him. "Of course. You're a doctor, after all, aren't ya?"

Was he? He didn't have an answer. "Have you heard from Arthur? Do you know where he is?"

"No. I can't say that I do."

Joseph had claimed ignorance as well, and John had received no answer from the note he'd sent Mrs. Wilcox. "If he comes here, find me. I owe him an apology as well."

"Of course."

John stroked Fortis' neck. "Can you saddle him? I think I'll go for a ride."

Several minutes later, John trotted Fortis down the gravel path toward the road. He was well out of sight of the house when he saw a figure in the distance running toward him. Miss Howard. His heart dropped. He dismounted and ran to her.

She was soon sagging in his arms, gasping for breath.

"What is it? What's the matter?" he asked. He took her by the forearms and gently pulled her upright. A metal band wrapped itself around his chest. Her face was like chalk.

She gripped the lapels of his coat. "My friend … Clara … Clara Bromley. She's sick."

"How? Is it cholera?"

"No, I think she drank something." Her hold tightened, and the panic in her eyes eclipsed to outright fear. If she, of all people, was afraid … "And someone has attacked her. Please come. I don't know what to do."

The gravity of her last statement plowed into him. The stillness was gone, and he felt himself sliding. He gripped her tighter. "Let me take her to the hospital."

"There isn't time, and we can't take her there."

"Why?"

She looked away for a moment. "Because we can't. *Please!*"

"Penelope." He clenched his jaw and swallowed. "I thought I made it clear I don't deserve to be a doctor."

She locked her eyes on him, her fear receding as they quickly welled with compassion and something else he didn't dare hope to name. "The only thing you made clear to me was that you are a soul in need of grace and healing."

She didn't go on. She didn't need to. He mounted Fortis and pulled her up in front of him, wrapping an arm around her waist and pressing her back against his chest. Her hair, loosed from its bun, brushed his neck and cheek as they rode. Lavender and roses. *My grace is sufficient … Please don't let us both regret what I'm about to do.*

They arrived within a few minutes. John eased her to the ground and followed her to the cottage. He stopped short at the door, gagging at the smell. He gripped the doorframe and coughed. "No. Not that."

"You know what it is?"

"Pennyroyal." Beth had taken it. Memories rushed at him. Maggie's crying, Beth's limp, pale form. Warm fingers grasped his hand, and he started.

"Come back," she whispered. "Don't let it paralyze you."

How did she always know? He drew in a deep breath and walked into the cottage. Miss Bromley lay on her bed. One eye was bruised and swollen shut. More bruises lay across her face and wreathed her neck.

"She was on the floor when I found her." Penelope held up a bottle. "This was lying beside her. Empty."

He took it from her, and his heart sank. It was the oil. Why couldn't it have been the tincture, the less potent of the two? "Do you know how much she drank?"

"No, but there was some on the floor near where she lay."

He took her pulse. It was there but weak and quicker than it should be. And despite her bruising, she was altogether too pale. At least there wasn't evidence that something more severe had been done to her. He rubbed the back of his neck. Was it the pennyroyal making her unconscious or the concussion she'd sustained?

He rubbed her wrist. "Miss Bromley? Clara?"

Her good eye opened for a moment and she lifted her head. Hope lifted in John's chest. She wouldn't be able to be roused if it was pennyroyal. But she wasn't awake for long.

"Students ..." she muttered and was insensible again.

He looked to Penelope.

"She runs the girls' school from here. They're due to arrive soon."

He picked Clara up. She was petite and light. With Penelope's help, he could get her in the saddle and climb up after her. "Come on."

Penelope preceded him out the door and brought Fortis to the gate. He lifted Miss Bromley, and Penelope somehow managed to keep her upright as John climbed up behind her. He wrapped one arm around her and steadied her as she slumped against him. He looked at Penelope.

"You can't take her to the hospital," she said.

"I know. This isn't the first time I've seen a woman use pennyroyal." Unfortunately, it wasn't the first time he'd seen a woman so badly beaten either. "I'll take her to Fairview."

"No."

"But it's closer."

"The fewer people who know about this, the better."

Why was she so resolute? He caught her gaze, but she looked away. Miss Bromley moaned slightly. Questions would have to wait.

"All right. I'll take her to the Hall. I think I can get her in unnoticed through the side door to the library." If he approached the Hall from the far side and around the gardens instead of the main drive, he could slip in that way.

"I'll enter through there as well, once I deal with the girls." She reached up and laid her hand over his. The warmth traveled up his arm, generating more heat in his chest. "Thank you."

"Don't thank me yet." He wouldn't lie to her. He couldn't.

"Why?"

"Neither of my last patients survived."

Fortis snorted. He didn't like being made to slow down as they made their way through the woods surrounding the southern part of the house. John guided him around tree roots and uneven ground until they could see the Hall across a short clearing. Miss Bromley had remained unconscious the entire ride, but she needed to get inside as soon as possible. He looked around the clearing and saw no one. He made for the library side door.

But how could he get her down from the horse without further injuring her? He'd have to take a chance with one of the servants. He rode close to the library windows, peering through them, hoping to see Parker or Joseph. A young maid was inside dusting, but how to get her attention?

Just then, she turned. Her eyes widened, and he motioned toward the library door. She walked out, dust rag still in hand.

"My lord? Shall I go for Mr. Parker?" she asked.

"No." He trusted Parker, but Penelope was right. As few as possible should know about this. The maid was young but tall and appeared strong. "Come here and help me ease her to the ground."

The maid threw the cloth to the side and walked up to the horse. He gently slid Miss Bromley into her arms. She held her upright until John climbed down and picked her up, ignoring the pain in his leg.

"I need to get her upstairs, quietly. Preferably to a more remote room in the house."

"Of course, my lord." She thought for a moment, then brightened. "I know just the place."

They made their way through the rear of the library and into his study, and from there into the morning room. There, she walked ahead of him and cracked the pocket doors leading to the rear of the entry hall. She peered through the opening and motioned him to follow.

They encountered no one on the stairs or as they walked down the hall toward the rear of the house to a bedroom in the northwest square tower. The maid shut the door behind them and turned down the covers so John could lay Miss Bromley in the bed. Sheets covered the rest of the furniture in the small square room.

He straightened and rubbed his leg. "Thank you..." He grimaced, unable to recall her name. "I'm sorry—"

"Ellen, my lord." She rested the sheet and coverlet across Miss Bromley's chest.

"Ellen, I have to ask you to tell no one that she is here, even Mrs. Lynch."

"Of course. You'll be needin' an emetic, my lord?"

He stared at her. "How do you know?"

"My granny was a midwife, so I know that smell about her," she said. "Mrs. Lynch keeps an emetic on hand."

"Good. Fetch it while I'm gone, and see if you can get any in her once you've loosened her stays. I have to see to my horse before anyone notices. I'll be right back."

Once Fortis was in the hands of a groom, he slipped up to his room, got his medical bag, and returned to the tower room. Ellen had done as he asked as well as uncover the washstand and the rest of the furniture. She rose from a chair next to the bed when he entered.

"I tried to get her to swallow it, but she woke for a moment and pushed me off." The girl looked at Clara's bruises with wide eyes. "Who did this to her, my lord?"

"I don't know, but I intend to find out." He picked up the bottle of emetic and the spoon that lay beside it and sat down on the edge of the bed.

"Do you need anything else, sir? I'll need to be getting back to my duties before I'm missed."

"Cold compresses if you can manage it. You can say they are for me if anyone asks. And Miss Howard will be arriving shortly through the library. Show her up here."

The girl bobbed a curtsy and left. Miss Bromley groaned and raised up on her elbows. One look was all John needed to know what was about to happen. He grabbed the bowl from the washstand and wrapped his arm about her shoulders as she got sick. It was not much, and it did not smell as strongly of pennyroyal as he would have thought. Thank the Lord. He considered a plan for her treatment.

When she was through, he set the bowl on the floor and handed her a handkerchief before easing her back down on the bed. She remained awake this time and darted glances about the room. Finally, she noticed him.

"Lord Turner." She covered her battered face and sobbed.

"It's all right." He sat on the edge of the chair. "You're at the Hall. Miss Howard found you on the floor of your cottage. Who did this to you?"

"Do you know, my lord? She had to tell you, didn't she?" She didn't wait for him to answer but went on. "I deserve what has happened to me."

His hands clenched to fists. When his jaw finally loosened, he had a hard time keeping the edge from his voice. "No woman deserves this."

She lowered her hands. "It was my choice to get myself in the state I am. And I deliberately tried to kill the life growing inside of me." She closed her eyes. "That is unforgivable."

"No. Nothing is unforgivable." She turned her head away from him, unconvinced, but he sat back as his own words washed over him. "No one is beyond redemption."

Penelope stood on the threshold with a cold compress in her hands. She walked over and stood over him. "Please say you believe that," she whispered.

He rose. "I can't." He drew in a jagged breath. "See to her."

He closed the door behind him. A solitary chair sat on the other side of the hall, and he sank into it. It wasn't that easy. Not for him. It couldn't be. He put his head in his hands.

Either a minute or a half hour later—he wasn't sure which—the door opened, and Penelope stepped out. "She's asleep."

He had to get away from her, but she blocked his path. "What you said. You're right. You have to believe that."

He had to tell her now. There was no way around it. He had to tell her all of it.

"I became a doctor with honorable intentions. Help the sick and hurt. Heal them. Rescue the dying. I went to war to fight all three, and I thought I was winning." He shook his head. "I didn't even come close."

She grasped his hands. "But the war is over now."

"It's more than that, Penelope." His fingers tightened around hers. "I should have stopped practicing medicine then and there. But did I? No. I thought I could redeem myself. When the war was over, I went home to Philadelphia and worked with the poor.

I didn't take a cent from them. I worked the docks during the day to earn my keep and walked them as a doctor at night. But the war wouldn't leave me alone. It haunted me in my dreams. So I drank. Then I met Maggie."

She dropped his hands. Good.

"She thought she cleaned me up. But I would still indulge, behind her back or after we fought. That's how her little sister, Beth, got attacked. It was my fault. One night while we fought over my drinking, Beth slipped outside to go for a walk." He stopped, bile rising in his throat. Heat rose in his cheeks and eyes, and he blinked. He choked out the next words. "Maggie recognized what a monster I was when Beth and her unborn child died at my hands."

She turned away. He drank it in. But she knew now.

"Am I still a doctor in your eyes?" When she didn't reply, he continued, "You once told me that pedestals were dangerous things. You were right. The one God placed me on when I became His child is the most dangerous one there is. I fell, and I'm still falling. For eternity."

CHAPTER 29

"Are you sure Miss Bromley did not say who she went to stay with?" Thomas frowned as he guided the cart to church Sunday morning. They were just approaching the lane that led to Clara's cottage. His eyes lingered on it as they went by.

Penelope sighed. "Yes, I am sure. All her note said was her illness returned, and when some friends came to visit, they insisted she go stay with them."

"If she writes you again, tell me." He urged the horse a little faster.

Should she tell him? He was certainly very concerned about her. No, it wasn't her secret to tell.

The story was not strictly a lie. It just wasn't the whole truth. Most people had accepted it readily enough, even Mr. Gregory. He decided to have Penelope close the school for the time being. With the harvest coming up, the girls would be needed at home anyway. Clara was still at the Hall, recuperating under her and Lord Turner's care. Penelope had gone each day since to help and to sit with her and try to cheer her. Ellen also came and assisted them, with encouraging words of her own. Yet while Clara's body was healing, her spirits were not.

As for Lord Turner, she couldn't be sure.

He had moments when he would look at Clara and then shake his head. She could not help but hope he was thinking back to the day they'd taken her to the Hall. *Nothing is unforgivable.* He'd said those words as if he might believe them. She longed to see him accept God's grace and make his spirit whole again. But inside that solution lay another problem.

If he were whole, if he returned to God, what did that mean for them? She wasn't a fool. She knew why he'd bared everything to her. He loved her. And she loved him. She drew in a slow, deep breath. Her heart would fly out of her chest if she didn't slow it. He had no business wanting her. She couldn't give him an heir. She had to encourage him to go. There was no other way around it. Best he leave believing she was the woman he imagined her to be. Not the ruined woman she was.

The church was not as full as usual, a stark reminder of the sickness which had swept through Woodley. But Mr. Gregory gave thanks that it was not worse and praised the efforts of those at the cottage hospital. He mentioned not only her but Lord Turner as well. While he was not there to accept their thanks, she accepted them on his behalf.

She had just finished speaking to someone when Thomas came to fetch her. "Are you ready? Hannah and Fanny started back several minutes ago."

"Lord Turner is absent again this week," Thomas commented as he helped her into the cart. "Has he told you why?"

"What do you mean?" she asked as he climbed up beside her. "How should I know why?"

He stared at her before urging the horse forward. "I mean you've been practically living at the Hall. You can't possibly be going that often and not know."

"I'm helping one of the maids with something. And there's the Harvest Dinner." Her cheeks heated. There wasn't a Harvest Dinner. In light of his departure, Lord Turner had called it off.

Silence followed. It was several minutes before her brother spoke again. "When will Lord Turner propose, I wonder?"

Her jaw dropped. "Propose? Why would he?"

"The question, dear sister, is why wouldn't he? Or are you blind to the way he looks at you?"

She clenched her hands. What could she say? She should deny it. It wasn't as if they had a future together.

"So you're not. Now the question is what will Miss Howard do when he does ask?" Fresh heat rose in her cheeks, and she was still at a loss for words. He continued, "Surely you will accept. Or are you still pining away for Mr. Kern?"

"No." She snapped her mouth shut. That answer had been far too quick.

"I thought not." His face was unreadable. He said nothing the rest of the ride home and was equally uncommunicative over luncheon. He left Fairview on horseback afterward, claiming something pressing had arisen at one of the farms and needed his attention.

Penelope paced in the parlor. Did he know about Edmund? And if he did, how had he found out? They had been careful, very careful. Not even Hannah knew or suspected. Why even bring him up if he didn't know something? More upsetting was the way he seemed to feel about her fall from grace. Almost happy. She sank down into her mother's chair by the fire.

A soft rap at the window had much the same effect on her as if someone had pounded against it. Ellen stood outside with wide eyes and a fist to her mouth.

Penelope flew to the window and, after struggling with the latch, opened it. "What's happened? Has Clara taken a turn? Has she lost the child?"

"Miss Bromley's gone and hurt herself. I went up as soon as I could after church. She'd gotten into Lord Turner's medical bag. He sent me to fetch you."

Oh dear Lord, no. She'd been prepared to talk to Clara for days now. Why hadn't she done so sooner? How could she have allowed herself to be so diverted by her hopes for Lord Turner. "Wait for me. I'll be right out."

Penelope latched the window and walked to the door of the parlor. The house was quiet. Since this was their afternoon off, Fanny and Hannah must have finished cleaning up from luncheon and gone visiting. She left a quick note in case she was still gone when they returned, took her cloak and hat from their hook, and let herself out.

When she and Ellen arrived at the Hall, they found Lord Turner in bloodstained shirtsleeves next to Clara's bed. He stood when he saw them.

"Sit with her for a few minutes, Ellen," he said, coming toward them. He led Penelope outside and shut the door behind them.

"What happened?"

"She found a scalpel in my bag and cut her wrists." He shook his head. "I didn't even know I had left something like that in there. It must have slipped down inside the lining." He leaned his head back against the doorframe.

She laid her hand on his arm. "My lord, this wasn't your fault." Would he believe that? Or would this push him back into the darkness?

"When Ellen found her, she was awake and frightened," he said. "I gave her a little laudanum, and she fell asleep. But I don't think she should be left alone."

"I'll go and sit with her. You should change."

He pushed away from the door and left. If the sight of his retreating back pained her, how would she ever be able to convince him to leave permanently? She pressed her hands against her warm cheeks before entering the room.

"You'd better go before you're missed, Ellen," she said as she walked to the bed.

Ellen nodded and gave Clara a kind, sisterly look before she quit the room. Her compassion was touching. Most would have been condemning.

Penelope removed her cloak and hat and set them aside. She lowered herself to her knees and propped her arms on the edge of the bed to pray. *Father, use me to bring her back. My past has ruined me, but it may help heal her.* When she was finished, she drew the chair closer to the bed and sat down, watching her friend's face. Painful experience played across her features even in sleep.

An hour or so passed. Lord Turner had not returned. Perhaps he had decided to retire to the library.

Clara roused and opened her eyes. They grew glassy when she saw Penelope.

"I am so sorry." A tear slipped down her face. She raised her hand to wipe it away, and more began to flow when she caught sight of the bandages on her wrist. "I don't know what I was thinking, Penelope. Truly, I don't."

"I know, darling," she soothed and wiped her face with her own handkerchief. "You've been so melancholy."

"I've been unsure of the state of my own soul." Clara closed her eyes. "What must God think of me?"

Penelope gently took hold of her hands. "God loves all His children. Even when they make mistakes."

"I know I should believe you above all people." She looked to the ceiling. "Does God really forgive women who've fallen as we have?"

❧❦❧

John watched the two women through the crack in the door. He couldn't have heard Clara correctly. Fallen? No. How was that possible? He focused his attention on Penelope. At the ruins, she'd said that God's grace covered not only his mistakes, but hers as well. Was this what she'd meant?

She answered Clara's question by pulling something from her pocket and laying it in the young woman's hand. A rock. Clara looked at her questioningly, almost fearfully.

"I used to be the apple of my father's eye," Penelope said. "But when I ran away with Edmund Kern and he violated me, Father gave me this."

Violated? The wood doorframe should have cracked. No, the whole door—the whole wall—should be giving way in the wake of the fire which burned through his chest. If this Edmund Kern was anywhere in England, he would find him and throttle him with his bare hands. For the moment, he'd settle for the doorframe. It prevented him from committing murder, but it also kept him from striding into the room. There was more. If he walked in now she'd never be able to say it. She needed to tell him without knowing she was.

"In his eyes, my fall was terrible. He gave me this as a reminder." She took the stone from Clara and turned it over.

The young woman squinted at it. "What is that carved there?"

"John 8:1-11. The story of the woman caught in adultery."

Clara stared at her.

"I don't understand," she whispered. "You're not an adulteress. He *attacked* you."

"Adulteress, loose woman—all the same in my father's eyes. He said Edmund only did what any man would do in his situation, and it was my fault for stepping into the carriage. My father gave this to me as a reminder of what I had done. As a way of keeping me from straying again." Penelope leaned back in her seat and clasped her hands in her lap. "I read that passage every day for years. Twice if I happened to see a handsome young man. I kept myself from forming any kind of relationship, in part because of that passage and in part because when I had my daughter, there were complications. I can't have children."

His hands fell from the doorframe. She couldn't have children? No. No, she was made to be a mother. Sadness tamed the angry flames and his arms ached to hold her close and never let go.

"Oh, Penelope, none of that is your fault."

"I know that now. It's funny how you can read something over and over and still not really read it. One day I read through it again, and I saw it."

"What?"

"The rock."

"Which one? Everyone has rocks in that passage, Penelope. They were ready to stone her."

"No, Clara. *The* Rock. Jesus, the Christ." She reached up and wiped her cheek. "He is the Rock I stand on every day. He is my sure foothold when I sin, and He does not condemn me. And He does not condemn you either."

Tears streamed down Clara's cheeks as Penelope drew her close.

John stepped back from the door, shaking. He gripped his head in his hands then swung them to his sides as he strode down the hall. His steps became a jog, then almost a run until he reached the library. William's Bible. It sat on a stand near the window. He scooped it up and took it to his study, shutting the doors behind him. He read the passage in John, not once, but three times.

… He that is without sin among you, let him first cast a stone … where are those thine accusers? … Neither do I condemn thee …

Neither do I condemn thee …

He sank down to his knees. *Truly, God? How can you forgive me? How?*

Grace. My grace is sufficient for thee. My power is perfect in your weakness.

This time he let the verse in. Its warmth wrapped around his chest and back like a father holding fast to his son, pulling him from the edge of danger. He gasped and laughed, his heart pounding out a joy which reverberated through every cell in his body. The endless pit, the freefall, was over.

He raised himself to his feet.

He stood on the Rock.

Always had and always would.

Robert had been right.

She had been right.

Penelope. He needed to see her. Tell her. Tell her everything. That he knew about her past and how little it mattered to him. How could it? After everything he'd done, how could he judge her?

He wiped his handkerchief across his face and opened the door to his study.

Penelope stood on the other side.

He didn't give her a chance to say or do anything. He swept her into his arms and held her. Her heart beat against his chest, and he let himself drown in her scent of lavender and roses. "It's over, Penelope. I'm not falling anymore."

She pulled away from him. "My lord?"

"No one is beyond redemption." He cupped her face with both hands. "You're right."

"Clara ... she ..." Penelope stammered. "She's sleeping. Again."

He swept a thumb along her cheekbone. "I'm glad you came to tell me that."

"I should go."

Why was she pulling away? Didn't she understand? Nothing stood between them now. He held her fast by her forearms. This day would not end without asking her to remain by his side until he drew his last breath.

"Did you need anything else, my lord?"

He bent slightly and could feel the sliver of air between them vibrate as he whispered in her ear. "You do know I have a name, don't you?"

She tried to step away again. He drew her closer. Bit by bit, he lowered his head until his lips brushed hers. She sighed and relented.

He drank her in, and she tasted sweeter than before. With a great deal of effort, he lifted his head and found the azure blue of her eyes. "To answer your question, yes, I do need something else. You. Always. Every day. And every night."

Penelope stared at him. What could she do? Or say? She was caught between sorrow and joy. He still didn't know.

"My lord—"

"I have a name."

The door opened, and they parted. Mrs. Lynch came in, carrying a ledger.

"Yes, Mrs. Lynch?" Lord Turner asked.

She walked past them and sat down in one of the chairs in front of his desk. "My lord, I need to speak to you."

"I'll leave," Penelope said.

"No, Miss Howard," she said. "Stay. This concerns you as well."

Her? Lord Turner took her hand and led her into the study, pulling her behind the desk with him. He sat, and she stood just behind his chair. Mrs. Lynch handed him the ledger.

"What's this?" he asked.

"It belongs to Mr. Howard, my lord."

After exchanging glances with Penelope, he opened the ledger. The more pages he scanned, the more his jaw tightened.

"What's wrong?" Penelope asked.

"He's stealing from me." He snapped the ledger shut.

"What?" She flipped the ledger back open.

Column after column, in Thomas' own hand, were entries which showed him skimming money from more than one source. The salary for his bailiffs in Somerset and the Isle of Wight were higher than what they were actually given, and he pocketed a portion of the profits from the holdings in Southampton. He had also stolen a portion of the tenants' rents by lying about the actual amounts being charged and pocketing the difference. A month prior, Ashford House had been let out, and he'd retained the entire amount.

It was as if her whole body had become a block of ice as shame leached the warmth from it. *Thomas, what have you done? How could you?* She pushed the ledger away and focused on the edge of the desk.

"My lord, I swear I did not know any of this."

Lord Turner shut the book. "I know."

His tone would warm her if she let it. She didn't.

"He betrayed all of us," Mrs. Lynch said.

"All of us?" Lord Turner asked.

"Miss Bromley most of all. Has she ever told you who the father was?"

Penelope started. "No. Harriett, how can you even know? Clara confided only in me."

"If you go to your brother's studio, you will find irrefutable proof that it's his. Though I warn you, it isn't proper in the least."

What was colder than ice? There was no word for what chilled her now. "You mean—"

"Yes. He never left his past completely behind. The rest, the money, was because of your uncle."

"I don't understand," Lord Turner said. "What proof? And how does William factor into this?"

Proof? Would Harriett say? A portion of her thawed as she answered.

"Except for the title, Lord Renshaw could have given all he owned to anyone he chose, in full or in part. Thomas was furious when he was left only Fairview and the promise that you would be encouraged to keep him on."

"He never acted as if that bothered him."

"My brother is a clever actor, my lord," Penelope whispered. "Though I thought I was close enough to him that he could not fool me."

Lord Turner grasped her fingers. Thomas' indiscretions reminded her of her own. The man next to her, attempting to comfort her as best he could, had to be convinced to leave before he knew everything. With a wrench to her heart, she pulled her fingers free.

"Do you know where he is now?" he asked.

"He's gone," Mrs. Lynch said. "He's done all the damage he can and left."

"How did you know all of this?" Penelope asked.

Mrs. Lynch worried the edge of her sleeve for almost a minute before answering. "Miss Bromley was not the only woman to be used by him."

Their conversation outside the pub, the tie pin. Neither had been innocent coincidences.

"Are you well, Harriett?" she asked.

"I was more careful than poor Miss Bromley. What will happen to her? Will her child be all right?"

"I intend to do everything I can for her," Lord Turner replied. "As far as I can tell at this point, the child is fine."

Joseph appeared at the door. "My lord, there's a messenger here from Hartsbury Manor. You're wanted there at once."

CHAPTER 30

Fortis was damp with sweat by the time John arrived at Hartsbury. He dismounted and threw the reins at the groom who rushed out to meet them. His leg throbbed, and he was obliged to pause at the bottom of the steps leading up to the house. Taking them as quickly as he dared, he rang the bell and walked inside as soon as the footman opened the door.

"Mrs. Baines is expecting me," he said.

He was shown into the parlor. The older woman was the only one in the room, and she sat in a high-backed chair, looking like the queen herself holding court. "Ah, Lord Turner. Good afternoon."

"Mrs. Baines."

He growled the words, but she apparently did not notice. "Won't you sit down?"

"Actually, I'd rather not." His leg begged to differ, but he ignored it. "If you could, please tell me why you felt the need to summon me here on a Sunday afternoon. I would like to hear it and return home."

"I see. I'm afraid I have received some rather disturbing news concerning Miss Howard."

He clenched his jaw and looked over the fussy, ornate room before returning his gaze to her. "And what complaint do you have against her now, Mrs. Baines?"

"Not a complaint, a confirmation." She pulled a letter free from where it was tucked in the cushion of her chair. "This was delivered to me not an hour ago. It is a letter to Miss Howard from a Miss Neale. Apparently, they met in London. In a lying-in hospital. As patients."

She held the letter out to him, and he snatched it from her hand. He skimmed the contents. Nothing new, but enough to confirm a spiteful old woman's suspicions. How on God's earth had Mrs. Baines gotten a hold of it? If only the fire searing through his body would ignite the paper and turn it to ashes. He folded it and she snatched it from his fingers before he could rip it to shreds.

She raised a brow at him. "Do you have anything to say about the contents of this letter?"

"No."

Her round eyes grew even more so. "No? What can you mean?"

He worked his jaw. When his classics professor in college had described a harpy from Greek mythology, he must have used her as a template. "I am aware of the situation Miss Howard found herself in several years ago. I know for a fact it was not her fault."

Mrs. Baines leaned back in her chair, her chin raised. "I see. But surely you must see how impossible it is for her to continue to represent the Hall in your name. Her character has been severely compromised."

"I'll thank you not to speak that way about my future wife."

She huffed at him like a locomotive. "You cannot possibly be serious, sir."

"I am very serious, Mrs. Baines."

The woman leaned forward in her chair. Were her eyes really gleaming with delight? "And what will happen if your tenants discover her indiscretion? Hmm? What then, Lord Turner?"

"If you so much as breathe a word of this, I will sue you for slander."

"You wouldn't dare."

"Try me."

Sir James walked into the room. "Lord Turner?" He frowned as he looked from him to his sister. His gaze settled on her. "I see you're still here."

"I am," she replied. "I told you I wanted to talk to you about this decision of Isabella's, and I meant it." She looked at John. "I'm very sorry, Lord Turner. I hope you will excuse us."

Sir James held up his hand.

"Wait a moment, Dorothea." He looked at John. "What brings you here, sir? I have to apologize for missing your arrival. I was seeing to some details regarding my daughter's recent marriage."

Mrs. Baines gave a sniff. "To a stable boy."

"You mean Arthur? Arthur Wilcox?" John asked. He had been here all this time?

"The very same," Sir James replied. "I sent for Arthur after he blew up the well. I was curious about this young man who had the audacity not only to defy you but to force his way into my house and be so open about his feelings toward my daughter." His eyes became tender. "I love Isabella very much. She's like her mother in many ways, and I admit I indulged her thirst for knowledge, not realizing how hard that would make it for her to marry."

"I tried to tell you, James," Mrs. Baines said.

"And at first I thought I should have listened, but I've come to realize she wouldn't have been happy. She wouldn't be our Isabella." He sat down in the chair opposite his sister and laid his hand over hers. "I came to see she couldn't marry an ordinary man. When I saw how clever your protégé is, Lord Turner, and how much he genuinely cares for her, I gave them my consent to marry. Mr. Gregory performed the ceremony yesterday."

"Much too sudden if you ask me," his sister mumbled.

"Which is why we did it quietly," he replied. "I courted Emma for less time than that, and we were very happy for the few years we had together."

Mrs. Baines gave him a wave of her hand but said nothing.

"Sir James," John said, "does Arthur still have plans to pursue a career in medicine?"

"I do."

All eyes turned toward the door where Arthur stood, coat on, hat in hand.

"Where is my niece, Mr. Wilcox?" Mrs. Baines asked.

"My wife hasn't come down yet, Aunt Dorothea." Mrs. Baines' mouth dropped open, but Arthur regarded John with cryptic eyes. "Lord Turner."

John stepped over to him. "Arthur, I'm glad to see you. I owe you an apology. I behaved very foolishly. And ignorantly. I'm sorry, and I hope we can remain friends and, one day, colleagues." He held out his hand.

He didn't take it. Had he pushed him too far? He would understand if he did.

"That is very good of you, Lord Turner."

The new Mrs. Wilcox entered and took her husband's arm. She gazed up at him, one brow delicately arched. Arthur's shoulders slumped, and the groom who had looked at the library with such fascination took John's hand. "I'm sorry too, sir. There was more than once when I was disrespectful."

"Not at all," John replied. He'd deserved it. "Things might not have ended well if it hadn't been for you. In more ways than you know." He clapped Arthur on the back. "And congratulations to you both. I assume you are off on your honeymoon. Be prepared to work hard when you return. Dr. Royston and I will not be easy taskmasters."

"I will, sir—wait. You *and* Dr. Royston?"

The young couple held such similar expressions of wonderment John gave a small laugh. "Yes. Both of us."

"You have my word, sir." Arthur threatened to shake his arm off.

"I hope you will allow me to help, Lord Turner," Sir James chimed in.

"Of course."

"All very touching to be sure." Mrs. Baines scowled. "But it would not be wise, James, to have too close a connection with this man."

She handed him the letter. John clenched his jaw. How much deeper would she attempt to dig her talons?

Sir James frowned as he read it. "You will remain silent about this, Dorothea. I won't have our name connected to a scandal."

"But James, this woman should not be caring for those in Woodley."

He ignored her outburst. "I have written to Charles. He is willing to accept his share of the responsibility as our brother in supporting you and is expecting you in York."

Without another word, Mrs. Baines rose and left the room, pausing only to embrace her bewildered niece and nod to her new nephew.

Her brother looked after her. "Miss Howard has done a great deal for the Hall and Woodley. I want that good work to continue. And I've certainly made my own mistakes." He handed the letter to John.

He took it, tension seeping from his neck and chest. Sir James would be an ally then. Good. He reminded him of Robert in many ways. "Thank you."

"We must be off, Papa, or we will miss our train." Mrs. Wilcox released Arthur long enough to embrace her father.

John and Sir James escorted them to the door and watched as they made their way down the steps.

Arthur paused at the bottom. "Lord Turner, that day at the Castle when you found the stone marker. I'm sorry I didn't tell you about it. I wasn't to tell. Ever."

"Don't let it concern you. I understand." John joined him. "I think you already realize how hard being a doctor can be. I'm glad you do because I didn't, and I nearly destroyed myself. Grace is powerful medicine. Dispense it generously."

They shook hands before Arthur climbed into the carriage with his new wife.

Sir James invited him to take tea with him, a request John felt he could not refuse in light of the man's promised discretion. But as soon as politeness allowed, he made his way back to Ashford Hall, albeit slowly this time. His leg protested all the riding and standing he'd done today. He paused on the drive and gazed at his inheritance. The Hall had never looked more inviting, the way it glowed in the light of the setting sun.

The library was dimly lit. And empty. He expected to find Penelope curled up in his chair by the fire, perhaps reading *Jane Eyre*. But the fire was cold, and the oil lamp was turned low, throwing off half-hearted light. He pulled the bell and found her favorite book while he waited. In all likelihood, she was checking on Miss Bromley. He allowed the tome to fall open in his hands and skimmed a few lines. Would he be able to persuade her to read to him before she left? No, she was sure to be tired. He'd read to her.

Parker entered.

"Where is Miss Howard?" John asked.

"Mrs. Lynch told me she went home, my lord," he replied. "She said she mentioned having a matter to deal with at Fairview."

"Oh, of course." If only things hadn't taken so long at Hartsbury. No matter. He would see her tomorrow. And every tomorrow after that. His chest warmed at the thought. "Go to bed, Parker. It will be a big day tomorrow."

Both brow and voice rose as he spoke. "Very good, my lord."

Parker had just reached the green baize door when he called out to John. "A message came to you from London, sir. George has it."

"Thank you, Parker. Good night."

"Good night, sir."

John climbed the stairs, still clutching *Jane Eyre*. He'd read a chapter or two before he went to sleep. How those blue eyes of hers would warm when he began to talk about it tomorrow. He hoped the message Parker mentioned wasn't urgent. Who could have sent it? Mr. Smith concerning some unexpected paper he needed to sign? He didn't know anyone else in London—he stopped at the top of the stairs. Reason told him he shouldn't jump to conclusions, but his heart urged his feet to stride toward his room as quickly as possible.

CHAPTER 31

The morning dawned crisp and bright. If only Penelope's mood could match it. Her evening had been spent unpleasantly. Ridding her brother's studio of the filth he'd painted, not only of Clara, but other women as well, had unsettled her stomach enough that she declined the food Hannah had offered. She refused to allow the housekeeper or Fanny to help her. They didn't deserve to see what, had Mrs. Lynch been less giving, would have surely ruined them all. It was fortunate his studio had a hearth large enough to allow fire to devour his indiscretions. Sleep had eluded her at first, and she worked far into the night, putting the rest of his supplies and the few landscapes he had painted in a large crate. By the time she finally slipped down to her room, there was little to indicate the studio had ever been an artist's haven.

Thomas had left no note. The only thing that indicated he was indeed gone was the absence of his clothes and his leather sketchbook. She could only pray nothing within its pages were as damning as what had been in his studio.

After breakfast, she sat at his desk in the study. Mrs. Lynch had given her the ledger when she urged her to return to Fairview yesterday evening. By midday, she had partially sorted out the mess he had made of the Hall's accounts. It seemed he had not been embezzling for very long, only since their uncle passed when he received Fairview alone as his inheritance. But he'd been clever enough to steal a great deal of money in a short amount of time. Money she could only assume he had taken with him.

She rested her head in her hands. Lord Turner hadn't sent for her. Mrs. Lynch told her she was sure he would first thing in the morning. And after what had transpired between them in the library ...

She drew in a shaky breath. A moment later, her mouth went dry, and she raced up the stairs. Stealing from the Hall might not have been the only crime her brother had committed. A search of her bedside table left her hands shaking uncontrollably. Edna's letter was gone.

She sank on her bed. He knew. No wonder he'd been summoned to Hartsbury. Thomas had given Edna's letter to Mrs. Baines. It was the only explanation.

"Miss Penny?" Fanny called from the doorway. "You're needed at the Hall."

Only death itself was quieter than Ashford Hall. The fresh flowers which always stood on the front hall tables were gone. Through its open door she saw sheets covered every stick of furniture in the library. He was leaving? Of course. He knew about her now. Why would he want to stay?

But instead of the library she was escorted downstairs. Why would he want to see her in the servant's hall? Because that's all she was to him now. Joseph led her to Mrs. Lynch's sitting room where the housekeeper sat at her desk and perused a letter with a sour expression. Penelope's chest tightened. Was it Edna's letter? Had Thomas really been that cruel? Where was Lord Turner?

Mrs. Lynch stood, laying the note aside, and grasped Penelope's hands.

"Good afternoon, my dear." Her tone was soft, almost too kind. "I'm not sure what to say."

"He's leaving, Mrs. Lynch. I can see that." Her voice felt thin, and she cleared her throat.

"Actually, he left last night, not long after he returned from Hartsbury. I understand he went to London." She pulled a letter from her pocket. "I'm supposed to give this to you."

Edna's letter. She took it and slipped it into her reticule.

"I understand." She understood she had failed him. His memory of her would be forever tainted. While hers of him would be purer than driven snow. In her heart, despite everything, he was the most honorable man she'd ever known.

"About Miss Bromley. Is she up to being moved? I don't mean to sound unfeeling, but I must close the house." The housekeeper's words scratched like a stiff broom.

"Of course. I shall take her to Fairview. Is it possible to borrow Ellen and the use of a coach?"

A short time later, Penelope was following one of the Hall's coaches home. From inside her heart, she watched a shade of herself going through the motions of life. Settling Clara in her mother's room, assuring Ellen she could visit whenever she liked, taking dinner with Hannah and Fanny, even completing the task of cleaning up the Hall's ledgers. It wasn't until the most silent, darkest watch of the night that she allowed her grief and regrets to well up and overflow onto her pillow.

The first thing that worried her was who would take her brother's place. But it seemed Lord Turner had already taken that into account. The bailiff from Somerset, Mr. Hale, arrived at Fairview's door in short order, and Penelope and Hannah spent two days taking him around to meet the tenants. He did not stay with them, of course. Arrangements had been made for him to room at the pub in Woodley, as he would be going back and forth between here and Somerset. The ambiguous story that Mr. Howard was gone for a time was not questioned. What she would say when the magistrate came to call she couldn't imagine.

Except he didn't come.

"He must not have contacted him," Clara said as they sat in

the parlor. It had been more than a week since Lord Turner left. She was up and about, and her thickening middle showed she still carried her child.

"He should have come by now to ask questions, to see if I know where he went." Penelope flipped through the pages of a book absentmindedly before shutting it with a snap.

"Is it possible he called at the Hall and found out what he needed from Parker or Mrs. Lynch?"

"I suppose." Penelope rose and placed the book back on the shelf. "I shall call there tomorrow and find out."

Clara nodded and regarded the fire. It snapped and popped as it ate away at a large log. "In the meantime, what are we to do about me? As big as I'm getting, I can't return to teaching."

"I know."

"Ellen told me her grandmother was a midwife." Clara fingered the fabric of the blanket lying across her lap. "She lives in a small village outside Hull and has told Ellen she would be happy have me live with her. She knows and understands my situation."

"Hull is a long way away."

"I know, but it will be for the best."

Penelope gave her hand a squeeze and settled back down in her chair. While Clara resumed her knitting, Penelope laid her mother's Bible out on her knees. It was time she rallied.

But the passage in John did not speak to her as it once did. It seemed so ordinary, so everyday. She flipped to Romans.

And we know that all things work together for good ...

But where was the good in all this? Thomas had been found out and was no longer stealing from the Hall. Clara had found a safe haven. Ashford was being well cared for, judging by the tenants' comments to her. Those were all good things to be certain, and she had no doubt God's hand was in them. But with regard to her, His goodness seemed to have dissolved.

No, that wasn't true, and she knew it. She just couldn't see where He was leading her.

Penelope had every intention of driving straight past the ruins on her way to the Hall the next day. But before she realized it, she took the lane to the Castle.

Her heart spun in two different directions. She longed to see her angel. And yet she couldn't bear the thought of being in the same place where she had been with Lord Turner. But something—her angel, most likely—coaxed her from the cart and to the base of the Angel Tree.

She swept the grass from the marker as she usually did and, pulling off her bonnet, settled down next to the tree, anchoring her shoulder against the trunk.

In her mind, a five-year-old little sprite played with the early oak leaves which had fallen from the tree. She smiled as she watched her gather them up and then throw them in the air for the wind to catch. For a split second, she could almost catch the scent of her hair and the music of her laughter. A gust of wind scattered the leaves and the image.

Her gaze drifted to the entrance to the cellar. It had been her angel's birthday. Lord Turner had quoted Longfellow, and she had told him she loved *Jane Eyre*.

Where was it that Rochester declared himself to Jane? Under a tree? How ironic. Here she sat, under a tree, where she and the man she loved had promised to forget about what they felt for one another.

That kiss.

She rose. It was time she returned.

"Where are you going?"

She started. Just her imagination. She'd imagined her angel. Now him. Letting out a humorless laugh she answered as Jane had. "To Ireland."

"Then the cord that connects me to you will snap, and I will take to bleeding inwardly." Lord Turner stepped out from the other side of the tree. "I think that's how it goes."

No. It couldn't be him. Another gust of wind would blow him far away. But the next moment his arms were around her, burying her into his chest. Searing heat and bitter cold shot through to her very core, and she shook. She lifted her head. "What are you doing here?"

He lowered his forehead to hers. "I came for you."

"Why? You left." Her voice hitched. "They told you about me, and you left."

"If you mean Sir James and Mrs. Baines, they didn't tell me. Mrs. Baines tried to, but I already knew. I overheard what you told Clara. I know, and it doesn't matter."

If she hadn't been in his arms, her knees would have certainly given out. He'd heard? "But you left."

"An old friend of mine, Dr. Robert Matthews, is in London with his wife. Sarah fell ill and he sent for me. I was the only doctor he trusted with her care."

"But Mrs. Lynch said—"

His voice darkened. "Mrs. Lynch lied to both of us. And she destroyed the messages I left for both you and Parker. This whole time she was covering for Thomas while he went to London to withdraw the money he stole."

"Why? He used her just as he used Clara."

"I wish I knew. It's possible Thomas was holding something over her head."

"I went over the ledger. He has a great deal of your money."

"No, he doesn't. While we were in London, George was out running an errand for me and spotted him. He's in prison waiting for his trial. And Parker told me Mrs. Lynch suddenly left the Hall last night. She must have heard somehow." He drew her closer still. "It's over, Penelope. There's nothing to stop me from making you my wife."

She shook her head, tried to push away, but he held her fast. He shouldn't want her. Not if he knew what she was and what she could never give him.

"Penelope, trust me, there isn't."

"But there *is*." She pounded her fists against his chest. She couldn't let him do this. "If you heard what I told Clara, then you know there is. My lord, you can't marry a woman who cannot give you an heir."

"John. My name. Is John."

Her lips parted, but words refused to come. They fled at the passion in his face, his arms, his very being. He didn't care. *She* was all that mattered. Her soul trembled and she buried her head in his chest. It was too much. Nearly everything her heart had dreamed could not possibly be in her arms at this moment. He lifted her chin and brushed her lips with a light and agonizingly brief kiss.

"Penelope, say it. Say you'll marry me. And use my name."

"Yes, John," she murmured.

EPILOGUE

One year later...

John wasn't surprised when his wife slipped away while he met with the new estate agent. He knew exactly where she'd gone. She'd wanted to stop on their way back to the Hall yesterday, but their train had been delayed and it was too dark by the time they arrived in Woodley. He watched her through the library window as she rode off. He would follow as soon as he could. The meeting was brief. He had been careful to stay in touch as they toured Athens, then Rome, and then during their stay in a remote villa in Tuscany.

As he saw the agent out, Clara walked into the entry hall. The man's eyes sparked with interest, and Clara twisted her fingers together when he introduced them. But she kept her face impassive, her manner reserved as she had whenever she had been introduced as Penelope's lady's maid in the past year. They escorted him out the door to the front steps and watched from there as he mounted his horse.

"Clara, don't put yourself in a box."

She watched the agent ride away. "I'm still not ready, John."

He drew in a deep breath. *Don't let her start down that dark path, Lord. Lead her to still waters.* He took her by the elbow and led her into the entry hall. "How is he?"

This time her eyes lit up. "Perfect. He's sleeping. The journey wore him out, and Penelope and I laid him down for a nap before she went out."

He nodded. "Good."

"Thank you again for what you are doing for us."

"You've said that already. Many times."

"I know."

"We'll raise him as our own, and no matter what happens, you will always have a place with us and with him." He tilted his head toward the door. "But that doesn't mean sacrificing your own happiness. He's a good man with a spotless reputation."

"I need to check on Matthew."

She climbed the steps. John sent another prayer up behind her.

Fortis carried him to the Castle in record time. Penelope was exactly where he knew she would be, reclining at the base of the Angel Tree, her riding habit billowed out around her. He watched her as he tied Fortis next to her horse, warmth flooding his chest. How was it possible that he loved her even more now than he had a year ago?

"I'm sorry we couldn't stop last night," he said as he walked up to her.

She smiled. Her hat lay off to the side, and a few strands of hair danced in the breeze.

"Matthew was sleeping, and it was too dark." She reached over and pushed back the tufts of grass that had grown too close to the angel marker.

He sat down against the tree's sturdy trunk, propping one leg up in front of him, and began to pull the grass away.

She laid a hand over his. Concern dulled her azure eyes. "Don't."

"Why?"

"People will see and ask questions." She squeezed his fingers. "She should remain hidden."

The sadness in her voice gave him exactly what he needed to tell her of the plans he'd been working on since Matthew's birth in Italy.

"She's not staying here."

"John—"

He pulled her against him and drank her in. He never wanted to see such worry and pain in those eyes again. When they eventually parted, she pressed her cheek to his chest, and he tightened his hold on her with a deep sigh.

"I'm going to have her moved to a place on the Hall grounds." He smiled when she raised her wide eyes to his and continued, "I've had the new agent working on a private garden while we've been gone. For you. That's where she'll be. No one will see her, and no one will ever have to know except us."

She swallowed. "Thank you."

A tear slipped down her cheek. He swept it away with the pad of his thumb. "We'll visit our daughter together."

Confusion wrote a V between her brows. "*Our* daughter ... but ..."

He silenced her with another kiss. A long moment later, he broke it resting his forehead against hers as he continued, "You said in our vows all that is in your heart is mine. That makes her my daughter too."

This time, as he pulled her close, he let the tears stream down her face unchecked.

THE END

Made in the USA
Lexington, KY
02 September 2018